# Without Tears And Other Tales

Michael Eisele

Other books by Michael Eisele:
Twelve O'Clock Sharp


Publisher: Michael Eisele

Printed and Bound in the United States of America

*To*
*My Wife*
*Renate*

# Contents

# A Way Out

Thirty years ago the east coast of Barbados was a lonely stretch of windswept land. One could pitch a tent amidst the dunes of Bathsheba without being bothered. Swimming below in the foaming sea could be enjoyed all by oneself; seldom would another being be sighted along that wave-washed strand. Only curious monkeys came out of the hills from time to time.

Further south lies Crane Beach, a rare beauty indeed. Travellers should be wary not to stay too long at that heart-captivating spot, lest they be haunted by memories for a long while. It is not easy to forget those stately palms, playfully, with an old world grace, inviting each other to dance in the wind. Once back home, who knows, they might still hear the droning, sleep inducing sound of an angry sea, impeded on its path of destruction by a long stretch of reefs. In pensive moments they might inwardly see huge, rolling waves breaking up over coral rocks, creating an extended foamy barrier between the shore and the open sea.

The moment Lisa Hermian laid eyes on that unrivalled spot, she knew the hands of destiny were beckoning. She was a solitary woman, intentionally shrouding her life in secrecy, disguising her past zealously. What did she have to hide? Nothing, except the fact that in twenty years of searching she still was, as it were, trying to find Kenna Quhair, that is 'Weissnichtwo.'

But now she had found it. Her instinct talked louder than reason, which tried to remind her of other times when similar sentiments had touched her. True, till now, after smiles of joy illuminated her face at the sight of new vistas, soon shadows of doubts began to obscure that newly found radiance again. But not this time, far from it. Finally at age thirty-five, she felt a most profound sense of belonging. Her wandering days were over, she knew. Gone were the nights when half asleep she would listen to that ominous crack of the whip, an imaginary sound equally loved and hated, which spurred her on to new quests. Here she would remain for the rest of her days, her instinct understood what no argument could dispel.

Of course the matter of subsistence had to be considered, if not immediately then certainly within the year. Living like a native in those benign times was wholesome and inexpensive. Her means would have sustained her easily more than ten years. But she was disinclined to do so, even thinking about it threw her into a dither.

Lisa Hermian preferred opulence to penny pinching. Next to luxury, if unattainable, she would settle for comfort: meaning sumptuous meals in gracious surroundings, and a home well decorated. True, the natives seemed to be sufficiently provided for, judging by their glowing health, strapping figures and friendly miens, not even mentioning the unfailing smiles. But she was not a native, and besides had no intention to live like one. In any case her money should last for a while, it had to sustain her in a half decent fashion, till something else came along, she figured. And it did.

Lisa Hermian was an attractive woman, not beautiful if measured with yardsticks of the new world, meaning plastic forms, studied poses and frozen grins, but she looked promising to any man with blood in his veins and stir in his bones. Even ageing Lotharios could not resist turning their aching necks when she passed them. She of course was not oblivious of this allure, but one could hardly call her ostentatious about it.

Three months had past since her arrival, a heavenly time, only obscured by a ripping awareness of her dwindling resources. Fate had led her to Utopia; now she had to find a way to prolong her favourite's sojourn in this strangely different and fascinating island. So far not a whiff of promise lay in the air, not even the faintest outlines of an opportunity appeared on the horizon. For one thing, however, she had time on her hands, which was applied to gain acquaintance with her surrounding.

Luck was still on her side; she found a suitable house with a beautiful setting right above the foaming ocean. The rent was surprisingly low, not even two hundred dollars a month. With not a moments hesitation she engaged it for six month. There she spent restful nights and pleasant days.

"This is life," she announced more than once to the blowing wind and breaking waves below.

At times she hardly managed to contain a surging jubilation. An all consuming exultation gripped her some days, which urged to embrace everyone in her path: young, old, black and white. It was the sweet life; if only that nagging uncertainty about the future had not been. However, an innate optimism kept her spirit up. Indeed, how could anyone, short of death's embrace, be disconsolate amidst the soft air of the Caribbean, where people's very gait express a contagious contentment. Where sleep comes easy at night, and dreams interlace with the rustle of palms and the inimitable cries of whistling frogs.

Not Lisa Hermian, who had found her destiny. She liked to stroll down to the beach, at times just to look at a half-hidden estate house sitting on a promontory above. It was walled in on three sides; the fourth one was protected by sheer cliffs which a pounding sea attacked with unceasing fury.

The place intrigued her, it bore an air of mystery, besides being ideally located. Despite a neglected appearance, it possessed an old world charm that no amount of imagination could have evoked. Every time Lisa passed by the wrought iron gates, she paused to look inside. A force greater than her natural reticence compelled her to do so. She never detected movements inside, though the cultivated grounds indicated human hands at work.

Irresistible this place began to cast a spell over her, it seemed like heaven on earth. It exuded a tranquillity among a pastoral setting, an air of calmness amidst seclusion but not isolation, which was meant for an independent spirit like hers. How she would love to live in there! she would do anything to become the mistress of that mysterious, alluring place. The view alone must be worth many sacrifices, she told herself, not mentioning sounds of a weird, yet soothing nature.

Vicariously she could feel the perpetual balm rendered her restless soul if she could live in there, all alone preferably. She could see herself sitting in one of the bowers by the gates, watching women on their way to market, colourfully dressed, carrying baskets on their heads, their sturdy hips swaying and tongues wagging, displaying a joy to be alive. Dream on Lisa, dream on, she sighed every time while walking by.

One day she could contain her curiosity no longer. Perhaps driven by faint hopes to experience a miracle, she went across the road to see Jaques Gratton, owner of the only hotel far and wide. After a bit of banter, in which that Montrealer delighted, interlaced with gasconades, she asked as if in passing:

"By the way, whose property is that over on the bluff?"

An inquiring glance, if not stare, preceded his answer.

"That place I know nothing about," she was informed in a tone of finality.

"But it is only a few stone's throw away, besides being a remarkable holding," she remonstrated laughingly.

There came the characteristic shrug of shoulders, followed by expressive arm movements.

"We hear rumours, some quite fantastic, but in my ten years stay in this area, I, nor anyone known to me, has any information concerning those grounds. Mind you, Miss Hermian, one does not inquire about such affairs in Barbados, where privacy is valued more than the Holy Grail."

"Oh, I did not mean to pry," she declared with an air of annoyance and a sigh of disappointment.

Gratton's quick empathy sensed her embarrassment, therefore he tried to reassure her:

"I am implying no such thing, Miss Hermian, it is just so unusual to be asked anything hereabouts. Come to think of it, indifference probably governs that fact more than good breeding."

After she had left none the wiser, the thought obtruded itself that Mr Gratton, in spite of his courteousness, had not told the truth; he concealed something which perhaps would have made him uneasy to mention. Indeed, that was so. But how could he know that his denial of any knowledge about the neighbouring estate's dark and dangerous history, would bring her no end of humiliation and sorrow. Divulging what he knew so well might have tamed her curiosity, and doused her sprouting hopes. As it now stood, the place fascinated her more than before.

An irresistible attraction grew into a downright obsession. It supplanted good manners and obfuscated good sense.

Henceforth she passed by the gates more often, moreover stopped frequently to peer through the picket gaps. Soon she became bolder. Pretending to take a needed rest, she sat down on a rock nearby from where the house could be clearly seen; her bashfulness shrunk by degrees. Like a thief, whose deeds remain undetected, graduates to further and greater thefts, so Lisa considered it her right, if not duty, to lift the veils of mystery from that stately property. Nothing could be seen or heard inside indicating the presence of human beings, although the fairly well maintained grounds suggested as much.

A month later her investigations, such it could be called by now, still bore no fruit. November neared its end. The rain, far more infrequent than on the Caribbean side, had practically stopped. Trade winds gathered strength, waves began to built up higher beyond the reefs, over which they were transformed into a strip of thunderous foam.

A wonderful time approached. The summer heat, muggy and oppressive at times, gave way by degrees to cooler air. Days became delightful, still warm without being enervating, while nights acquired a soothing quality. Pleasure seekers, that cloud on the horizon, had not yet arrived. Soon the island would be teeming with strange and boisterous people, visibly insecure, yet disturbingly rambunctious. Domineering women, overweighed and underclad could be seen, their men in tow, meek and browbeaten towards them, but loud and assertive among themselves. The atmosphere on the island would soon change; peace and quiet will be gone for a while. The soft voices and gentle ways of natives would be drowned out by strangers who romp through the narrow streets like dozens of juggernauts.

Lisa Hermian knew nothing about this annual metamorphosis, besides she would hardly have paid attention to it. Her interest was more and more captivated by that plantation house on the promontory. An all consuming fascination with it made her oblivious to wind, waves and changes in weather. Even the sudden disappearance of pesky insects escaped her attention. She knew more than ever that destiny was calling. Especially since the day she became privy to exciting news.

It happened a week ago, after spending most of the night tossing and turning from here to there, plagued by gruesome dreams, trying to find a few hours rest. Although the wind blew unobstructed through her sleeping chamber, despite the cool night air, she was bathed in perspiration. The rustle of palms beside the house, always before perceived as a good night, sleep well encouragement, bore an ominous message.

Finally she rose, while still completely dark, much earlier than usual. What compelled her to dress and start walking she could not have said. Mysterious, but irresistible forces led her steps towards that house. A burning excitement had gripped her, whose cause soon revealed itself. There was movement in the garden. Two shadowy figures appeared to be in conversation, which sounded more like an argument.

Her first impulse called for a hasty retreat, yet that inescapable coercion, governing much of her life lately, dictated otherwise. Stealthily, without further compunction she took position behind one of the gate pillars. The rustling and scraping palm trees vexed her to no end, she could have hewed them down with her own hands, since they drowned out the words from inside. They were upset, so much was discernible in the approaching glimmer of dawn. Interrupting their slow walk at times, one or the other cut the air with outstretched arms, then punctuated his words by smashing a clenched fist into the palm of his hand. Words reached her ears occasionally, indicating that one was berating the other for being there.

Then suddenly both turned, pointing their faces towards her. Startled, she pulled back quickly, yet in that fleeting moment she received a jolt to the core. One of the men was Jaques Gratton.

"But that is impossible," she murmured repeatedly while practically running back to her house. For she remembered distinctly the Quebecois' words:

"That place I know nothing about."

She recalled vividly how positive he seemed, besides somewhat irritated.

"I must be mistaken," reason whispered in one ear.

"No, I am certain," countered instinct into the other.

By now she had reached an intersection where a lane sloped down to the beach along an embankment grown over with trees and bushes. Feeling hidden from view she halted in order to think. One idea more confused than the next raced through her head. Without realising it, she clambered up the ridge and crouched low behind a cluster of bushes.

Meanwhile the sun's rays started rising above the water, setting the eastern sky ablaze. It was a welcome sign, which lifted her spirit as quickly as the sun crept up on the horizon.

Suddenly the whole affair took on a different aspect; it made her chuckle, thinking about her silly notions. Even if it was Mr Gratton whom she had seen in the garden, what of it. And why attach so much importance to his testy denial?

As daylight flooded sea and land, she almost laughed aloud over anxieties which deserved not the slightest attention.

She went back to Amhara, as she called it, just to prove a point. This time the gates were wide open. A man, a fine figure to be sure, was talking to on older native, who repeatedly nodded his head without saying a word. The man waved at her and called out:

"Good morning Miss Hermian, and a beautiful day it will be again."

She was taken aback. First because he hailed her with such enthusiasm, but more so since he knew her name. While still trying to collect herself, the man approached the gates, smiling from ear to ear. Proffering his hand he introduced himself:

"My name is Arthur Bowles. I understand from Rufus here that you have been showing some interest in my place," he said in a droll way which made her smile amusedly.

"You know my name as I notice," she observed somewhat surprised.

"But of course Miss Hermian, after all we are practically neighbours. I would have introduced myself sooner had I been here. I was abroad for the past months. May I invite you inside?"

She liked Bowles immediately. He was well built, had an open face, and evidently possessed exquisite manners. He was of European extraction, but by all appearances a man with local roots. Life had obviously treated him benignly, which should hardly come as a surprise in a climate always soft and warm; surrounded by people whose unhurried ways are balm to the soul, where a breath of far away Africa still fills the air.

He was deeply tanned by the omnipresent Caribbean sun, and the trade wind that never rests. She was touched by his courteous demeanour, strangely elevated, almost exalted. He appeared to be her own age, perhaps a few years younger, although his confident bearing would have done honour to a much older man.

There began a courtship, not stormy by any standards, but steadily leading to matrimony. They were married at St. Michael's Cathedral two months later. When she tried to invite Jaques Gratton to the wedding, he was found to be abroad. Thinking perchance to postpone the wedding a few days, she asked the man behind the counter:

"How long will he be absent?"

"At least two months," she was advised.

It turned out to be a quiet ceremony, without festivities or even guests. When she asked for a list of attendants and people to be invited, Arthur gave her a strange look. Never before had she seen that expression on his face. First came surprise, then shadows of annoyance flitted over his handsome features, followed by a flash of pure aversion, albeit quickly suppressed. She had neither time nor cause to be disconcerted over this sudden manifestation of malevolence, for instantly his face took on its usual affable air.

"I had a simple wedding in mind Lisa, with your consent just the two of us would suit me nicely," he declared with his loveable smile.

Hiding her astonishment she answered:

"No objection from me darling, my concern is meant for you. I imagine you must have a host of friends and acquaintances locally, who might be miffed if not invited."

"Let them be offended, you may have noticed that I am not much of a society man; two, to my mind is enough company for any occasion," he declared.

Indeed, she had perceived as much. He seldom left the property, nor did he receive visitors to her knowledge. Beyond daily appearances of Rufus, the old gardener, she hardly ever saw anybody else there. Rufus, along with the odd native woman, supplied him with necessities. Produce and fruit was locally grown. No, gregarious he could not be called by any stretch of the imagination which, however, she found in harmony with her own propensities. She could have lived entirely alone in this fabulous place, without experiencing a day of boredom.

Just tending the extensive garden could occupy an idle mind. Should a desire arise for further diversion, one could always observe the activities on the beach below. True, the predictable antics of waddling, lobster-red, and clamorous tourists will do little to disperse ennui, but it was worthwhile to walk a bit northward, where a beholder could be in for a treat hardly believable.

Between two large outcrops lies Shark's Hole, a deep ground cavity not more than fifty feet from the beach, where youngsters carry out an unusual sport. Incredible it may sound, but some boys dive down and snare a shark by the tail fin, which others, perched on rocky ledges, pull up. Admittedly, these sharks are small, the natives call them 'Baby Sharks', but nevertheless it is quite a spectacle to watch. Of course, after the boys had their fun, the sharks would be released.

Lisa Hermian, or Mrs Bowles, as she called herself now, had finally entered Amhara, her private paradise. She was walking on air, a lifelong search had come to an end. To be mistress of this wonderful estate surpassed her most ardent hopes. Her husband proved to be a most solicitous mate, as indeed she had expected. After a month of their lives together she still experienced nothing but pleasantness from him.

A trait about him, call it reticence, define it as introversion, repelling to some people, appealed to her sense of propriety. He was a man of reserve, but not taciturnity. Yet concerning his past he seemed closer than a clam. Did he love before, was he ever attached to a woman, had he suffered reverses whose recollection at times clouded his handsome features? She did not know, besides was too genteel to ask. However, his circumstances he had explained to her unreservedly.

His parents, who died ten years ago, came over from Guyana. Being the only offspring, he inherited this property, plus considerable holdings in Georgetown and Patricia. All were held free of mortgages. No doubt he could be called a rich man, but with equal emphasis a recluse, which as mentioned agreed with her own disposition to some extend.

Not a whiff of disharmony clouded her days. Initial concerns that marriage, while freeing her from anxieties of a livelihood, might curtail her freedom, possibly even chain her to that chimera obligation, proved unfounded. Arthur's broad-mindedness quickly dispelled such misgivings. His lack of intrusiveness touched her like a gift of the Magi. He never crowded her, nor made any demands on her time or private life. She welcomed this admirable trait in her husband, as much as the absence of want. He had opened a bank account in her name with sufficient funds to cover her needs of a lifetime.

Their first disagreement, mild as it was, came over an innocent habit of hers. Quite by accident she had discovered a small library on the premises of Sam Lord's Castle, a short walk away. Almost daily she sauntered over to that beautiful facility with an unsavoury past. On the way there her spirit always soared, which contrasted with her mood while walking back. Why so? Because of the librarian, a well-read woman, refined and soft spoken, and bestowed with an aristocratic air, who exhilarated and disconcerted her at the same time. Her calm, unobtrusive demeanour, besides an extensive knowledge in literature, acted as an irresistible attraction. Lisa realised how uplifting good conversation can be.

Unfortunately this elation was dimmed by shadows of sadness that hovered around the librarian, who seemed burdened by perpetual sighs which she dared not vent. That alone, however, did not unsettle Lisa. The woman's furtive glances discomforted her most, they were probing, evidently triggered by an anxiety to speak. Lisa could not dispel a notion she either wanted to warn her, or express commiseration.

But warning her made no sense, for she had no enemy on this peaceful island, where in any case violence was practically unknown. To pity her would even seem more incongruous, since she had not a care in the world. Yet this woman, gentle to her fingertips, appeared to hover on the edge of committing an indiscretion.

On the way back Lisa's ill humour dissipated as usual in proportion with increasing distance between her and that mute Cassandra. She must be an eccentric, she thought, with peculiar notions which best remain unexpressed. In any case, why wrangle or brood on such a beautiful day, surrounded by signs and sounds of perpetual summer.

Walking along the beach her eyes wandered from an azure sky that seemed to vie for attention with a blue ocean. She could hardly believe her luck of finding not only Amhara, the perfect spot on earth, but also a wonderful husband, loving and solicitous, who never pried or begrudged her anything. Then she remembered Christmas, so near, yet worlds away. She felt not the least bit nostalgic, Santa Claus belonged to a forgotten time of ice and snow.

Her train of thought was suddenly interrupted by a strange foreboding, which at first she hardly heeded. But soon these inexplicable misgivings grew stronger, they forced her to stop and listen. But that was silly, she admitted; who could hear anything in such noise, caused by breaking waves on the sand.

When she walked on, a suspicion of being followed took hold of her, that made her laugh and cringe at the same time.

Nevertheless, a benumbing pain crept up her back, which for an instant reminded her of legendary Jettators with their evil eyes. Against her better judgement she turned around, albeit not quickly enough. She could barely see a shadow disappearing behind a rock. She called once, twice, but for some reason dared not walk back. "Imagination old girl, pure fancy" she murmured while hurrying towards the estate. All the while she could have sworn to feel a focused thrust of evil intentions from head to toe.

When she arrived at the estate Arthur could nowhere be found, which seemed odd, since he proved to be such a homebody. Not that she intended to say much, certainly nothing about an imagined encounter with a lurking spy, which within the secure walls of their home looked puerile, to say the least. Even less would she say about her visit to the library, in view of an unpleasant incident. She could never explain his surprising conduct that day. When she came home, almost out of breath for joy, she called out before even seeing him:

"Arthur, Arthur, guess what I found."

"What my darling?" he wanted to know with an indulgent smile.

"A bookstore and library, over at the Castle," she announced triumphantly, while holding up some of the borrowed books.

She would never forget his reaction. Wahela, Lot's wife could hardly have grown stiffer than he. Arthur virtually cringed. She could not believe her eyes and ears. Arthur Bowles, an equable man who never raised his voice or became indignant, practically bellowed at her:

"You should not go there."

To call her surprised would not even tell half, she was outright shocked, startled and stung as never before.

"But – but, Arthur, why?" she barely managed to stammer.

His face, transformed abruptly into a mask of petulance, smoothened as quickly again. Still morose he became apologetic:

"Why, you ask? I can not tell you now, but reasons do exist," he advised somewhat stilted.

Regaining his accustomed urbanity he added:

"Forgive my rudeness darling, of course you must always follow your own inclinations."

After he went his way she stood there for a while. Rude, he called his outburst, to be sure, frightening would have been a more apt description, she thought. But nevertheless she still went to the library, although sort of on the sly, or a better interpretation would be circumspectly. Before disappearing behind the bend she always looked back. Sure enough, Arthur invariably stood at the near corner of the property, leaning over the parapet, seemingly absorbed in the white crested waves far out. Several times she waved at him, but he never responded.

Then things began to happen. Strange they were, possibly fortuitous, even fanciful, but nevertheless more and more disquieting to Lisa. At first she paid scant attention to these occurrences, she shrugged them off like that illusory spying incident, but they persisted. Sensations or not, she was unable to shake off the feeling of being watched.

True, common sense dictated that it could not be, certainly not around the estate, which was only frequented by her husband and old, gentle Rufus. However, no amount of reasoning or self-criticism accomplished what she strove for, namely to dispel the perception of being slowly sheathed in a web of evil intentions. Arthur's conduct gave little rise for concern; his devotion, expressed in words and gestures, appeared genuine; his deportment towards her exemplary. Since that little tiff a while ago, not a single cloud darkened their conjugal firmament.

Mind you, as time went by she discovered a few idiosyncracies about Arthur, but none were disturbing to any degree. His reluctance to accompany her outside of the estate seemed odd. She sometimes gained the impression that he was averse to be seen together. To be sure, it could be attributed to his tendency towards reclusion. She hardly gave it a second thought.

More disturbing she perceived his dislike, bordering on loathing, of the librarian over at the Castle. In her estimation that surprisingly cultured woman deserved anyone's esteem. Why a man, poised at all times, should lose his composure at the mention of her, was incomprehensible. When Lisa expressed a desire, half in jest, to celebrate upcoming New Year's Eve together at the Castle, he flared up momentarily:

"I will not set foot on that property, ever," he practically cried.

Taken aback, she tried to appease him:

"But Arthur, why such a hubbub over a simple innocent question. After all the Castle is a wonderful place, besides being so close."

Placated he said:

"I know, I know, it's just that a few people over there are highly unsympathetic to me. Some day I shall tell you why."

In the next instant his imperturbable personality showed itself again. He laughed and invited her for a walk around the estate.

Privately Lisa had to admit that something was odd about Miss Jenny, the librarian. Her manner of looking at her now and then, furtively mind you, she found disquieting. As if she were on the verge of saying something, which a delicate disposition prevented. After one of those contemplative glances, quickly turned aside when reciprocated, she could not refrain from asking:

"Miss Jenny, do you want to say something to me?"

The woman reddened from temple to temple, averting Lisa's eyes she stammered:

"No, no, Mrs Bowles, nothing, I was just admiring your dress."

"Oh, is that all?"

It was not, as it turned out later. But for now nothing further was said about it.

One night Lisa almost had a serious accident. She was sitting on one of the balconies facing the ocean, while Arthur worked in his study on the floor below, with a view of the garden. She sighed, not from sorrow, but out of sheer happiness. As could be expected this time of the year, it was a clear night. Eerie sounds of whistling frogs filled the air. Piercing, yet soothing, these mighty cries from tiny throats never failed to lift her spirit. The locals say that after a while one becomes oblivious to them, but Lisa hoped it would not happen to her. For these haunting calls, almost fierce, embodied an appeal to be courageous. She closed her eyes and leaned back, letting the wind tussle her hair, and the sound of breaking waves over the reefs play in her ears.

Suddenly she heard a crushing sound down below, which startled and alarmed her.

"Arthur, what happened, is that you?" she called out, while at the same time rushing to the edge of the balcony.

As she grabbed the balustrade with both hands to lean over for a better view, it gave way and fell down. Jumping back horrified, she could not avoid seeing a dark shape disappearing behind bushes.

That was the beginning. Her husband was terribly upset when he heard and saw what happened. He blamed himself for being irresponsible, but to her surprise, Jaques Gratton over at the Crane Hotel received a stream of scathing criticism.

"What has he got to do with it?" she asked perplexed.

"A lot Lisa, if not everything."

"Really Arthur, I don't understand you," she remonstrated.

"Right now I'm too upset to explain, let us leave it for another day."

"Of course, of course," she agreed.

Arthur continued:

"First we have to engage a contractor to inspect the premises from cellar to roof. Best will be Da Costa, a most reputable firm. I can assure you that every door, window and railing will be examined and secured. Just thinking about your near miss makes me shudder. Imagine falling off that balcony, good gracious darling, it could have been fatal."

It took a bit of wangling to convince the company that this was an emergency, or even necessary. They finally consented to dispatch a team the following day. Four men showed up a week later. They rattled and hammered through the house for four days. Upon leaving, the foreman affirmed that not a nail or screw was missing anywhere.

"Everything is fastened down solid, no more accidents will happen," he confirmed with beaming confidence.

Yet they did. Scarcely had they left when Lisa stepped on a loose tread and tumbled down the stairs. Luck was on her side once more, she only sustained contusions and abrasions. Two tradesmen came back and fixed it. After they left she could not help overhearing what sounded like an argument. One of the workers was saying:

"I tell you sir, nails were removed forcefully from that tread."

"What are you implying?" her husband asked testily.

"That they were pulled out deliberately," the tradesman insisted.

"Impossible," Arthur exploded.

"Improbable maybe, but not impossible. If you can come with me, I will show you hammer and crowbar marks."

Lisa had heard enough, obeying an undefinable urge, she quickly tiptoed away. The worker's unwavering assertion, sounding more like an accusation, set her head into a whirl.

From thereon she slid inexorably towards the clutches of distrust, which became difficult to avoid. Even most insignificant incidents took on a sinister aspect. Stubbing over a stone in her path was deemed an intentional obstruction to inflict injuries on her. A falling roof tile turned her mind towards a dangerous missile hurled by an enemy plotting her demise. But who could it be, since she had no foes, certainly not on the island.

Then she remembered Jaques Gratton, the affable owner of the Crane Hotel. His puzzling assertion, probably a lie in view of her discoveries, not to be in the least acquainted with the estate, seemed portentous. And did Arthur not impute him with gross negligence concerning maintenance of this place? She recalled her husband's promise to explain his baffling accusations against him that evening. This would be a good time to obtain enlightenment, she thought.

After the tradesmen had departed, she went to his study for a chat.

"Remember Arthur, you faulted Jaques Gratton for that loose rail at the balcony," she asked him in her most inveigling manner. "You were going to tell me why."

"Indeed, I did. He is turning out to be quite a nuisance, I can assure you."

"Why, darling?" she asked more surprised than ever.

"It's like this. In my absences, frequent and prolonged before our marriage, he managed the estate for me. For a consideration of course, I might add. Now, all maintenance, improvement and contractual awards came under his bailiwick for many years. Expenses were paid out of a fund set up by me, but dispensed by him.

"When I returned after an extended sojourn from Guyana, just before our marriage, the fund was depleted, yet the estate seemed in disrepair. I am not talking about trifles, but a considerable sum."

"Are you saying he cheated?" she asked astonished over her own words, because that high spirited Montrealer did not in the least strike her as a scoundrel.

He hesitated before answering, looking here and there, but avoiding her disbelieving glances.

"Not necessarily. That can only be ascertained after a full accounting has been submitted."

"Is Mr Gratton refusing to give it?"

"So far, yes."

Lisa now lived in constant fear, which no amount of reasoning could banish. She tried to laugh it off, explain it as elaborate images of inflamed anxieties, yet all endeavours led nowhere, she felt the sword of Damocles hanging over her head. It will fall, she knew, when however, was a matter of conjecture. Strange enough she did not confide this growing dread, at times bordering on terror, to her husband. Despite her suspicions that these mysterious incidents, now almost a daily occurrence, were machinations of someone with evil intentions.

Only after a peculiar frightening experience did she mention her inner turmoil. One of the rails along the high ridge failed, it was another near miss, when it leaned over to her touch. She rued even alluding to it, when she noticed his cavalier attitude. He looked at her with eyes of a wise, albeit condescending Mentor. She evidently appeared to him as a whimsical woman in need of being humoured. He said smilingly:

"Darling, you must not ascribe too much importance to trifling matters which overly stimulated imaginations render significant. But just to calm your nerves, I shall call Da Costa's tradesmen back."

Taken aback, actually shocked, she concealed her anxieties thereon from him.

Next morning on the way to the Castle, she could not help wondering why Arthur should not be affected by these dangerous conditions. Did he lead a charmed life, was he spared by a fate benevolent to him, but pursuing her with inexorable wrath? Hardly, she mused, it is probably just coincidence or luck. But why then laugh at her in view of irrefutable facts, impute her with being whimsical?

She stopped and stamped her foot on the sand: No, someone is either trying to chase her away, or is engineering her demise. With a heavy heart she realised how friendless she was. With the possible exception of Miss Jenny at the library she could trust no one.

Today she intended to talk with her, draw out some information about the area and its inhabitants. She would proceed cautiously of course, inquire unobtrusively about the locals, their habits and predilections. The conversation could drift inadvertently towards the Crane Hotel and its owner, yes, even to the estate and her husband. She was embarrassed to let on how little she knew about Arthur, certainly next to nothing about his past.

Since he showed no willingness to be communicative in that respect, she assumed it contained no unsettling memories or loathsome antecedents that could haunt them. Bygones were of little interest to her, provided they did not deleteriously effect the presence and future. Now however, she regretted her haste to have consummated a union which might well drag her to Golgotha. Without saying it aloud, she realised that nothing would induce her to leave this enchanting place voluntarily.

All carefully rehearsed plans to wangle information from the librarian proved superfluous. Hardly had she finished greeting Miss Jenny, when she was asked:

"Mrs Bowles, was it you that swam out to the reefs yesterday?"

"Yes, I do it quite often," she replied.

Miss Jenny grew ill at ease, she looked disapprovingly at Lisa, then said with a frown:

"You should never swim out that far."

"Oh, don't worry, I'm a good swimmer, besides my husband is with me most of the time," she explained.

Now Miss Jenny grew agitated, her mien acquired a pallor which penetrated far beneath her skin.

"Don't, Mrs Bowles, don't," she gasped.

"Don't what, Miss Jenny?"

"Do not ever go swimming out there with Arthur," she was exhorted.

"But he too is a good swimmer," she declared nonplussed over a relative stranger's solicitude.

"True, quite true," she almost lamented.

"You know my husband by the sound of it," Lisa said in a casual tone, meant to conceal her surprise.

"I do," came a reply dripping with abhorrence.

Lisa could never have imagined that two words, the shortest possible, could be uttered with so much venom. Taken aback she said:

"You don't like him, it appears."

Miss Jenny did not respond immediately, she just viewed her visitor closer, with eyes that expressed suspicion and disbelief. Is she putting me on, her glances seemed to say, does she know all, but only likes to have some sport with me? Visibly garnering resolve she said:

"You are aware of course that there were deaths by drowning near those reefs."

"No, I am not," she was answered.

Now Miss Jenny eyed her with outright incredulity.

"Arthur never told you about it?"

"He did not. I guess he knows nothing about them. Don't forget, he had been absent quite frequently."

Miss Jenny became quite upset, shaking her head continuously, she walked to and fro between bookshelves while muttering disjointedly:

"He does know. More and better than anyone else."

Her irrational behaviour frightened Lisa, for the first time she saw the staid librarian discomposed. Suddenly she confronted Lisa once more with that hunted look. Emphatic, more insistent than before she said:

"Mrs Bowles, I implore you not to swim near those reefs, especially not where I saw you yesterday."

"But according to my husband that is the safest place along the whole stretch," she blurted out defensively.

Miss Jenny stamped her foot and cried out:

"It is the most dangerous spot south of Bathsheba. A treacherous undertow, not easily recognised, can carry even a dolphin far out to sea and leave him there."

"Ah, Miss Jenny, it is only water, true a bit tossed up, but in my estimation fairly harmless, certainly to a proficient swimmer. Carry a dolphin out to sea, indeed, what next. My husband told me that he crossed that channel several times, and there, he is still alive and chipper," Lisa protested.

Then she added:

"I am a better swimmer than you think."

These words, not at all meant as a boast, would ring loud and clear in Miss Jenny's ears later. Yet she never mentioned it to anybody.

Just then several tourists from New York, boisterous as ever, entered the library. Annoyed, Miss Jenny gestured Lisa not to leave, but her signals were not heeded. She left without a further word, because she simply could not stomach these boorish, half-naked people.

On the way back she lingered. Shambling on the water's edge, reluctantly setting one bare foot before the other, her thoughts stayed with the librarian. Miss Jenny was about to reveal what evidently burned the tip of her tongue for some time. Telltale signs pointed towards nothing else. Her probing glances, conflicting facial expressions, as much as sudden, twitching movements, indicated as much.

She sat down to ponder, yet also to avoid seeing her husband just now. Her mind was in a turmoil, which grew more profound as incident after incident passed before her inner eye. They were not easy to explain, even less to banish from her thoughts, pitted by doubts, and corroded by suspicion. One thing, however, was certain: they had lost an innocent meaning. As Arthur's advise for instance, given so forcefully, to swim unhesitatingly in an area which Miss Jenny described as most dangerous, where people apparently drowned before.

Obeying an urge she jumped up. Her mind was set; she would forthwith return to the Castle and continue their conversation. Miss Jenny seemed prepared to reveal what weighed heavily on her thoughts, which once disclosed might shed light on her predicament, or even be of assistance.

She approached with alacrity, albeit cautiously, making certain the librarian was alone. After ascertaining that this was so, she entered resolutely. Miss Jenny hailed her with joyful anticipation. Silently she locked the door, then turned a shingle in the window, so that the 'Closed' inscription faced outside.

"Let us make sure we remain undisturbed this time, especially by mouthy tourists, who are looking for trashy books, and get belligerent when they find none."

Turning to Lisa she pointed to a table surrounded by chairs.

"Please take a seat," Lisa was invited. "I am glad you came back," she added with that gentle, knowing smile.

"I had to," Lisa said quietly.

They sat silent for a few moments, gauging each other's intentions and sentiments. Lisa read in Miss Jenny's eyes sincere sympathy, whereas the librarian sensed mounting concern in hers.

"Miss Jenny, you mentioned that people drowned out on the reefs."

"Yes, exactly at the spot where I had seen you yesterday."

"Who were they, do you know?"

After drawing a hand several times across her brow, Miss Jenny asked a question, or rather made a statement in return.

"Mrs Bowles, you are aware of course that Arthur was married before."

Lisa started surprised, turning red under her tan, and visibly abashed she replied:

"No, I am not."

"I can tell you, he was married at least twice before," she was informed.

"But – but, that is impossible, he – he would have told me."

"Well, a rumour is circulating that he was also married in Guyana, but that is hardly worth mentioning, the fact is he was married twice before, right here in Barbados."

A more genuine expression of amazement, mixed with disbelief, could not have been portrayed by the greatest masters, as appeared on Lisa's face.

"Where are these – – – wives now?" she managed to stutter.

"They died," came a terse answer.

"I see," whispered Lisa crestfallen, still too aghast to say more.

Then gradually the fog lifted, a presentiment, unthinkable at first, forced her to ask:

"How did they die?"

"By drowning."

Lisa was about to ask where, but she instinctively guessed the answer, she just nodded several times. Miss Jenny understood her mute reaction, nevertheless she could not refrain from repeating:

"The currents there are deceiving, I'm told, the waves look inviting, but their undertow is perilous."

Lisa first intended to protest, argue that it could not be a danger spot in view of her husband's assertions and recommendations. However, a terrible realisation paralysed her tongue. Silently she slumped down on her chair, where she sat burying her face in both hands, muttering incomprehensibly. After a while she lifted her head and said:

"Miss Jenny, tell me everything. First, who were these women?"

"Suzanne Gratton was one of them."

"You mean Jaques's sister?"

A nod answered her question, she then asked:

"And the other?"

"Amelia Watteau, my sister," she replied, while tears filled her eyes and slowly rolled down her cheeks.

"Oh my God," Lisa moaned, then reached over and enclosed Miss Jenny's hands warmly with her own.

After the librarian had calmed down, Lisa cleared her throat, then said:

"I will ask you point blank, do you believe Arthur had a hand in their deaths?"

"In my sister's case, yes. Concerning Suzanne I am less certain. I did not know the woman, they came from Guyana, she and her brother that is, some years ago. I must stress how little one knows about neighbours or anybody's personal life in this area. My sister and I were not even cognizant of her marriage to Arthur, till shortly before Amelia's death. It came as a surprise to us, to say the least."

"How can you be so sure about your sister?" Lisa queried almost against her better judgement.

"Amelia and I were very close. Much younger than I, she habitually confided in me more than I wished at times."

"When did she marry Arthur?"

"About a year after Suzanne's death, I believe. I see, that you raise your eyebrows. You are probably wondering how someone can be so casual about a matter so important and close to her."

When Lisa made signs of protest, she raised her hands reassuringly:

"You must remember, that we arrived after Suzanne's death. Amelia, as I said, was quite a bit younger than I, moreover far more impressionable. Arthur dazzled her from the moment they met. Add to his charm the allure of that old, but truly enchanting estate, the rest can easily be imagined."

"I know, I know, " Lisa said under her breath.

"For a while she trod on air and inhaled the ozone of bliss. But soon things began to happen."

Pretending not to notice Lisa's mute, but vigorous acknowledgement, she continued:

"Incident after incident occurred at and around the estate. They seemed innocent enough at first, admittedly queer, but explainable. A falling roof tile from an old house is no rarity, even less a shaky banister or loose stair treads. Just the same Amelia told me about it. As I mentioned, she entrusted me with the most trivial happenings. It was her nature to impart any of her little secrets to me.

"Now I regret my nonchalance, of which I reproach myself almost daily. I shrugged off what I considered idle chatter, closing my ears as it were, when she started talking about them. When she insisted that someone was following her clandestinely, I just laughed and teased her: 'It is probably your own shadow,' I twitted."

"Whom did she suspect?" Lisa interrupted.

"She could not say in the beginning, but later she maintained it was Arthur. Regrettably I paid scant attention to her increasing recitals, which I considered a product of her fertile imagination. I laughingly called her hyperbolic, you know what I mean, having a tendency to overstate frivolous occurrences in order to be heeded. Little did I know," she muttered with unspeakable bitterness.

"Did anything else happen?" Lisa asked.

"It certainly did, but first let me say that Amelia had a stubborn streak in her, moreover she was a plucky, fighting gal that did not readily cut and run. Once challenged, she hardly ever ducked. Nevertheless she got careful and alert, nothing eluded her sharpened senses, she touched everything before pushing or leaning against it. She probed treads before stepping on them, and moved speedily from point to point. Rails began to give, more roofing tiles fell, small rocks seemed to be hurled at her from nowhere. But her circumspection, as much as heightened alacrity saved her from harm."

"So nothing happened."

"Not at the estate. Strange as it may sound, Amelia liked this cat and mouse game, contrary to myself who still believed she was imagining most of it anyway. Then suddenly all these mysterious incidents, life threatening at times according to Amelia, eased and then stopped completely. She relaxed, her life became normal again, soon everything was forgotten. Arthur could now as then be termed the perfect husband and companion. Amelia found him solicitous, understanding and charming. She came close to admitting that I was right, she might have suffered temporarily from paranoia, which she had overcome. We both were happy till that fateful, unforgettable day when she went out swimming with Arthur and never came back. Only he returned, bathed in crocodile tears and lamenting his loss."

"Was there an inquest?"

"To be sure, but I would call it a routine performance of tired old men, muddleheaded, with preconceived ideas and verdict."

"You were a witness I assume?"

"Yes, so was Arthur of course and Gratton, who was only subpoenaed upon my insistence."

"How did it go?"

"I related Amelia's experiences and complaints, which by then appeared no longer fanciful to me. However, they were viewed with jaundiced eyes, and I was looked upon as someone deserving to be mourned."

"What did Arthur say?"

"Ha, you should have seen and heard him. There he stood, a picture of contrition and anguish, forced to carry out a painful duty, which appeared to push him towards the edge of despair. Alone his subdued, sepulchral voice, so well trained, stole my thunder. He made me look like a revengeful schemer. Then he described, what he called his wife's, – his heart bled while having to say it – neurotic attacks, which he was sorry to say seemed to be hereditary. This disclosure, reluctantly made, judging by his facial expressions, was accompanied by a glance in my direction."

"Did the previous mishap, after all a repetition according to you of that one, not incriminate Arthur?"

"Not in the least. Their opinions were prisoners of a narrow horizon, incapable of expansion."

"Could the coroner not see a connection when Jaques Gratton testified, which I assume he did. He surely must have had much to report."

"Ha, that fellow. He is a scoundrel and traitor in my opinion," Miss Jenny said in a voice laden with disdain.

She then observed Lisa sideways for a moment, not sure how much exactly she should say. Deep down she felt her visitor's dilemma, which she judged to be an extension of her sister's. She seemed not only worried, but outright terrorised. Nevertheless she still was Mrs Bowles, who an hour ago tried to defend her husband, a man, who she discovered wielded considerable influence with the authorities in Bridgetown.

"Gratton's deposition exonerated, rather than implicated Arthur," she concluded.

Lisa looked at her puzzled.

"How is that possible in view of what you told me," Lisa wondered.

"What I described is true, I made certain that it came to the surface at the inquest, where I was deemed the devil's advocate. In fact I questioned witnesses myself, the rules allow this, you know. Arthur's presence was established in both cases, he was right there when it happened, but of course only he knew what happened. I alone testified against him, I told them everything I had learned from Amelia, including the fact that he lured her to the very spot where she found her appalling end."

"Did she actually say he enticed her to bathe there?"

"Not in these words, but she wondered out loud, not just once mind you, that he exhorted her never to swim near the reefs except in that one spot. His words were always: 'There you could almost wade across without being endangered.' Amelia told me several times how odd that seemed, considering her own findings. You must remember, she knew that whole stretch from here to the Crane Hotel like the back of her hand. But as mentioned, he always insisted whether alone, or with him, to bathe there and nowhere else."

When she saw Lisa shift uneasy in her chair, she smiled knowingly and said:

"He probably does the same to you."

Lisa did not answer, there was no need, her countenance said it all.

"Tell me Miss Jenny, why would a man, a gentleman from head to toe, decidedly generous, benign and tolerant, want to be rid of his wife after a few short months, in any possible way to boot."

Miss Jenny could hardly hide her satisfaction, for Lisa's words contained a confession that supported her contention about Arthur.

"He is a man who indeed shows overt respect, bordering on reverence towards women, but covertly fears and hates them, and for that reason seeks to harm them wherever possible. But that is only my opinion. In any case Mrs Bowles, I urge you not to go near the reefs again, particularly not with your husband."

Lisa looked down, then up and around. She appeared to be on the verge to let Miss Jenny in on a secret, but decided otherwise; she just said:

"I can tell you again Miss Jenny, I am a better swimmer than you and others think."

On the way back many thoughts raced through Lisa's mind; ideas that made her head glow under the burning Caribbean sun. She was oblivious of the unfailing trade wind, it could not put a damper on her inflamed senses. What she had just learned lent credence to a nagging suspicion, steeped in uncertainty and fear. More than that, it raised the spectre of terror. Where would it end? Her life stood in danger, that much could be no longer denied. An inexorable destiny neared with steady strides. Would she be the third victim of a man afflicted by an ill-fated mania, which a healthy mind was unable to understand?

She shuddered when she espied Arthur up on the grounds, leaning over the parapet rail, pretending not to see her. It was just as well, since she harboured no desire to acknowledge his presence. Far weightier matters occupied her now, vital to her well-being, if not her life. She had to be careful not to go near him with a face still flushed by excitement and darkened by suspicion. The knowledge just gained needed to be effaced from her countenance.

Arthur was sensitive she realised, forever leery of her visits to the Castle, especially today after an unusual long absence. He knew of her whereabouts, no doubt about it, because she had been shadowed again. Today he might forget his tact and ask her some pointed questions, for which she prayed to have ready answers.

Time was ticking away, a solution had to be found before she lay either crippled for life on a bed, or cold as clay in a coffin. Leaving was out of the question, she had no place to go. Talking to Arthur straight from the shoulder, as it were, would be futile. He seemed stuck in a mire that pulled him down deeper by the day. There was no way out, neither he nor she could escape the march of destiny.

But Lisa had an indomitable spirit. Having led a roller coaster life, up and down, down and up, she learned early not to throw in the towel at the first sign of adversity, even if it seemed fatal. Certainly not without a Herculean struggle. According to her she had neither failed as a human being, nor as woman and wife. True, her husband never possessed her wholly, for part of her belonged to this enchanting island and wonderful estate.

But on account of it her spirit soared, enlarging a hitherto more confined horizon. Therefore having just part of it, should count more than completely possessing a narrow one. To be sure, she was a devoted wife, loyal and true, which in her estimation made no difference to him. Whether she be a Griselda or harridan, a man in the clutches of misogyny obeyed orders from powers unknown to her.

Lisa found her husband in his study, absorbed with a book before him. Without preamble she said:

"You know Arthur, from now on I will visit the library in town for books and information."

He looked up surprised but pleased even more. For an instant she thought he would leap up from his chair to embrace her affectionately, but he must have remembered in time his solemn nature, which considered effusiveness tantamount to weakness. With satisfaction written all over his face he said:

"I commend this decision highly. First you have a far greater selection there, second I will not hide the fact that I have great reservations about the librarian over at the Castle. Don't take it from me, ask Jaques Gratton or others, that woman is the most vicious gossip on the island. Her tongue is steeped from tip to root in slander and defamation. I bet she has been trying to denigrate me and others with you."

"Never, Arthur," she lied.

"I am astonished to hear it," he said with raised eyebrows.

"If you don't object, I will go to Bridgetown tomorrow, there are a few books I would like to take out," Lisa changed the subject.

"Shall I go with you?" he inquired.

"I would say better not, it would be too boring for you, because once I get engrossed with a mass of books, I forget time and possibly you too," she countered.

At the library in Bridgetown Lisa made a thorough search through law books and registers. It took a while to find out what she was interested in. When she read excerpts from one and the other, a smile stole around her mouth that did not diminish all the way back. She gave the impression of a woman whose soul had been freed of a great burden. She chuckled between tunes which she hummed to herself. At times she interrupted herself to say:

"And yet there might be a way out."

Arthur too was in high spirits, he almost forgot himself and became playful and demonstrative.

"Darling, did you find what you were looking for?" he greeted her from afar.

"I believe so," she replied.

"Now let's see what the lady is reading," he said mimicking the manners of a stern lecturer.

When he saw her selection, a whistle forced itself from his lips.

"The laws of Barbados," he sang out.

Whether approving or criticising her choice, could not be discerned.

"The lady intends to do some profound reading," he quipped.

"I hope the gentleman does not mind," she replied in a similar vein.

"Not at all, not at all," he confessed, then added:

"Since we are on the subject of law, you probably know that ours are governed by British statutes in practically all respects. I say this for the single reason that our inheritance regulations do vary a bit. In Barbados for instance, without a proper will stating otherwise, the wife is the sole heiress of a husband's estate."

When she tried by means of gestures to silence him, he answered:

"No, no, you should know that, in spite of our law, I have ensured that no one can contest your inheritance. A will to that effect has been deposited with my lawyer, I should say our lawyers, Goldstein and Murlay on Bank Street."

"Come Arthur, let's skip all that and talk about something else," she remonstrated.

"All right," he acquiesced. "What for instance?"

"I would like to go swimming with you more," she intimated.

"Well, that can be arranged easily, just say when and where."

"Down at the reefs again, perhaps even starting in the morning," she suggested.

"I'm game," he confirmed with barely concealed eagerness.

They went to the spot recommended every morning for five days, laughing, frolicking and daring each other out further and further. On the sixth's day Lisa came back alone. No one seemed to notice her frantic flailing and brandishing of arms out there, nor did anyone hear or pay attention to her desperate cries for help. Finally some youngster on the beach took notice of her violent struggle in the waves. Like most natives they were good and intrepid swimmers. One after the other raced into the water and swam towards her.

Lisa in the meantime had succeeded, in spite of her ebbing strength, to free herself from the crunching waves over the reefs. She made but a half-hearted effort to reach the shore. She seemed beside herself, while thrashing and screaming like a woman gone berserk she pointed in the direction of the foaming sea. The youngsters did at first not understand her raving, only when she cried repeatedly:

"My husband, my husband is out there, save him, go save him!" did they catch on.

But they shook their heads in unison, for one and all were aware of the hazards around those reefs. Fishermen only in well built keel boats crossed them daily. Not a single one showed inclinations to enter that raging strip of water, infuriated by obstructions in its path. They practically dragged her out by force, she was fighting them right to the beach, where she was left gasping and panting, still moaning about her husband.

"Your husband is beyond help," she was advised, which indeed was true.

A fisherman found his corpse three days later far out to sea.

The resulting investigation clearly revealed that Arthur Bowles died by misadventure, that is, he drowned at the very spot where his two wives also had found their demise. The water there was described as a veritable Charybdis, which any sane man would avoid.

Lisa's statement was terse and illuminant. Ignoring her entreaties, she deposed, her husband swam far out, beckoning her to follow. Then suddenly a huge wave crashed over their heads, throwing them to and fro for several minutes. That was the last time that she had seen her husband alive. When she got her head above the churned water for a moment, he was gone.

Their combined statements, Lisa's and Miss Jenny's that is, confirmed what the authorities suspected already. A picture of a man was painted, stroke by stroke, who lay in the grip of a strange compulsion. Some uncanny force, like an evil spirit, appeared to lure him to that perilous place. Why his three wives should have shared this urge, remained a mystery. Lisa maintained she simply satisfied her husband's desires, but the police did not believe her. However, she was held entirely blameless of his death, she had done her utmost to save him.

This exoneration, coupled with the deposited will, cleared the path to an unchallenged inheritance. Lisa Hermian, as she called herself again, had finally found her Amhara. Incontestable by fate's vagaries, unassailable by privations, and save from a husband bent on her destruction.

Months passed, spring arrived, prolonging days and shortening nights. Mosquitoes came back, slowly to be sure, but nevertheless making their pesky presence felt. Clouds gathered far out over the restless ocean, which the now more erratic trade wind gradually drove towards land. Soon the rains would start, pleasant days and cool nights were about to disappear for eight months.

Miss Jenny and Lisa gravitated towards each other more and more. They became friendlier almost as quick as the unsteady, turbulent weather neared. Many tea parties were held after sundown amid rustling palms and fragrant jasmine shrubs. They sat out on the patio, feeling save and comfortable with each other, at times lost in reveries as if under a spell. Below them they heard rushing waves breaking over sand, lustrous under a full moon. Out over the reefs the churned sea send droning sounds with the wind, loud enough to hear, not intrusive however to annoy. Slowly, they were at times lulled into a feeling of euphoria.

Miss Jenny never mentioned passed incidents, although she had since made a startling discovery. She had to be careful not to betray her esteem for Lisa, whose cause she would never disclose.

Some weeks ago a tourist from Montreal left a newspaper behind upon departure. 'The Montreal Gazette' it was named, an English daily by the looks of it. Flipping listlessly the first page over, she was struck by a familiar picture. Under the title: 'Where are they now?' she recognised Lisa's picture. A subhead read: 'Lisa the Dolphin.' Reading on, her eyes popped and her ears rang. The short of it was this:

Lisa was reputed to have been at one time one of the best and most daring swimmers. When quite young she earned title upon title in Quebec and elsewhere. Her most astounding feat however, could have been termed the crossing of the Lachine Rapids. In these perilous, if not murderous waters, many a sturdy and seaworthy boat smashed to pieces. But 'Lisa the Dolphin' swam twice across without sustaining a scratch. This performance had neither before, nor after been repeated.

Miss Jenny burned that page instantly, because she remembered Lisa's words:

"I can tell you Miss Jenny, I am a better swimmer than you and others think."

These unforgettable words had taken on a more profound meaning.

# Tolerance Stretched

The green Island of Montserrat rises abruptly out of the sea. It is one of the few remaining gems in that area, unspoiled and pristine. The Wade Inn at the northend of town had over the years become the meeting place for expatriates who, with few exceptions, were North Americans and Britishers. They met every evening for a sundowner, in accordance with a time-honoured habit of colonial days. Hardly had the whistling frogs begun their loud and cheery concert, when up rose filled glasses to everyone's lips. So it went nightly amid the eerie, yet peculiarly soothing cries of these tiny frogs with such mighty voices, till the owner announced the last call at eleven o'clock.

The Wade Inn was ideal for such gatherings, being conveniently situated, besides under the management of an affable publican, whose portliness alone ensured an atmosphere of geniality. The habitual frequenter's manners and speech could be called informal, if not frivolous. They met to exchange ideas, express opinions, swap experiences, or simply to feel the friendly proximity of similar natures. Arguments did at times arise, but they were never too serious or heated, just compliant, more like a co-operative banter. Right or wrong hardly mattered in that obliging circle of public-spirited men and women, whose highest ambition was to be considered regular and nice.

Without exception they prided themselves to be tolerant and open-minded. Colour differences in people, that is racial features to them, did not exist, in the same way as prejudices. They had long ago risen above such base sentiments, all averred. They abhorred them unequivocally.

A casual observer would have been struck by a curious discovery, namely they all resembled each other like menechmians of old. To be sure, they hailed from different, far apart countries, spoke or grew up in various languages and dialects, had skins of contrasting hues, but surprisingly they sounded and appeared to be alike. The fact is, had you met one, you met all.

Now, how could it be possible to find people from opposite corners of the globe, born to different backgrounds, diversely educated acting so similar, and even at first glance look alike? What cemented these divergent individuals into astounding uniform beings? Which secret power engendered in such diverse human beings, who never before met each other, this startling Dromio effect?

"Tolerance," they would have cried; "open-mindedness, a liberal spirit towards the views and actions different from our own," an inquirer would have been advised.

"Freedom of bigotry glues us together," announced Bradley King, a mulatto from New York at every opportunity.

He was glad to have escaped from the clutches of mean-spirited prejudice and destructive hatred, which stymied one like the other, and dragged them all gradually into an abyss of no return. Here, amid an atmosphere of impartiality he felt at home, he cherished the Wade Inn's relaxed ambience, as much as the matey company, whose leader, as it were, he had become.

So it went for years until Andrew Mair arrived, a Scot from Montreal, older than most with a few exceptions, notable the owners and a Dutchman from South Africa. Bradley King, the mulatto from New York, disliked Mair on sight. The lass from Glasgow found him unappealing after a second glimpse, he was certainly not her type. Hinrich Bruges, the Dutchman, turned up his nose and looked the other way. Even Don

Camden made a wry face when he caught sight of the new arrival.

He was a newcomer from England, of a rather staid disposition, which as time passed, underwent a gradual, thorough metamorphosis. Initially taken aback by the group's come-hither attitude, to this day unable to emulate them, he nevertheless found it likeable. His hinted displeasure could have well been nothing but an echo of the other's instant resentment.

None among the regulars felt comfortable in the presence of Andrew Mair. Within two weeks they wished him a thousand miles away. His visits, although irregular, affected them adversely, as much as his absences, which plagued them with a dithering anticipation. Will he show up tonight? their uneasy glances seemed to ask. Glimmering hope, doused by gloomy resignation now ruined their hitherto pleasant evenings. Fun had flown out the window, anxiety stood at the door, their much vaunted tolerance began to crack at the seems.

What engendered that state of alarm, if not panic, in a group of people dedicated to indulgence and open-mindedness? Did Mair reveal a contemptible characteristic, like intemperance in behaviour or speech? Was he perchance overbearing, or, god forbid, prone to prejudice, perhaps even practising racism? None of it; on the contrary, his appearance could be termed a sight for sore eyes. Adorned with colourful clothes, blessed with a confident bearing, furthermore soft and kind in speech, he radiated nothing but cheerful confidence. To be sure, this contrasted somewhat with their own drab, carelessly slipped on raiment, no less than their indifferent deportment.

"But what of it, after all we live in a colony," reminded Camden in good spirit.

True, it irked them, but it caused no dismay. Trouble however was on its way.

One evening as the frogs whistled their little hearts out, and the trade wind rustled through the hibiscus trees, the whole company grew maudlin and disputatious. Something was brewing, the assemblage seemed preoccupied with selfsame thoughts. Mair sensed a gathering of clouds, heavy with discord, which were at the point of bursting over his head. To disperse them he started to sing, which immediately took the bite out of their ugly mood. Heads came up, eyebrows were raised, some out of curiosity, others because they were annoyed by an unwelcome distraction. But all grew silent and listened. Hinrich Bruges stirred first, he started to fidget, visibly irritated he grumbled into his glass:

"What a silly thing to do. What an unmanly demonstration."

Then suddenly his head snapped up, for the young lass from Scotland had chimed in. Bruges looked challenging at each member of the inner circle, before his accusing stare wandered from the girl to Mair. Since this did not daunt the singers, he bounded from his chair and moved towards the exit. It proved too much for his virile temper. Growling he stumbled into the Caribbean night, although not before he turned and barked contemptuously:

"I will not set foot in here again until this harum-scarum is off the island."

That was the beginning of a surprising development, which took a while to manifest itself. The group's much vaunted commitment to liberalism ran into difficulties; its foundations started to tremble as if built on shifting sand. The presence of Andrew Mair became a thorn in their flesh. Not only did his irregular visits at the Wade Inn disturb their equilibrium, but his very presence on the island pitched their lives onto a disquieting path. Try as they may, avoiding him even away from the Wade Inn proved not easy. For Montserrat, lush and serene, is a small place where pretty well all business and social life is concentrated in two or three narrow streets, through which Mair seemed forever to wander.

Bruges, the Dutchman came back, his precipitate promise to shun the place proved too onerous to keep. These nightly, till recently so convivial gatherings, meant more to him than he realised; they had become part of his life. On the first evening after his hasty retreat, he instinctively strolled towards the Inn, but checking his steps he turned around. On the following night he forced himself to stay home. Although tormented by recurring desires to struggle to his feet and hurry down the hill, he managed to use restraint.

Came the third evening when his mind was aflame with irresistible urges to go there. No, chided his pride, yes, cajoled his yearnings. Before he knew it, he was wandering several times past the Inn. Mind you, on the opposite side. On the fourth evening, later than usual, he stepped over the threshold of the small barroom, when he immediately froze to a statue.

Two things caught his eyes at once. Ignoring loud greetings, paying no attention to effusive invitations from all sides to join them at their table, he stood transfixed, like Balaam of old must have done when out of the blue his ass rebuked him for blessing the Israelites. To see Mair sitting in a corner all spruced up, very well, he expected as much, but never the neatly stacked books lining one of the walls. They were not just any old, well-thumbed paperbacks, far from it, volumes upon volumes of ornately bound editions brightened the sparse room.

"What in god's name," he muttered repeatedly, all the while casting reproving glances in every direction, and finally a long one at Mair, whom he rightly suspected to be responsible for this. Most prominently displayed were obviously much used dictionaries and encyclopedias, for reasons that could easily be imagined.

Bruges felt an inexplicable danger arising from these shelves, aiming squarely at the core of their beings. He sensed a portentous shadow encroaching, bearing a puzzling, but nevertheless unwholesome message in its wake. He stood there staring perturbed at these ponderous books, as always around this time three sheets in the wind, swaying lightly, muttering confused. He was a very tall man, once proud and erect, but now shrivelled and flabby. He had some time ago lost all physical stamina and mental alertness. One from dissipation, the other from associating solely with people cut from the same cloth, woven of platitudes and embroidered with spiritlessness.

A harsh realisation seemed to creep towards him, which he tried to stave off with trembling gestures. Bradley King, as much as his other cronies, recognised fate, that inexorable spinner of life's threads, as she was showing her hand. King rose and led his comrade silently to his table.

As usual Mair left early today. In his lively, somewhat abrupt way he wished everybody a pleasant evening and restful night, however, with a peculiar twinkle in his eyes which did not miss its mark. For earlier, when the evening was still young and the mood gay, he managed to rattle them to the core. It sort of crowned an ambience of lingering suspicion and wariness on their part. There was neither love nor liking for Mair in the hearts of this self-appointed elite before, but now their antipathy turned to intense aversion.

Till now they took it for granted that his sojourn on the island would be of short duration. True, nothing but hope supported this assumption, but it served them well. Despite his otherwise communicativeness, he remained tight-lipped concerning reasons for his visit, as much as length of stay. They endured him because of self conferred assurances that their ordeal might end any day, which now, however, proved a fallacy. He had advised them unceremoniously about his plans to remain at least a whole year among them.

What made Andrew Mair so insufferable?

"His haughtiness is insupportable," said Udhal Sindh, a young Trinidadian of East Indian descent, who drank neat rum from the time the whistling frogs fell silent, till after midnight. He was a self-conscious, breezy man, sensitive to slights, imagined or real, furthermore on the lookout for deprecations.

"No, no, it is his pretence at knowledge that rankles," averred Bradley King, the mulatto from New York, who felt upstaged by Mair.

Before this Montrealer showed up, he was cock of the walk in more than one respect. Arbitrator of disputes, oracle in need, Mentor to all members of the group, he rightly considered himself. But look at it now, he said to himself, instead consulting me, they open his confounded dictionaries, probably just to spite me. These dratted books of knowledge took half the fun out of their jovial evenings, till recently so eagerly anticipated by every one. Mair got somewhat involved with every argument, which he invariably won. His books, almost reluctantly opened with a rueful smile, proved him right. Bradley, as much as the others, was not well read. Besides, they followed the tenets of that famous Michigan writer, expert in flippancy, who boasted never to have opened a dictionary in his life.

They became quite intolerant towards Mair, to the extent of sheer persecution. Bruges was the first to stir up the chimera of vengeance, he felt it was not only his due, but expected of him, for he was the oldest and most travelled among the group. First he had a word with Howard Fein, the publican. One fine morning, just before daybreak he paid him a visit.

"Howard, you are going to lose customers, unless that fellow Mair stays away," he announced without a preamble.

Fein knew of course about the many hands that shook the tree of discord, but he paid little attention, since it happened twice before. He knew that crowd well; wishy-washy to the core, glorifying mediocrity, hiding a deep seated feeling of insecurity and inadequacy under a mantle of tolerance, which however went only one way, namely towards the more miserable, whether deemed so or real.

But anyone with lofty desires, plus a mind of their own and brains to boot, was soon awash under a torrent of envy and spite. But of course he was a man of business, with bills to pay and banks to satisfy. After all, this substantial crowd served him well. True, they were loud, a nuisance at times, but they paid cash. Granted, they were his horns of dilemma, on the one hand keeping him and his wife afloat, on the other spinning an insidious cocoon around his ambition and initiative.

"What exactly is he doing that is so annoying?" he asked, knowing beforehand that this question is unanswerable.

Like those two men earlier, he just did not fit in. However, they got the drift quickly and showed enough sense to stay away. Not so this Scot from Montreal, he was obviously carved from hardier wood. He showed no inclination to avoid the place; on the contrary, just a few days ago he made inquiries about one of the guest rooms upstairs, which he considered for a long stay. Bruges gave a few evasive reasons concerning their plight with Mair, plus an insinuation that their crowd would be more than welcome at the 'Quarterdeck'.

"I will leave it with you Howard, for the rest of the week in any case," he advised upon leaving.

Now, Fein was nobody's fool, nor a poltroon. He had an open, strong face, which bespoke obduracy and an adherence to certain convictions, despite acting as host to this crowd of

'Weeping Philosophers'. He had a good mind to tell this Dutchman, so big in body and small in mind, where to go. But he was a businessman first, a man second.

A week later Fein woke up one late night bathed in perspiration. Never in all his years on the island did the nightly whistlers outside sound so shrill and ominous. He shook his wife till she bolted upright.

"What is it Howard?" she cried alarmed.

"I can't help it Berta, I have a premonition that something terrible happened. There, can't you hear it?" he almost shouted.

"Hear what, you silly man."

Indeed what. He opened the door and listened with strained nerves. Nothing was stirring in the building, not a sound could be heard. Only the little frogs outside made a din as if Doomsday had arrived. They are mocking me, he thought, hooting because of my baseless excitement. But nothing could deter him, he had to go down and investigate.

"Come Berta," he urged.

"Whereto?"

"To the bar, woman, to the bar," he almost cried.

"Go back to bed," she said laughing, albeit a bit concerned over his unwonted agitation.

"No, I'm going down to look, alone if you don't want to come."

Shrugging her shoulders, she slipped something over and accompanied him. An unimaginable sight awaited them in the barroom.

"Oh no!" Berta moaned.

"Maniacs, maniacs," Howard could only whisper, while leaning against a wall. All the books, so beautifully bound, collected with great care and considerable expenses, lay strewn in tatters over tables, chairs and on the floor. Howard Fein could only mutter repeatedly:

"I guess their tolerance was stretched over the limit."

# Sangaree

When Franz Ebert received the telegram he did not hesitate a moment. With dextrous hands and nimble feet he started packing. To see his old friend and comrade again filled him with glee. Regrettable that joy was tinged by apprehension, easily understandable upon learning the facts. The communication read:

"I need help, come at once. Ask for Rinaldo at the 'El Rancho' in Petionville, Haiti. Signed: Sangaree."

"I wonder what that Canuck is up to now," he muttered to himself.

Doubting the authenticity of the message was out of the question; the term Sangaree gave it the stamp of genuineness. It was their code chosen long before that memorable night, when they said farewell down at the Montreal harbour.

That was some years ago, but still vividly anchored in Ebert's mind. There they stood, heedless of the rain, embracing and bawling like two motherless children, swearing eternal loyalty and everlasting friendship. Flight seemed the only way out for Baldwin, who feared for his freedom and very life. The law was surely going to pursue him, failing that, Karel Gabari's relentless arm would find its intended aim.

They had known each other since time immemorial; memories, both joyous and sad, bound them inextricably together. Chuckling, Ebert mused:

"Just like him, ask for Rinaldo. He never could pass an opportunity at levity, it always tickled his fancy."

They met as arranged. To say that Ebert was distraught when he laid eyes at his friend, would have made light of the fact that he was shocked. Baldwin looked confused, if not hunted. The neat, handsome man of the past had undergone an unfavourable transformation. Once well groomed and smiling, he delighted the hearts of the ever susceptible Canadiennes. Dishevelled and grouchy he now stood before him. The hand, always so steady, hung limp in his grip. He seemed to be in the throes of advancing old age, prematurely and rapidly.

"Art, are you ill?" he could not refrain from asking.

"Not physically, nothing wrong with my body," came a cryptic answer, which Ebert ignored tactfully.

He quietly followed his friend to a lounge, sensing without fail that a lot of turbid water had flowed under Baldwin's bridges lately. Furthermore that he struggled in its currents, barely staying afloat. A voice from heaven knows where, admonished him to be careful, not to besiege his friend with probing questions. He seemed unwontedly sensitive, on guard as it were, thus bearing witness to a gnawing grief caused perhaps by material want. The ring on Baldwin's hand did not escape Ebert's notice. After they had sat down at a remote table, he alluded to it:

"I see you are married," he remarked in a cheerful tone.

"Was Franz, was."

"Oh, what happened?"

"My wife died a month ago," came a reply in a voice neither indicating regret nor satisfaction, but unmistakable expressing a reluctance to say more.

This was odd, considering the circumstances. After all they had not seen each other for years, nor had been in contact since the day of Baldwin's precipitate departure. Added to that the matter of an urgent message, signifying nothing less than a call of distress, Baldwin's behaviour could indeed be termed peculiar.

However, Ebert pretended not to notice his friend's queer deportment, neither did he show signs of a rising discomfort within himself. How different he looked, transformed into a veritable caricature of his former self, he conjectured. Some great sorrow, stoked by fear which he tried to conceal, appeared to be ploughing him into the ground. Thinking that soon he will learn all about it, Ebert allowed himself to be drawn into reminiscences concerning their mutual past.

"Yes, we spent a turbulent youth together," he agreed, and then added:

"But our later years were in no way less eventful."

"Not only that, but they were crowned by success," confirmed Baldwin.

"Talking about the subject, how are your finances?" inquired Ebert, before he was able to bite his tongue.

Deep furrows appeared on his friend's brow, he heaved a sigh that would have moved a cynic to pity. Edging away from that subject quickly, Ebert remarked:

"I suppose you know about the outstanding warrant for your arrest?"

"I do."

"It is international now."

"I am aware of that also, for which reason I refrained from contacting you."

Ebert then chuckled as if trying to ridicule his next announcement.

"You might also be aware of Karel Gabari's contract on your life."

Baldwin shrugged it off.

"I was not conscious of that, but it does not surprise me. How much?"

"One hundred thousand dollars."

That made Baldwin snicker:

"Thanks for cheering me up, old man, I need it."

Surprising enough that was so, Baldwin visibly took heart.

"Franz, that is beside the point. Canadian law can't reach me here, moreover, that crazed Gabari concerns me no longer. To begin with, he and his whole family lack the funds to even take a bus to Kahnawake, let alone finance a venture two thousand miles away.

"If I were not so dignified, I would roll on the floor laughing. One hundred thousand dollars, indeed. They could not raise one thousand, even if all signed with their blood. The whole clan is bankrupt, besides being in hiding from the underworld."

"That concures pretty well with my assessment," Ebert agreed.

The outburst had a beneficial effect, it raised Baldwin out of the doldrums. The glow of past years returned to his face, his features took on a livelier hue. But shadows remained, they were clear signs of a lingering irresolution. While he visibly groped for a way to overcome this hesitation, Ebert looked discreetly the other way. His eyes fell on the medley outside. A smile lit up his face as he marvelled once again at an inexplicable phenomenon before him.

How such disarray was capable to create an almost soporific ambience, eluded his comprehension. What caused this redeeming feeling? People moved different here, they walked as if they had been borne on their feet. But that in itself hardly accounted for this peculiar impression of being sheltered, he surmised. Perhaps their inevitable smiles and unrestrained laughter were responsible.

But no, he thought, it must be the women who create an atmosphere of bliss. They always touched his soul when he watched them passing along, utterly sure of themselves in a truly feminine way, their colourful dresses lifting and falling in harmony with their swaying hips.

His reveries were interrupted by a deep sigh coming from the depth of Baldwin's breast.

"Franz, I'm in trouble."

"Well, tell me all about it."

"Deep trouble," he moaned.

"That is what I am here for, to help sorting it out. But would it not be more convenient to retire to your house, or wherever you live?"

"Indeed, it would."

After a long drive they arrived at his dwelling. It turned out to be a humble place, maybe dingy would have described the little house in the middle of nowhere more aptly. However, it was exceptionally private. Not a sign of further habitation could be seen, nor could sounds be heard except that of breaking waves whipped up by prevailing trade winds.

Ebert concealed his surprise with admirable composure, not a word of disappointment rolled over his tongue at the sight of this dismal abode. He remembered only too well Baldwin's extensive holdings in Quebec, which he himself converted to cash and gilt-edged securities. Even in retrospect his breast swelled with pride at the thought of his ingeniousness. He had acted with utmost deliberation, leaving nary a trail behind, nor an opportunity to trace a single dollar to its final destination; meaning the hands of Baldwin. It was quite a fortune, surely enough to purchase a tract on the island with all appurtenances. And then some, he would have not been shy to add.

They settled down quickly. Looking at his friend expectantly, Ebert was unable to fend off an impression that Baldwin stood at the threshold of a nervous breakdown. He noticed pictures, resembling carefully prepared portraits, the moment they had entered the bungalow. They showed a woman of character, that in turn bestowed an image of beauty. Not in the dolled-up sense, far from it, yet she possessed a charm that invited the beholder to look again.

"Your wife, I presume?"

"Yes."

"Quite young, as I can see. How did she die?"

"Franz, what I am going to tell you is most astounding, as much as disquieting. Anita, my wife, was exceptionally healthy and active until some weeks prior to her death."

"Did something untoward happen then?"

"Not at all. Certainly nothing outward. But suddenly her demeanour changed, she became fidgety, testy and totally inactive."

"Did she visit a doctor?"

Baldwin's head came up in a single movement.

"She refused, maintaining there was nothing amiss."

"Strange, but not so unusual. How long had you been married?"

"Scarcely six months, blissful months I might add. There was never so much happiness in my life. I had just bought an estate of some renown, over in Caraco at the Atlantic side. The place, all walled in, suited us perfectly. Maintaining the extensive grounds occupied our days, and our evenings were filled out with reading and conversation."

"But then your wife suddenly became ill."

"Not really ill, just notable languid, almost weary of life. In a few short days she was unable to rise to her feet."

"No doctor examined her, you say?"

"Yes, I called one against her will, behind her back, as it were, but he found nothing wrong. Just a lack of spirit, he declared, that would soon pass."

"But her condition did not improve, I take it."

Baldwin snorted contemptuously:

"Within twenty four hours she stopped breathing."

"You called the doctor back of course."

"Not the same one, but two others from Cap Haitien, who were highly recommended."

"What was the cause of death?"

"Heart failure, which was confirmed by a third consultant, whom I had called in."

Baldwin fell silent, which suited Ebert very well. For he was vexed by a rising discomposure, whose source he could not pinpoint. An inexplicable compulsion drew his eyes again and again towards the wall, where one of Anita's pictures hung.

Evening was approaching fast, the western sky took on a spectacular hue. Flaming colours started to drape the blue horizon. Soon the sun would disappear, giving the signal to voices of the night to start their concert. Ebert, however, paid no attention to the striking transition from day to night, he still was unable to free himself from the compulsion to stare at the pictures on the wall. This fixation came to a sudden end, when he heard a most astounding exclamation:

"Franz, I am being persecuted."

For an instant Ebert was undecided whether to laugh or be irritated.

"Man alive, by whom, and why? You said a moment ago that the law's arm can't reach you here, moreover that Gabari's threats are comical at most."

"True enough, but I am not referring to either one."

"Who then?"

That question elicited a long stare, accompanied by groans from a tormented breast.

"Indeed who then, who then. I simply can not guess. But one thing is certain, someone with evil intentions is pursuing me. A sworn, relentless enemy has undertaken to destroy me in body and soul. That is why I called you. I'm at the end of my rope."

For a terrible moment Ebert thought his friend, always so imperturbable and plucky, was going to break down and cry. Wavering between embarrassment and anger, he barely managed to keep his composure. An image of misery sat opposite him, the like he had only seen in a mental institution before. For an instant Baldwin appeared to be sliding into regions where demons reign and the afflicted howl. But he checked himself with super human effort.

"Let me hear all about it," Ebert urged, visibly annoyed by now.

"Be prepared, what I tell you is the gospel truth. About a week after Anita's funeral I went to the bank in order to rearrange my affairs. I had spent little of what you had procured for me through sales of my assets. It was a considerable fortune, as you well know."

"Some must have been eaten up by the acquisition of the estate," Ebert interrupted.

"Only on paper really, since we merely made a down payment of ten percent, and contracted to pay the balance at a later date."

"We, you said?"

"Yes. I mean Anita and myself, we were engaged by then."

"Hm, I find that puzzling, knowing your tenet to avoid interest payments."

"Quite true, but Anita insisted."

To conceal his frown of disapproval, Ebert asked quickly:

"How did it go at the bank?"

"Not good at all, there was nothing left to arrange."

Taken aback, Ebert repeated:

"Nothing left to arrange? But there must have been a small fortune in deposits and bonds."

"Should have been, my friend, should have been. But it all had disappeared."

Ebert jumped up.

"That is beyond the pale of my comprehension."

"Mine too. The account was practically cleaned out, and the safety deposit boxes were completely bare."

"But were you not the only one with signing authority, as much as keys and passwords to satisfy safety requirements?"

"Not really, Anita had full power of attorney concerning all matters, including keys. She was privy to passwords, moreover personally known at the banks."

"You are talking plural numbers."

"Indeed I do. Money and securities were deposited in three major banks."

Anticipating his friend's next observation, Baldwin announced:

"Yes, the same had happened at the other places."

As Ebert expressed silent disapproval about putting one's whole fortune at the mercy of someone else, wife or otherwise, he suddenly realised why these pictures on the walls fascinated him. Anita, Baldwin's wife, looked familiar. He was all but certain that he had met her previously, or at least knew a close blood relative of hers. But his attention was diverted again by his friend's startling announcement:

"I tell you Franz, someone cleaned me out."

Raising both hands to forestall his friend's anticipated reaction, he said:

"Before you jump to conclusions, be advised that everything happened four days after Anita's burial, I am sure of that. It was impossible, besides being fraudulent. I put up quite a row at the bank, till the manager along with his entire retinue showed up. Trying to calm me down proved hopeless, I pounded the counter and stomped the floor until the president appeared."

"What did he have to say?"

"Not much for a while. He started talking in sort of a patois, which I only half understood, prior to asking me plus four or five of his employees, to accompany him to his office."

Interrupting himself, Baldwin cast the strangest look imaginable at Ebert. Amazement mirrored itself in a sea of disgust and unfeigned abhorrence.

"What I learned there curdled my blood and raised my hackle. Hold on to your seat Franz, here it is: All of them maintained that Anita made the withdrawals, moreover it was she who they admitted to the vaults, they insisted."

"So help me, someone must have impersonated your wife," Ebert interjected.

"That is what I said, but the president rejected such frivolous notions, as he called it. He explained indignantly that the signature was authentic. The teller, although recognising Mrs Baldwin, nevertheless called the manager to obtain his approval. After hearty greetings, he knew her of course, Mr Cote, the manager, co-signed the transaction.

"When I asked, in a rebuking manner I fear, whether he did not consider such singularly large withdrawals odd, he viewed me with utmost surprise.

'Why, Mr Baldwin, your wife did most, if not all bank transactions. I had neither cause, nor the right to interfere,' he advised.

'But my wife was buried four days prior to these withdrawals,' I screamed at them."

"What was their reaction?"

"They shrugged their shoulders and smirked, assured that I was either drunk or hallucinating."

"Did you make a police report?"

"Not immediately, I needed time to think. But on the following day I paid them a visit. Armed with all pertinent documents, including the death certificate, funeral confirmation and heaven knows what else, I presented my case."

"You got nowhere, I guess?"

"They were politely bowing me out through the door."

"In other words, they saw you coming."

"By all appearances, yes. The banks must have forewarned them, most likely dropping hints about my shaky mental state.

Who could have blamed them considering the facts. 'Imagine officer, insisting that his wife lay buried in her grave, yet we met her days after. How can such a man be trusted,' they must have said."

It was getting late. Ebert felt tired in body and weary in soul. The sounds of the Caribbean night, eerie but pleasing, hitherto a source of elation to him, now jarred on his nerves. The rhythmical rush of the surf, always worth a strenuous climb and long treks, deemed him like Thor's hammer pounding his bare skull. He hovered between a world of reality and fancy. His physical being grappled with changing images.

His eyes beheld his friend's well-known countenance, his ears recognised the familiar voice, yet his mind refused to admit that it was really Arthur Baldwin sitting beside him. He felt confused and exhausted, ready to fall into bed. Before retiring however he wished to clear up a point or two.

"I am just curious Art, how you can be so sure that your money and securities disappeared after your wife's death. Mind you, I'm not insinuating anything, but to err is always possible."

Baldwin viewed him with a rueful smile, as if to say:

"You too, my good friend."

"As mentioned before, I am absolutely certain of it. Two days before her death Anita insisted, for some whimsical reason, that I should make the rounds at the banks to check our assets. She refused to accept my assertion that an exact tally can be learned from our books. Since it evidently meant so much to her, I completed the errand. All was extant to the last penny. Hearing it, she smiled contentedly. Since that day she never stepped out of the house. Two days later she lay cold in her coffin."

"Art, I believe your wife has crossed my path before. I'm certain to have met her."

"Not likely, she led a totally secluded life."

"Then it must have been close relatives I met."

"Impossible, she was an orphan."

Noticing his friend's exhausted state, Baldwin remarked:

"You go and turn in, I will follow soon."

Horrendous dreams disturbed Ebert's sleep, he felt himself chased by spectres of various ferocity. All were women, everyone resembled Anita Baldwin. They all mocked him mercilessly, cawing in his ears one challenge after another.

"Who am I, scoundrel? Friend of a rattlesnake, you think you know me? Remember quickly before it is too late; he will die, do you hear, die, perish before the end of the month."

His subconscious knew it was a nightmare, yet it all seemed so real. Especially when the pictures on the walls started to grow. They took on enormous proportions till reaching life-size dimensions. A scream, his own, woke him up, for out of each enlarged picture frame stepped a figure. Nerve-racking hee-haws issued from every throat. Each countenance was twisted by hate, and they all pressed towards his bed. That sight was enough to hurl him out of his trance. He bolted upright, which was more a reflex action than a conscious effort.

Bathed in perspiration from head to toe, he stared at the half-open door. Not a sound could be heard in the house, with the exception of the muffled drone caused by the surf down below. The rousing concert, given nightly by tiny whistling frogs, was rapidly subsiding. He knew the signs; the sun had started to climb over the eastern horizon.

As he shook off the last vestiges of a benumbing lethargy, he realised why Anita, Baldwin's wife, looked so familiar. Perhaps he never met her, but he sure knew her bloodline now, which pointed across the mighty Atlantic, all the way to the lively city of Montreal. Her face bore the signs of a Gabari. That come-hither air of Zoltan and Karel Gabari was indelibly imprinted on her countenance.

He should have detected the resemblance at first glance. Alone the sardonic smile, consciously suppressed, yet forever present on the brothers' lips, predicted kinship. Added to it the sloe-eyed features, as much as that characteristic aura of resoluteness, reinforced the assumption that all three sprouted from the same family.

He knew the Gabari brothers fairly well, especially Zoltan, now dead of course, shot by persons unknown, buried under the shadows of his beloved Mont Royal. Karel Gabari blamed

Baldwin for the deed, whom the authorities wanted as a material witness.

More confused than ever Ebert rose, slipped on something light and walked down to the beach. It was a glorious morning, the rapidly climbing sun chased the early morning mist up the mountains, quicker than the eye could follow. The view across the sea became unobstructed for many miles. The sight of dancing water, playfully rising and falling under a friendly sun, inspired him with increasing optimism. A new day lay before him, twelve hours of bright sunshine amid a world of lushness and bloom, a world that never failed to set his heart afire.

Quickening his steps while savouring this new found confidence, he slowly walked into the foaming surf. The tickling, cooling spray cleared his head, his thoughts were no longer obfuscated by higgledy-piggledy images. Baldwin, his friend, had been swindled, that was the short of it. Someone cleverly had purloined his fortune, at the same time perhaps sending his wife to her grave. It could not have been otherwise, yet by what mechanism remained a riddle, a mystery made intriguing by Anita's involvement. She had to be part of the scheme, to what extent he could not even guess. In his views her participation, whether wittingly, or as a mere dupe, led to an early grave.

His reflections were interrupted by Baldwin's appearance. His demeanour spoke volumes. He looked frazzled, as if evil forces had chased him through gauntlets of snarling spectres every hour of the night. In a flash, triggered by pity, he decided against mentioning his suppositions about Anita.

"Let's go for a walk," he suggested.

Strolling along the edge of the surf, neither man spoke for a while. Ebert gained an eerie conviction that Arthur wrestled with himself whether to say more. He meant to draw it out of him, by means honourable or otherwise. After all they were friends, in Aristotle's words a single soul in two bodies. This affair reeked of evil machinations, that not only rendered Baldwin a pauper, but was dragging him onto the threshold of mental ruin. He, Ebert, would not look on while this happened.

"I suppose your property on the other side is still intact," he remarked.

"It is lost," came a curt reply.

Noticing his friend's bewildering expression, he exclaimed:

"Full payment was due two weeks ago. Lacking funds to settle, the property as agreed reverted back to the vendor. The man, French to his fingertips, behaved quite decently, meaning he was willing to wait. But I could not hear of it in view of recent developments. He insisted however, to reimburse part of the down payment as a token of his appreciation. After all, he maintained, we improved the grounds and repaired some of the neglected structures. That allowed me to rent this place and keep myself above water."

"Don't worry about that, I can provide for both of us," assured Ebert.

Baldwin's reaction was a prolonged silence. After several attempts at further conversation, which amounted to nothing more than throat clearing, he finally blurted out:

"I would never live in that house again; never, never!"

Taken aback, Ebert nevertheless nodded sympathetically:

"That is understandable considering the painful memories you must be plagued with. But time will heal these scars, no matter where you live."

"You are misinterpreting my reasons."

"Tell me what they are."

Pointing to a spot higher up on shore, Baldwin suggested:

"Let's find a quieter place away from the surf."

They sat down without saying a further word. Then Baldwin started talking:

"Yesterday I mentioned being persecuted."

"Yes, I remember, by persons unknown apparently."

Baldwin expelled another of his harrowing groans:

"I did not relate everything. About a week after Anita's burial, I was strolling along Fisherman's Wharf in Cap-Haitien, when turning round I caught sight of a figure that froze the blood in my veins."

Chuckling because of his friend's colourful language, Ebert asked:

"Who was it?"

"Anita, I thought for a moment, till I recalled were she was."

Ebert tried to be accommodating by saying:

"That happens sometimes under these circumstances. It is called autosuggestion. What occupies the mind intensely, the eye is liable to perceive. Nothing serious, I can assure you."

"Wait till you hear all. As I turned and stared obtrusively by now, I am afraid, the woman stopped also. When I walked towards her she disappeared behind a building. I searched high and low, but was unable to get another glance of her. Even asking sailors on the quay whether they had seen a woman with such and such features, proved fruitless."

"Pursuing a woman helter-skelter has never been part of your character," Ebert could not refrain from saying.

"The woman was wearing Anita's dress," Baldwin announced.

"You mean one similar."

Shaking his head vehemently, Baldwin repeated:

"Franz, it was her dress. Not only that, it happened to be the one which Anita wore when we laid her inside the coffin."

Dismissing that assertion with a wave of the hand, Ebert objected:

"Coincidence, nothing but coincidence."

"Have it your own way, but what followed right after convinced me otherwise. Arriving back at the estate I found the gate unlocked. Now, that is a sturdy device, forged by craftsmen of the old school. If you ever saw the locks used in Canadian prisons, you have an inkling what I mean. Latch-keys would sooner twist into coils than budge that plunger. But here it was, a touch and the heavy gate creaked in its hinges."

Ebert interjected:

"You had forgotten to lock it, is that it?"

"I had locked it alright, but someone found a way to open it, or of course had a key. My suspicion was aroused. Proceeding with utmost circumspection towards the house, I found the entrance door unlocked as well.

"Thoroughly alarmed by now, I armed myself with a stout cudgel. Remember, this happened not long after my encounter with that mysterious woman dressed in Anita's clothes."

Raising his hands to nip in the bud his friend's anticipated snorts of disbelief, he exclaimed:

"Call me whimsical, neurotic if you like, or roll in the sand laughing over my silliness. When I pushed back the door to the living room my nerves snapped. Was it I who cried? 'Anita, Anita darling, you are back,' or a voice from the outer spheres? I can not even say today."

Seeing his friend's pitiable state, Ebert searched for words of condolence, which evidently were not anticipated. Baldwin continued:

"Standing in that room, I was overcome by a fragrance which I knew so well. The smell of Anita's favoured, never absent perfume filled the air. Its redolence awakened sweet memories in me, but not for long."

"Why, what happened?"

"You have noticed those self-propelling ceiling fans, I take it?"

"More often than once."

"There in the middle of the room, suspended from such a fan, hung Anita's dress, swaying in the afternoon breeze, performing a veritable funeral dance."

"That sounds weird," admitted Ebert; then he added as an afterthought:

"One of the housemaids probably had pinned it up for airing."

"You forget, I had no servants at all, besides it was the dress which that elusive woman wore. In other words Anita's funeral dress."

Noticing his friend's intent to raise objections, Baldwin quickly added:

"That was not the end of it. On the table below the grotesquely swaying garment stood a finely carved fruit bowel, emptied of the fruit I had placed there in the morning, but containing now a ring quite familiar to me."

Here Baldwin paused suggestively, before he announced:

"It was her wedding ring. I see you shrugging your shoulders."

"It was done involuntarily. Just the same, there might be no mystery to it."

"You don't understand Franz, that ring was on her finger when we laid her to rest."

"It all sounds unbelievable," granted Ebert reluctantly.

"But true. What I just related is one of the reasons for my aversion to set foot on those premises again."

"There are more?"

"Indeed, there are. Next morning the main gate stood wide open. Don't say I did not lock it, for surely compelling motives existed to secure the grounds, and more so the house. You can well envision my rampant suspicions, culminating quickly in panic. I dared not leave the premises, for fear of being assailed by a terrible calamity."

"Did you not change the locks?"

"What for, the property stood in the throes of repossession anyway. Moreover, who wants to be a sitting duck for some slinking villain, imbued to the gills with mischief. My cup was full, I cleared out."

"Did anything similar happen since you moved?"

"No, I think my tracks have been lost."

It was an astounding revelation, disturbing and inexplicable. How much to accept at face value, Ebert could not decide. Some facts nevertheless were indisputable. His friend, while undoubtedly rattled, if not shattered, neither sounded nor looked unhinged. Therefore much of what he learned must be accepted as bearing the mark of truth. For one his fortune was gone, irretrievable so it seemed, as much as the estate at Caraco.

In any case bemoaning these deprivations had become secondary to his friend's recovery of peace of mind. A stupendous fraud was committed; by whom, by what means might be unravelled later. The key to the mystery, in Ebert's opinion, lay in the grave across the mountains. Did she infamously betray him, was she in turn ignominiously deceived?

They might never find out, besides for the time being his friend's health, rather his mental equilibrium needed to be addressed first. A change of scenery figured foremost in his mind, moving far away for months, or a year, to a place where people looked and acted like him. But this should not be done in a helter-skelter fashion, but well planed and gradually set in motion. The best time to lay the cornerstone for such a venture was the present, in Ebert's opinion.

"Art, why don't we take it easy for a spell, sort of mosey along without exerting ourselves. Let's forget the past and start living in the present. For one thing I like to read some of the books I noticed on the shelves. This is an ideal place to lose oneself in such pursuits."

Baldwin's interest could not be roused, he sat there brooding, staring vacantly ahead. His friend's sudden burst of enthusiasm did not suit him at all, he felt annoyed. A man steeped in misery, although hated, yet lonely without it, feels disinclined towards distractions. Unhappiness, Ebert knew, demanded constant nurture, attempts at diversion are greeted with indignation. Nevertheless he stuck to his guns, insisting that Baldwin come along to the house. He finally followed him, albeit reluctant and morose. Stretching out a hand he said listlessly:

"There they are."

Then in a tone even more languorous, he added:

"More can be found in those boxes on the floor. They were Anita's, I just brought them along for nostalgia's sake."

"Meaning you don't like them."

"I can't say I do. But you go ahead and look, I'm taking a walk."

Ebert was unable to control an urge, inexplicable to be sure, to race to that corner. He instantly got on his knees and started unpacking. Soon a listener would have heard mutters and exclamations of surprise, as his astonishment turned to amazement. Every title skimmed over dealt with the occult. Loading his arms without delay, he carried a stack of books to a spot outside, where a table surrounded by easy chairs stood under stately palms swaying in the wind.

In no time did he forget where he was, a cloud of mysticism draped its veils, enshrouding him in a world of voodoo and ouanga, that greatest of all enigmas. One book in particular captivated his mind. It was written by an European who had lived, perhaps still lives, among Morne La Salle people. He professed to be fluent in their patois, as much as having had first hand knowledge about practices no white man had ever witnessed before.

He wrote about hair-raising experiences, which even a pragmatic man like himself found difficult to name fact or fancy. True, at times the author narrated in a style that could be called tongue in cheek, but raillery was conspicuously absent.

He came to a section in the book that literally took his breath away. In descriptions, vouched for by sundry people, men and women were rising from their graves, or rather were dug up almost immediately after burial and resuscitated by dubious means. Zombies, these unfortunate creatures were called, walking corpses, brought back to life by sorcery for the purpose of exploitation. That elicited a chuckle of disbelieve from Ebert, and a satisfied grunt upon learning the author's unreserved scepticism.

However, as he reached the end, a short epilogue followed, which engendered a surge of excitement. The author, Timothy Sandor, related how he met professor Marteau at a gala gathering. Real Marteau, a medical doctor, was the foremost scholar in voodooism. Soon they were embroiled in an animated discussion concerning the island's mysteries.

"I read your book Mr Sandor, a most discerning work, I must confess," the professor announced.

"Praise from you professor, is worth more to me than all the glowing reviews the work received."

They were talking for a while about this and that, agreeing with each other mostly, till the subject of Zombies arose.

"You might be off your mark there," Dr Marteau remarked.

"Surely professor, you are not implying that Zombies exist."

"Not really Mr Sandor, certainly not in the form depicted by you."

"I am puzzled, could you be more explicit?"

"You refer to them as walking corpses, which is a misnomer to begin with."

"You mean…?"

"Nothing of the sort exists, Mr Sandor."

"In other words, if true what I have been told, these people were in a state of suspended animation."

"Something similar, yes."

"But how would someone know that, they certainly can not dig up all the graves in the country," Sandor expostulated.

"There is no need for it, if one creates such trances in the first place."

"What you are saying professor, someone with ulterior motives, versed in ouanga, induces a lethargic coma in a person, digs him up right after burial, revives him again and exploits him thereafter. Impossible, I say, preposterous. Do you really believe it?"

It appears that professor Marteau made no reply, he just shrugged his shoulders and smiled.

Seized by a growing excitement, Ebert read and reread that part, for he sensed a connection between the professor's insinuation and Baldwin's plight. Anita's evident fixation with voodoo and the occult sealed their fate. She proved an easy mark for unscrupulous operators.

Did Arthur not express his amazement at his wife's sudden languor accompanied by a morbid secretiveness? He distinctly recalled his words:

"I will never understand Anita's drastic change. Several weeks prior to her death she became morose, defensive and outright belligerent. That was before signs of a lingering illness appeared. Her frequent absences surprised me the most. These excursions, usually lasting all day, were never alluded to, neither by her nor on my part, since she would fly at me like a wildcat at the mere hint at it."

That is what must have happened, Ebert surmised. Anita was doped and duped, heaven only knows by what means, and afterwards sent to her grave. A worthy theory indeed, yet marred by that disquieting resemblance to the Gabaris. Jumping up he defiantly cried into the wind:

"I know it, she is a Gabari."

Then an idea struck him. Anita's body must be disinterred, an autopsy had to be performed. But reality dampened his enthusiasm quickly. To begin with, Arthur's signature was required, and even then the authorities might balk. Compelling evidence of a crime committed had to be substantially proved, a feat that looked like a Herculean chore to Ebert.

Baldwin came in sight. Shuffling along, his head bowed, it seemed to take him forever to reach the house. He looked dispirited, like someone having reached a bottomless pit, from which he, Ebert, would free him. It won't be easy he realised, but certainly worth the effort.

First the peculiar circumstances of his wife's death needed attention. It was necessary to wean his friend from the notion that he had married a loyal Zuleika, whom he just happened to meet, and after a short courtship was lucky to gain her hand. How easy it is for a man living in apprehension to be deceived, Ebert thought. The truth would come as a blow to his upright friend, in all likelihood it would shatter his concept of probity.

"Art, where is Anita buried?" he asked Baldwin, who in the meantime had reached the house.

"In a private cemetery in the Morne La Salle area."

Ebert started as if stung to the bone.

"Why so remote?" he exclaimed.

"Anita asked to be interred there. She left a letter behind, where among other requests this received particular emphasis. And why not? It is a beautiful place, high up in the mountains, private and cool."

Cool, why cool, Ebert meant to ask, but he bit his tongue in time.

"I take it that access is not granted to everybody."

"No. The grounds are walled in, moreover well guarded day and night."

Then looking at Ebert sidewise, he inquired:

"Why the interest, did you want to visit her grave?"

Ebert gave no reply. His thoughts took a hike up the mountains behind them, where Timothy Sandor, the author, might still be found. He decided to search for him, starting out in the morning. The truth could well be hidden there within the shadows of those lofty peaks.

When Baldwin mumbled something about needing a rest, it suited Ebert fine. It offered an opportunity to put his thoughts in order. Baldwin's notion, unwholesome to say the least of Anita's innocence, defied all logic. In his opinion it was nothing but woolgathering at its best. No doubt she wove, or helped weave a web, which became her iron shroud. Such assumptions were more than justified by irrefutable facts. Yet the slightest allusion to it triggered an outbreak of rebuttal from Baldwin. Blind loyalty it deemed Ebert, had dulled his friend's senses.

However, brooding about it would achive nothing; intrepid action was preferable, haste expedient. Disinterment, although informative no doubt, appeared to be a pipe dream. Obtaining Baldwin's consent, along with the authority's permission could prove impossible. After all, two separate death certificates, issued by reputable doctors, clearly stated that she died of natural causes. Heart failure they called it, conveniently forgetting the woman's youth and sturdy health.

Removing her remains on the sly stood not a ghost of a chance, in view of what he had just learned. Thus pulling up stakes and trying to forget everything, remained the only alternative. First, however, he wanted to have a word with Sandor and Dr Marteau.

That was easier said than done, in the case of Sandor for sure. Finding professor Marteau was not much of a chore, every loafer in town seemed to have heard his name. Gaining access to the scholar proved to be more cumbersome, for the professor showed no inclination to meet a stranger.

A ruse ultimately opened his doors. Ebert let him know that he was calling on behalf of Timothy Sandor, the famous author. That fib soon brought the doctor out of his chambers.

"I will not say that I am pleased to meet you, Mr Ebert, but since you are here, do come in," Dr Marteau said, stretching out his hand.

After a few niceties were exchanged, the professor wanted to know:

"How is Mr Sandor?"

"Professor, I have a confession to make. The author's name was only used to gain admittance. The fact is, although I read two of his books, I never met the man."

He scanned the doctor's face for signs of annoyance, but detected none. On the contrary, a broad smile illuminated his dark countenance, as if something had just tickled his fancy. Growing visibly relaxed he chuckled:

"What are you after, Mr Ebert?"

"Forgive me, professor, for being unceremonious, so here it is: In an epilogue of Sandor's book he mentions a conversation between him and you, highly revealing and intriguing, I thought."

"Refresh my memory Mr Ebert, remember I do say many things."

Moving quickly, Ebert produced a book from his briefcase, which he opened with a sweep of the hand at a spot previously marked. It revived the professor's recollection.

"Yes, yes, I do remember the exchange. Which part excited your interest?" he asked.

"Your cryptic remark concerning death-like comas, induced by mysterious means, from which a person can be revived at will."

"First a question, Mr Ebert, why are you interested in this?"

When Ebert hemmed in obvious embarrassment, Dr Marteau continued:

"Be advised that I entertain no wish to be a harbinger of sensationalism, nor do I want to serve as a medium of someone's quest for notoriety."

'Take that rebuke and leave,' the doctor's mien seemed to say, for he assumed that opposite him sat another satiety plagued idler, seeking cheap thrills.

Ebert shook his head convincingly, he started to explain the reason for his visit. Names were omitted, but nothing else. The professor listened with rising interest, which soon changed to visible concern. At the end Ebert accused Anita roundly of complicity, hoping to elicit a revealing comment from his host.

"I am almost certain she had a hand in it, still has for that matter, considering recent developments. But how did she managed it?" Ebert wondered.

His inquiring glance had little effect, the professor did not even raise an eyebrow, much less made a reply. He walked to a shelf lined with books. Ebert could hear him muttering about never finding what you are looking for, but just the same he soon returned with a well-bound volume in his hands.

"You read French, I suppose?" he asked.

"With ease," Ebert replied.

Handing him the book the professor said:

"This is the Criminal Code of Haiti, look at article 249."

It was a short paragraph, containing an amazing interdict that removed the scales from Ebert's eyes. It read: 'Giving a person substances, although not causing actual death, which produces a lethargic coma, qualifies as attempted murder. If such a person has been buried, the charge will be murder, regardless what happens after.'

"Professor, what does it mean?" Ebert gasped.

There followed another of Dr Marteau's cryptic remarks:

"That, my dear sir, is for you to decide."

The tone of finality was not lost on Ebert, he took his leave. Before he reached the door, the professor asked:

"Did you ever read Mr Sandor's pamphlet 'The Cemetery of Empty Graves'?"

Turning around Ebert replied:

"Is it of interest?"

"It might be. You see, Mr Ebert, he is writing about the private graveyard up in the mountains of the Morne La Salle area."

Stunned, Ebert walked out. In the shade of a blooming jasmine bush he sat down to collect his thoughts. A burning question surged through his mind. Was Anita, or whatever her name should be, still alive? Did she, or someone conspiring with her, indeed persecute his friend? If so, to what purpose.

Images of evil unleashed hovered before his eyes. Notions of snarling ghouls made him shudder in the tropical heat. The sweet scent all around failed to soothe his chaotic feelings. He no longer doubted the existence of a fiendish plot, yet the motive continued to elude his grasp. Was greed the driving force, or vengeance?

Judging by the risk that woman took pointed to the latter. Unspeakable horror crept through Ebert's veins at the thought of someone consenting to be buried alive, as it were, just to pay back a man who never wronged her, but rather treated her with loving kindness. How twisted such a mind must be to ever consider that step.

Her demonic plan evidently bore partial fruit; his friend's entire fortune fell into her hands. Yet the final stroke was still to come. Rest assured, Ebert mumbled to himself, the robbery was only setting the stage. It was meant to soften him up for the slow journey into a living hell. Insanity, nothing less was planned. A world of unceasing terror, where the weight of a feather crushes one like a ton of iron, had been chosen for him. He decided to hurry back.

When he arrived at the house there was no sign of Baldwin. He must be inside, taking a rest, Ebert told himself. He paid no heed to the wind stirring in the bushes and trees, nor did he pay attention to the splashing waves below. His concentration was focused on the house and the man presumable inside. His resolve had reached a point of no return. Baldwin had to leave the island, today, if possible.

Expecting the door to be locked, he was about to call out, when he noticed it moving on its hinges. That seemed odd, for as of late his friend barricaded doors and windows, whether he was inside or on the grounds.

The moment Ebert stepped across the threshold, he grew uneasy. A peculiar scent lay in the air. His nostrils were tickled by a seductive fragrance reminiscent of beautiful women in evening dresses, flirting with men of wealth and stature.

Then he remembered Baldwin's account of the swinging dress amid whiffs of perfume. It hastened his heartbeat and quickened his steps.

"Arthur, Arthur," he called out.

Not a sound was heard in the house. As he walked on, the smell became stronger, but also different, more acrid, as if incense mixed with a pungent substance had been burned.

In the back room he found Baldwin slumped in a chair, sleeping soundly it seemed. But why did he hold a pistol in his hands?

"Look at the hero," Ebert chuckled, "he is scared of his own shadow."

Then he became aware of the fumes trying to dissipate through every crack. The pistol had been fired recently, Ebert surmised, but why, and at whom?

These questions found a ready answer when he noticed the prone figure on the floor, wrapped in a fragrant vapour. Who it was deemed him no mystery, but he stooped down to investigate anyway.

"Anita Baldwin, the hellcat of Morne La Salle," he expelled through his teeth.

Groans from the direction of the chair diverted Ebert's attention. Baldwin stirred into live. His countenance, distorted by terror, with distended eyes he gasped:

"What have I done, God forgive me, I have shot my wife."

Ebert managed to calm him down enough to be made privy of the whole episode.

Baldwin was resting in his favoured chair, where he must have fallen asleep. Soon nightmarish dreams disturbed his slumber, dreams that gradually drifted into the realm of reality.

"A familiar aroma began to excite my senses, which grew stronger by leaps and bounds. Trying to rouse myself proved difficult. Nevertheless I must have managed somehow to lay hold of the pistol beside me. Although still in a stupor, I distinctly realised who was in the room. True, one side of me refused to accept such notions, since I remembered to have secured the house, yet the other, more prosaic, pronounced it a fact.

"As more than one wild idea raced through my mind, still veiled by the fog of sleep, I heard a report, followed by screams and a loud thud. Realising what I had done, I fell into a deep swoon. That is how you found me."

Then he started moaning again.

"Franz, what will happen? I killed my wife, I did not mean to, but yet I killed her."

Ebert gave no immediate answer, yet his face, dark a moment ago, brightened visibly. He smiled, then chuckled and finally broke out in peals of laughter.

"Art, you have killed nobody," he assured him.

Bewildered Baldwin pointed at the figure on the floor.

"You are talking nonsense, there she lies, dead as a door nail."

Ebert could not refrain from smirking:

"Maybe so, but tell me, how do you kill someone that is lying in her grave long enough to be no more, explain that to me."

"I don't understand you."

"Of course you do. Destiny has spoken, you are free again. Gird yourself and onwards we go."

"But – but, what about her, what shall we do with her?"

When Baldwin noticed his friend's suggestive glances from the prone woman on the floor to the grounds outside, he understood. A smile, the first in weeks, lit up his face.

# The Signal

Lucien Menard was strolling down busy Ste. Catherine Street in Montreal. It was the first beautiful spring day of the season. Somewhat late in arriving, but nevertheless welcome. As always he lingered around a band of musicians playing at a street corner. The wonderful, melodious sounds never failed to captivate him. These youngsters played, how should he describe it, well, like Quebecois. He had wandered right across Canada, from Cape Breton to the Charlottes, where every major city boasts street buskers, but none could compare with the ones in Quebec. True, some places like Victoria in the west, and a few eastern towns merited closer mention, however, equals they were not. No amount of facial contortions, loudness, or foot-tapping, could hide their lack of earnest endeavour so characteristic of these young French Canadians.

He was about to surrender himself to the lovely sounds, a Mozart piece he knew, when his attention was diverted by newspapers hung up around a nearby kiosk. – Terrible tragedy at the Forum – the headlines said. Menard generally paid scant attention to newspapers, which he rarely read, be they French or English. In this case, however, his attention was caught by a picture prominently displayed. Walking a few steps closer, he stopped in his tracks, for he recognised the man in the picture. No doubt about it, it was Harpal Sindh, the renowned trainer of ferocious tigers. His performances in every major city drew crowds, each presentation could expect to be fully booked in advance. What Sindh had accomplished with Simun the tiger, eclipsed any other wild animal act.

"History will bear me out Mr Menard," he was told at the docks of Bombay, where they stood one afternoon in sweltering summer heat, that in Menard's opinion must have made hell a place of fun.

"But tigers have been tamed before, and for all I know this might still be done," Menard countered.

"Quite true sir; Marco Polo mentioned that the Khan of Tatary had trained them for hunting."

"So, where does that leave your claim to fame?"

"Aha, I am glad you asked, it is this: My tigers are taught to do tricks, moreover astounding ones, if I may add."

"You mean stunts like in a circus?"

"Exactly. I am giving shows at the Gateway. Here are some free tickets, don't miss it, you will not be disappointed."

Yes, he remembered Sindh and his tigers well. They stayed at the same hotel where they spent many pleasant hours together at the lounge. Besides, he visited not one, but three unforgettable performances at the Gateway. Sindh also introduced him to his nephew Harminder and his leading actor Simun the tiger, whose sight sent flashes of terror through him. How anyone wanted to go near that sneaky looking beast, even while behind sturdy bars, exceeded Menard's comprehension.

History did bear Sindh out, he became not only famous, but wealthy too. From time to time Menard read about his amazing feats and successes. But now he was dead, mangled by his coddled tiger Simun.

To say Menard was saddened by Sindh's demise would have been sanctimonious, however, his curiosity was aroused. For he recalled the unstinting authority that Sindh exerted over the huge and wild animal. Simun always obeyed with a surprising pliancy and alacrity, bordering on amazement. Every exercise from handsprings to somersaults were promptly carried out. Even gruesome snarls and friendly gestures could that astounding handler elicit from the enormous cat, which appeared to be awed by Sindh.

So what happened? How could an animal, ferocious to be sure, but licking his trainer's hands, as it were, suddenly attack that same man and maul him to death in front of a terrified crowd, for no visible reason to boot.

Menard decided to investigate. Buying a few newspapers, English and French, he went home to read. What he learned shocked and bewildered him. The short of it was this:

The show took its expected course, the tiger behaved and performed admirably, he complied with every instruction expressed or indicated. The much publicised mock attacks had just commenced when things went awry. There was Sindh grappling with the tiger who retreated while snarling, yet seemingly frightened. It was a well-coached display that thrilled and scared simultaneously.

Tussling along they reached the ring's perimeter when Sindh froze in his tracks. With dilated eyes he stared ahead, while mopping his brow and starting to mutter refraining words that nobody rightly understood. In the next instant all hell broke loose. Uttering a piercing scream, as if wrung from a soul in anguish, he turned and fled towards the exit, which he never reached. The tiger was quicker, gnarling savagely he pounced on his master who with one final shriek succumbed to the agitated beast. What followed defied description.

As expected the newspapers had a field day; they were quoting freely, surmising wantonly, and exaggerating true to form. Sensational statements by witnesses, contradictory from start to finish filled their pages. Something, however, manifested itself clearly, Sindh's behaviour resisted all logic.

Who would expect a veteran handler to panic, particularly in the absence of any visible reasons? What induced an intrepid man of his experience to flee in terror from non existent dangers, knowing full well the disastrous consequences. His repeated utterances prior to turning and running afforded no clues; they sounded to some like 'armender,' to others more like 'horrender.' They made no sense to anyone, thus the papers did not expound on them. Sindh was a foreigner, so heaven knows what he was trying to say, they surmised.

Menard too was baffled by Sindh's singular behaviour. He tried to collect his thoughts, which were on the verge of growing tumultuous. He needed time to think. It seemed odd that Harminder, the nephew's name, did not appear anywhere in the newspaper reports. He surely must have been present as always, sitting just outside at his usual spot. For he remembered well Sindh's bizarre fixation with his nephew's imagined influence on the tiger, believed to be transcendental by the uncle, who deemed Harminder essential to his show. But why was not a word said about him?

Menard's mind wandered across two oceans to far away Bombay, a city he could never forget. Not so much on account of Sindh and his tiger, but more so because of an experience which left him shaken for weeks. He met Sindh shortly after returning from the Towers of Silence on Malabar Hill, whose significance is well known.

These towers, five in all, completely walled in, serve the Parsees as funeral sites. They neither bury nor cremate their dead, but lay them on gratings on top of the towers to be devoured by vultures. The sight of these abhorrent, bare necked birds of prey sitting around the parapet walls, waiting silently to be fed, haunted him many a night. Closing his eyes he could see them soar above their newly arrived feast, and hear their ghastly swish while swooping down.

Sindh and Menard became quite friendly during his stay in Bombay. Despite a vastly different background, even a divergence in race and language, they instantly felt kindly towards each other. They spent many an hour in the comfortable exotic lounge of their hotel, appreciating each other's company, talking unconstraint about many subjects. No, Menard could never erase from his memory that wonderful spot above the shimmering water of Back Bay, where the view is unobstructed, and the atmosphere unexcelled.

Their last evening together entered his mind, it might have engendered an elation never felt before. The next day Sindh and his retinue planned to be on their way to Europe, where an extensive tour was scheduled.

Sindh became expansive, wine seemed to loosen his tongue, along with Menard's sympathetic air it helped to overcome an inborn reticence. Noticing Menard's repeated glances in the same direction, Sindh asked:

"Would I be overly inquisitive if I inquired what fascinates you across the bay? The Towers of Silence perhaps?"

Menard's face took on a darker hue, and lowering his head, which the next instant was raised again, he said:

"They repel rather than attract."

He told Sindh about his recent visit to that sinister place, which in his words filled him with revulsion ever since. Sindh laughed:

"How peculiar the white races are, so needlessly cruel in many ways, yet invariably squeamish in matters concerned with nature."

Menard did not expound on it, he quickly steered their conversation towards more agreeable subjects.

Soon they were in the midst of discussions about the subliminal, leading in no time to fatalism, which Sindh defended as if driven by an ulterior motive.

"You mean to tell me that life's course is predestined?" Menard asked incredulously.

"I am certain of it," insisted Sindh.

"That, sir, is nothing but superstition, an excuse for people in the clutches of defeat," averred Menard passionately.

Taken aback by the Quebecois' sudden vehemence, Sindh argued no further, he just smiled. Though embodied with an oriental soul, he nevertheless understood the prosaic mind of the West. While observing Menard obliquely, he leaned forward and wanted to know:

"You rebut fatalism, so be it. What is your attitude towards the supernatural?"

Menard recalled a growing impression that Sindh was leading up to something which had preoccupied him all evening. Shaking his head, he answered:

"It is hogwash in my opinion, I am convinced that all phenomena have logical explanations. Believing in magic or miracles? not I."

Sindh looked at him like a father glances at an errand, but beloved son. Tilting his head, he said:

"You have met my nephew Harminder, I believe?"

"Why certainly, you introduced him to me," followed a somewhat perplexed acknowledgement.

Sindh then adopted an insinuating air:

"What do you think of the lad?"

"He appears to be a normal youngster."

"So you have not noticed anything peculiar about him?"

"Not that I could say. He does strike me as a bit too serious for his age, but apart from that I find him average."

Sindh eyed him with pursed lips and knitted brow. His countenance took on an expression of doubt, as if irresolute whether to go on or talk about something else, when Menard, more to say something than anything else, added:

"Now, Mr Sindh, surely your nephew is not endowed with anything supernatural."

Sindh began to act mysteriously, looking around like a conspirator, then bending forward he practically whispered:

"You are the first man I am going to tell this, and you will also be the last. Harminder exerts an amazing influence over Simun."

"You mean the tiger? Well that does happen sometimes; however, I don't see the connection between that and the supernatural."

"Yet there is. Harminder wields total power over my tiger, it is uncanny, I seriously believe they possess one and the same soul."

Menard remembered how he was unable to suppress a guffaw, which probably offended Sindh, although he showed no sign of it.

"Let me assure you that in Harminder's absence Simun is completely unmanageable. In fact I would not dream stepping in the ring with him, unless my nephew is present."

Thinking his companion had enjoyed a glass or two too many, Menard expostulated:

"Harminder was not even in the ring when I attended your shows, so how could he be essential to the performance as you seem to imply."

"He never is inside the ring, but always, I repeat always, sits outside in a conspicuous place."

"You are not really serious," Menard uttered while shaking his head.

"Indeed I am. Let me explain and perhaps you will understand."

Menard, undecided at first whether to dismiss Sindh's allegations as outright hocus-pocus, determined otherwise. Reclining deeper in his chair, he signalled his readiness to listen.

Annoyed as he was then, he soon thanked his stars for humouring Sindh on that memorable evening amid eerie sounds and strange sights. For the day arrived when recent events, so dreadful and inexplicable unravelled before his eyes.

Information imparted on that sweltering night ultimately gave the only clue to a terrible accident. Sindh's conviction about his nephew's suzerainty over Simun was the key to the puzzle in Menard's mind, whose ears were still tingling from that fantastic revelation. Even today, far removed from that awe inspiring environment, he had difficulty to digest it all.

Sitting here two years later, he could almost feel the sultry air rising from the tranquil water, adding to his discomfort while listening to Sindh's grotesque tale. Every detail came back to him, from the ghostly Towers of Silence looming high and sinister up on the hill, to ships moving in and out of the harbour, ablaze with lights whose rays danced over the water. Sindh began to relate:

"I bought Simun when he was very small, with the intention of training him for the circus. Even at a tender age he proved to be a little devil, hissing and spewing like a volcano prior to eruption. I showed extreme patience and indulgence with that recalcitrant rascal, who rapidly grew into a menacing rapscallion.

"When after many extended tribulations that hell-bent ball of fury still rebuffed every attempt at domestication, I gradually saw my life's ambition sustaining a crushing defeat. It dawned on me that no chance existed to make that tiger perform even the crudest tricks. I grew discouraged, then resentful, and finally hateful. Of course my aversion only exacerbated the situation, it made me overly critical, and Simun even more rebellious."

When Sindh paused to catch his breath, Menard felt obliged to say something:

"But the tiger is now performing admirably."

"Quite true; here is why. One day after a particular strenuous session with that ornery beast, I was ready to give up, even to shoot him, when suddenly, out of the blue that fiend changed his ways. Gnarling a moment ago threateningly at me, he now obeyed every command willingly. Was I surprised at the miraculous transformation? No doubt I was.

"Simun from thereon behaved like an ingratiating dog, the demon of minutes ago turned into a friendly, tractable big cat. My head was in a whirl. How could a Nemean brute transmute itself into an obliging medium, I thought, while Simun pranced and danced to my bidding."

"I guess the tiger finally got to his senses," interposed Menard.

"I would have thought so too, had it happened gradually. But this sudden metamorphosis, as it were, bordered on a miracle, which unravelled itself momentarily. Lifting my head, I saw my nephew Harminder standing outside the ring. I was surprised to see him, although not overjoyed, since we considered him a black sheep in the family. He appeared changed to me. True, we had not seen each other for quite a while, but still his looks, perhaps aura would be a more apt description, seemed remarkably transformed."

Menard vividly recalled that moment. Even now, more than two years later, sitting in his Montreal flat, upon closing his eyes he could see Sindh's enraptured face drawing closer, acquiring an apocalyptic expression as he revealed the unthinkable:

"As I looked from Harminder to Simun, an overpowering realisation gripped me. I can not explain it, yet it took my breath away. Before my eyes Harminder and Simun turned into similar shapes, neither human nor animal; I was in a daze. Was it a vision sent by the divine triad, or had I lost my senses? When I recalled the miraculous change in Simun, by Siva, I understood. It was an augury pronouncing my terrible fate at Simun's claws unless Harminder stays nearby. There and then I vowed never to step in the ring again with Simun in my nephew's absence."

It was a fanciful tale, grotesque to the last word, yet firmly believed by Sindh, an experienced and greatly admired handler.

All came back to Menard, all but the sense of it. However, in view of the recent event, the thought obtruded itself that Sindh's hypothesis warranted closer consideration, for it might furnish a clue to the mystery. Intuition told Menard of a connection between the handler's outlandish notion and his cruel demise. All pondering and rumination led nowhere.
One sentence, however, gained significance in his mind:

"You are the first and last to learn my secret," Sindh had announced that evening in Bombay.

Viewing Sindh's fear as a mere chimera, which it might well have been, counted little. His inexplicable headlong flight mattered, it triggered the tiger's bloodthirstiness. The question therefore was: Why did he run?

Menard decided to visit the forum in the hope to meet Harminder, or at least to become privy to more information. The newspapers were of little help, they contained sensationalism but no substance.

When he arrived at Montreal's symbol of hockey power, there was not much going on. With the exception of two policemen, plus a few never failing reporters, only regular day staff seemed to be milling about. Then his eyes caught Harminder standing among a small group of men at the far entrance. He sure was glad to see him, for by now he hungered for more news. Hurrying towards him, he called from afar:

"Harminder, Harminder."

Getting closer, however, he found out to his surprise that it was not him, but someone resembling the youngster he had met some years ago. Lowering his proffered hand, Menard blurted out:

"Forgive my impulsiveness, I thought you were someone else."

The young man addressed thus evidently harboured no desire to become acquainted, he quickly slunk away. Nevertheless Menard introduced himself to the others, who were all elderly East Indians. When he told them about his acquaintance with Sindh and his act, one man in particular grew quite interested.

"So you know Harminder, as I understand?" he was asked.

"Yes, I met him, his uncle, and Simun the tiger some years back in Bombay," Menard explained, then added:

"As you probably noticed I mistook the young man with you for Harminder."

The man chuckled, then said:

"Small wonder, they are first cousins."

"Where is Harminder? I like to meet him and express my condolences. A terrible mishap, I must say, moreover quite inexplicable."

"Indeed that is so," acknowledged the stranger not exactly effusively.

Menard could not help thinking that the man eyed him with more than a tinge of suspicion. His inquiry about Harminder's whereabouts received no attention, it seemed to have entered one ear and exited through the other.

"I am Indi Jadh, a friend of Harpal Sindh," he introduced himself reluctantly. Then followed another oblique glance.

"How well do you know Harminder Saan?" he wanted to know.

"Not well. As I mentioned we stayed at the same hotel in Bombay, where we met daily," Menard advised.

Jadh nodded while commenting:

"Well, he is a rich boy now."

"Oh, he is?" Menard remarked not in the least interested.

Jadh's glance became more scrutinizing, it made Menard feel quite uncomfortable, for which reason he felt obliged to say more.

"How did he become rich?" he asked, while wondering at the other's enigmatic smile.

"He inherited his uncle's fortune, that is how," Jadh said.

"Good for him, but where is he?"

"Probably back in India by now, securing his legacy," Jadh observed, shrugging his shoulders in a deprecating way.

Before Menard could say another word he was hurrying to catch up with the others.

Annoyed over their cavalier treatment, he looked around for more amenable faces, when someone called:

"Sir, sir, just a moment please."

Turning towards the caller he spotted an older man approaching rapidly. Judging by his manners he appeared to be a reporter, intent to have a word with him. Indeed he did.

What shortly after ensued strengthened his resolve to investigate, for another piece to the puzzle came to his knowledge. Even before he talked to the reporter, he sensed that the key to the solution of this baffling occurrence lay in his hands.

By now the reporter, poised with pen and paper, stood before him. Pulling out a calling card he announced:

"I am with La Presse, could I ask you a question?"

"Yes, go ahead."

"When you entered the arena, you called out to a group of men in the back."

"I might have, what about it?"

The reporter by the name of Francois Cloutier hesitated, he seemed in no mood to divulge more than necessary. However, when gazing at his opposite invitingly elicited no further information, he hemmed, then hawed a few times, before saying:

"You know of course about the terrible accident right here at the forum."

"I read something about it," Menard admitted, still on guard.

"Let me tell you, I sat in the first row when it happened. What I experienced will follow me to my grave. The handler was almost within reach from me, when he suddenly panicked and fled. Not however, before he called out repeatedly identical words, which you used a moment ago. Though I neither understood his outcries, nor could I explain them, I swear they were the same utterances as yours. Now the question is, what do they mean?"

Menard's ears pricked up, at the same time he became more congenial.

"I called out Harminder, Harminder, it is the name of a youngster I once knew."

"Could I impose on you to repeat it a few times more. Just to make sure, sir."

When Menard obliged, the reporter nodded vigorously.

"That is what the tamer was saying, over and over again, prior to flying shriekingly towards the exit."

Turning his head upward he then asked:

"Do you understand any of this?"

For an instant Menard felt a temptation to reveal his acquaintance with Sindh and Harminder. But many years of mistrust towards the media dictated otherwise. He never liked reporters; their forced affability went as much against his grain as their intrusiveness repelled him. He shook his head and answered:

"Nothing at all."

Then he turned and left. He should have been more responsive, for once swallow his aversion, it might have earned dividends. Because the reporter had witnessed more than Sindh's inexplicable terror, as much as his unmentionable end. However, he paid no attention to what appeared to be a trifle, totally overshadowed by the calamity that followed.

Had Menard been more talkative, who knows, the presumed accident might have acquired a different aspect right there and then. Nevertheless as luck would have it, the reporter had mentioned that seemingly insignificant occurrence to the investigating police officer, who dutifully recorded everything.

Summer, as so often happens in Montreal, arrived suddenly. A few days ago people walked around shivering in light clothes, which they wore out of anticipation and not because of mild weather. But this had suddenly changed. There was a festive mood in the air, as much as scantily clad people on the ground. Never dull at any time, the city had taken on a carnival spirit. Even a seasoned traveller like Menard felt affected by the colour and vivacity on the streets. The people's incomparable charm, so despised by 'The Others', warmed his heart. Only his hometown Quebec, some hundred miles upriver, displayed so much gaiety without being rowdy.

Today was Sunday, a time for aimless wandering, ending with a visit at the Irish pub, listening to the sons of the sod exchanging banter, watching their skill in tickling the Blarney Stone; but Menard felt disinclined to leave his flat. For no apparent reason he started to rummage through old papers, when he came across clippings of that terrible mishap at the forum. Despite a disquieting presentiment that it was more sinister than it appeared, he tried to forget the whole affair. But looking at the picture of that kind and brave man, his subconsciousness refused to give him a rest. Sindh's notions, delusive no doubt, obtruded itself on his mind. Indeed, that man harboured an odd believe, bizarre from beginning to end.

Mulling over what he was told that muggy evening in Bombay, he grew more bewildered than ever. How an otherwise prosaic man could foster such outlandish convictions, sounded incredible. Believing in a cruel end at his tiger's jaw if in the ring with him, while his nephew is not nearby, defied all reason. But Menard was unable to shake off a feeling that Sindh's erroneous hypothesis was connected with his death. The two were linked, how, he could not explain.

He began to ponder, delving into the past against his better judgement. The realisation of knowing something that in all probability no one else, except Harminder, even suspected, spurred him on. Sindh's phobic fear, coupled with a presumed talismanic protection provided by Harminder, had to be somehow connected with his panicky flight and resulting death. His outcries "Harminder, Harminder" meant nothing to Menard, till he called into mind the lad's inheritance.

Now, there was a thought. No doubt this legacy, surely known to the nephew, might have roused many a taunting imp, whispering heaven knows what in his ears. But even if he wished his uncle's untimely end, there was a long way between desire and fulfilment. Of course Harminder must have been aware of his uncle's incomprehensible infatuation, for he hinted as much to him more than once.

Menard could not free himself from further ruminations. The youngster at the forum appeared before his eyes. By golly, he did resemble Harminder, albeit only from afar. Stepping closer, that likeness disappeared however. Their characters evidently were not cut from the same cloth. Harminder possessed a pinched and veiled countenance, in contrast to the other's open and boyish face; he never was enamoured with Harminder.

Contrary to what he indicated to Sindh in Bombay, his impression of the nephew differed from it. He instantly disliked the somewhat stooped youngster, who seemed to look through a layer of haze with eyes ringed by furtiveness. The habit of tilting his head upward while observing one with lurking glances, could hardly be called endearing. A message to be on guard seemed to emanate from those crafty features. What Menard dared not think before, he now said aloud:

"Harminder had his hands in his uncle's death."

However, how he circumvented his uncle's vigilant eyes, required further explanation. Sindh knew his trade, moreover he possessed singular qualities to carry it out in safety. He told him more than once, chuckling and smiling all the while, of many ticklish situations that he had faced in the ring, which only a stout heart and composed mind prevented from turning ugly, if not fatal.

"Never loose your nerve, under any circumstances give in to fear," were his repeated words.

"You may believe me or you mighy not, but there is always a communication, like among animals in the wild, between victim and assailant."

"I don't understand," Menard had admitted.

"The quarry, I say, signals his readiness to become a victim prior to the attacker's pounce. That is what happens in the ring; the animal senses the handler's willingness to be assaulted and consequently obliges."

Strange theories uttered by a remarkable man, Menard thought. How did Harminder contrive to scheme against an alert uncle, thus inheriting a sizeable fortune? Menard doubted the ascendancy over Simun, but not the uncle's fixed idea, whom in any case he trusted to extricate himself from any sticky situation.

Had Harminder been absent, Sindh would have left Simun in his cage and conducted his show with other tigers, whom along with two or three lions he had trained very well. Sindh's fixation only applied to Simun, all other animals in his menagerie he faced alone with astounding intrepidity.

Putting aside his bias towards authorities, Menard resolved to make a report at the police precinct. On second thought he dismissed the idea, for fear to be laughed at.

Then he remembered his friend Hector Julien, inspector of the Surete. Talking with him appeared to be advisable, yet not at the presidium, but across the river at their club. Yes, Julien was the ideal man to approach first, he could help unravel a mystery which increasingly looked like homicide.

Their acquaintance was solid enough to render face saving unimportant. Sure, Julien might laugh and scoff at his conjectures, it would not diminish his prestige, nor make him feel absurd. After more than a decade of playing golf together and uncorking more bottles than either cared to count, their threshold of taking offence sat pretty low.

Wednesdays the inspector usually played and dined at the clubhouse and spent convivial hours in the lounge. Rain or shine, he rollicked from bunkers to greens, spreading his infectious humour, making caddies laugh and weary members chuckle. Menard was cognizant of his friend's rule, never to discuss official business at the club, but rules are made to be bent or broken, he thought.

When Menard arrived at the clubhouse Julien was already there. That he knew before he laid eyes on him, for one could feel his presence. His exuberance, contagious without being overbearing, filled the air. It put spring in the steps of men, and smiles on the lips of women.

He found him soon after, and a game of golf between them was forthwith arranged. Menard tried with every ruse at his command to strike up a conversation, but more so to steer it towards the recent mishap at the forum. Noticing whence the wind blew, Julien showed no interest, he skilfully averted his friend's repeated attempts. Finally Menard blurted out:

"Hector, quit being so dense."

"I wonder what could be meant by that remark," Julien parried innocently.

"I have something to tell you," Menard continued.

"You mean about the accident at the forum?"

"Yes, but it was no accident."

Julien's head come up, he examined his partner with an air of annoyance mixed with interest.

"Well my friend, so reads the official report as I recall," he objected.

Looking closer at his friend and noticing his more receptive demeanour, Menard ventured to say:

"Hector, I appreciate your reluctance to speak about official business on your day off, but I do have something to reveal."

"What is it?"

"Sindh, the trainer and I met some time ago in Bombay."

When the inspector shrugged his shoulders to express indifference, he quickly added:

"Something was imparted to me then, weird to be sure, nevertheless it puts a completely different complexion on the incident."

"All right, let's hear it after the game," Julien agreed.

Soon after the final stroke, half-heartedly made, they took seats at a remote table in the lounge.

"Now, what is it you want to tell me," demanded the inspector to know.

"Harpal Sindh was murdered," Menard blurted out, unsure how his announcement would be received.

"Now, that is a mouthful, quite contrary to the department's finding, as already mentioned. But out with the evidence."

Menard hesitated prior to saying:

"It is hardly conclusive…"

"Aha," interjected Julien, grinning broadly, "but please do continue, tell me who murdered him," he requested a trifle sarcastically.

"Harminder Saan."

"Who is he?"

"His nephew and sole heir," Menard announced.

"My friend, there was no one near the trainer, thousands of eyes can attest to that. Except the tiger of course, who out of the blue attacked him," protested Julien.

"So it appeared, but appearances can be deceptive. Hear me out Hector, just hear me out," Menard requested.

He told all, from his encounter in Bombay to Sindh's outcries at the forum, and Harminder's shifty personality.

Julien listened patiently, first with lowered eyelids and puckered brow, likely to divert from the presence of imps dancing in his eyes, yet soon he turned thoughtful, and finally grave. At the end he said:

"What you say, the trainer momentarily lost his nerve for reasons unknown, which emboldened the tiger to attack."

"Not exactly, I maintain that he sent a signal to be attacked."

Julien snorted.

"To the tiger?"

"Yes, to the tiger."

Observing the flabbergasted inspector calmly, Menard remarked:

"You might remember Sindh's theory about animals in the wild, where prey and assailant follow various cues to communicate each other's intentions."

"In other words a mutual agreement is silently reached."

When Menard nodded, Julien neither scoffed nor laughed, because he too had heard about tales of a similar nature. He asked:

"You believe therefore that Sindh had sent a signal to Simun to be attacked?"

"Precisely."

"But why?"

"That I do not know beyond a strong inkling, it is somehow connected with Harminder, the nephew. It was his name Sindh called out several times in utter anguish, while staring fixedly outside the ring."

"You are certain of that?"

"Reasonable so. A reporter with whom I spoke attested to it. Moreover, he termed these outcries resonant with sudden grief, mixed with abject humiliation. The man, the reporter I mean, sat not more than five steps distant from Sindh, when he abruptly stopped and gazed thunderstruck at him."

"At the reporter?"

"So he thought, though little sense can be made of it."

The inspector grew reflective, his face took on a troubled look. Bizarre, Menard's tale might sound, but somehow he sensed a whiff of truth. He too was never quite satisfied with the department's conclusion, but he raised no objections, despite his better judgement. To his knowledge a tamer of Sindh's calibre simply does not cut and run, particularly in the absence of cogent reasons.

He had read and heard about mock attacks by lions for instance, who lunged at their trainers, however, missing as if by design. He never heard of a trainer jumping aside, or even flinching perceptibly, for they knew that showing fear could prove disastrous. He resolved then and there to reopen the files.

"Allow a few days, Lucien, I promise that I shall search through the records personally. In view of your disclosure, this whole affair now bears a different stamp. You will be contacted soon. If nothing else, your statement will be added."

That was on a Wednesday. Came Thursday evening, a message arrived at his flat. – Could we possibly meet you tomorrow, any time after lunch – it read. Signed: Hector Julien.

Menard needed no second bidding, he showed up promptly at the precinct. Julien was evidently waiting for him; but not alone, somebody stood beside him, whom he introduced as sergeant Victor Kahan.

"Sergeant Kahan conducted the investigation, he speaks Urdu, the language of Sindh and most of his retinue."

Following the introduction all sat down. One glance assured Menard that the policemen were on the alert, a vital discovery had been made perhaps. The inspector explained:

"I have related everything you told me to the sergeant, including your hypothesis concerning Sindh's alleged signals given to Simun, the tiger."

Turning fully towards Kahan, Menard asked:

"What do you think of it, sergeant?"

"I believe it," came his surprising response.

When Menard glared, half reprovingly, half triumphantly at the inspector, Julien reacted with an indulgent smile, while saying:

"Mr Kahan still thinks like an Oriental in some ways, which at times is disconcerting to our sober minds, but in this case I am inclined to concur."

"Indicating that you discovered supporting evidence, or gained further knowledge," Menard interposed.

"We did," admitted the inspector, while the sergeant nodded.

"May I hear of it?"

Julien expounded:

"You see, Lucien, we were groping in the dark. Not knowing anything beyond what some spectators described, terribly contradictory I might add, we had reasons to consider it an accident. Your information, however, changes the whole affair, it puts an entire different construction on everything. When I mentioned the substance of a conversation you had with a reporter, the sergeant almost did a tap dance right in front of my eyes. Out came his files, in a twinkling two pictures lay on the table, and he practically cheered:

"That is who Sindh was staring at, not at the reporter."

Saying so, Julien pushed two photographs towards Menard.

"There is your Harminder," he announced.

One look sufficed to convince Menard otherwise.

"That is not him," he said.

Both policemen looked up startled. Surprise, as much as disappointment was written all over their faces, since it thwarted a mutually arrived at conjecture. They were convinced that the picture portrayed Harminder, the obvious object of Sindh's terror, prior to stampeding towards the exit. True, it did not explain the reason for Sindh's self-destructive behaviour.

"Who is it then?" Julien asked.

"It is the youngster I met at the forum, who resembles Harminder to a considerable degree. I was told they are cousins," Menard replied.

"Another veil over the mystery," sergeant Kahan moaned.

"Not really, the shrouds are lifting," countered Menard.

Chuckling satisfied, he rose from his chair.

"Perhaps I omitted to tell you, Hector, or you have forgotten, a peculiar description given me by Francois Cloutier, the reporter," he added.

"I can't recall what you mean," Julien replied.

Menard stepped over to the window where he could see the broad St. Lawrence, busy as ever, flowing under its bridges. In a way he welcomed his omission concerning the reporter's observation, for it accorded him time to reflect. What he was told appeared outlandish no more. In view of what he had just learned, the reporter's description took on a profound meaning.

Menard returned to the table, but refused to sit down. When Julien pointed invitingly to a chair, he shook his head and said:

"What I intend to relate is better said while standing. You see, gentlemen, the mystery is unravelling."

When neither made a comment, Menard continued:

"The reporter, no doubt a trained observer, mentioned something which now has acquired a significant aspect. It was this:

'Before Sindh panicked he looked at the tiger, just a fraction of a second. That glance, however, spoke volumes. Suddenly all life seemed to drain from the trainer's terror stricken face. The next moment he uttered an unearthly shriek, at the same time he turned and fled.' These were the reporter's exact words, I firmly anchored them in my mind."

After a short pause, the sergeant remarked:

"A moment ago you mentioned a profound significance."

"I have. After seeing the picture the reporter's words became more revealing, moreover inferences can be made with greater authority."

"What are they, Lucien?" interrupted his friend.

Menard explained:

"Sindh, we might agree, stared at the youngster in the picture, who sat beside the reporter. He of course thought it was Harminder at his usual place. As I mentioned they look strikingly alike, certainly from a distance."

"I still do not understand," interrupted Julien.

Menard continued:

"What exactly happened might never be known, yet one can guess."

Neither policemen spoke, they just viewed him expectantly, anxious to hear more. Menard obliged:

"Sindh had made his nephew, whom he dearly loved but not approved of, sole beneficiary of his fortune, perhaps just recently, following a whim, or obeying a deeper sentiment. There might have been a preamble to that evening at the forum, disagreements perchance, maybe ugly quarrels, recriminations, who knows. Therefore when Sindh noticed the deception, he assumed the worst. His dear nephew, loved despite his faults, was scheming against him. Clear signs of betrayal stared him in the face, dastardly conceived machinations, nourished by hopes that he would perish in the ring. The realisation must have devastated this high-minded aristocrat of the heart."

The inspector became visible restless, he started tapping on the table, not intrusively, nevertheless expressing a desire to make a comment.

"Are you not surmising too much? After all you were not there," he remarked reprovingly.

"Quite true, but someone was present, who possesses a keen eye and decades of training," Menard retorted.

"You mean the reporter Francois Cloutier," interjected the sergeant.

Menard replied:

"Yes. He left no doubt about Sindh's transformation, in the few seconds while staring ahead, into a statue of anguish, changing to shame and humiliation, and finally culminating in resignation. All life seemed to drain out of him when he turned to face the tiger, who appeared to be in a dither by now. He was under the impression, he told me, that Sindh's gaze carried a silent plea for help, a mute appeal to be freed from unspeakable grief."

When Menard paused, the sergeant wanted to know:

"Was it then that the trainer fled?"

"No. Again I repeat Cloutier's narrative. Sindh suddenly shuddered as if awakening from a dream. While straightening up, waves of terror convulsed his whole being, the like that experienced and hard-boiled man had never witnessed before. Then Sindh screamed and ran."

Julien leaped from his chair. Turning first to the sergeant, then towards Menard, he remarked:

"Quite a tale my friend, an amazing story, I admit, but is it true?"

“We can not be certain,” Menard answered. ”Yet I believe that Sindh pronounced his own death warrant, unwittingly mind you, but making eye contact with Simun at that critical moment, sealed his fate.”

“I understand what you say. Realising that he had committed the unthinkable, the trainer raced towards safety.”

“Leaving the tiger no alternative but to come after him,” completed Menard.

Silence crept into the room, each man followed his own thoughts, which he would have been averse to share. Sergeant Kahan rose from his chair. Looking nowhere in particular, he muttered:

“Yes, Mr Menard, we will never know for sure.”

# Without Tears

Napatuk worried them. Despite feverish avtivities, and the incessant pursuit of food, they glanced contemplatively at him. It happened in the fifties, when the European culture pounced on Canada's north with a vengeance, where it swept like blood poisoning over the tundra. Merciless it rampaged in the land of the great, white silence. Insatiable like Moloch of Gehenna, it assaulted men and beast, until the smiles froze on the faces of the unsuspecting Inuit. Promises of a higher order lay in the air, a new wind blew from Baffin Island to the Amundsen Golf. It scoured the immense barren land. Ahead it drove the strange tidings of civilisation.

"Those are astounding men," it was whispered.

But then one morning the truth stared into their drowsy eyes; they were no longer free! They had been tricked! This realization broke their hearts, it robbed them of the will to resist. Shame joined their sadness, a paralysing indifference weakened the hands, which not long ago wielded spear and bow, but now possessed hardly enough strength to accept proffered alms.

Of course not all succumbed to the influence of progress. A few scorned the gifts of the 'Big Eyebrows' and fled to a remote bay, near Igloolik, where they continued to lead the old life. Unmolested from the chilled hands of Christianity and the sting of civilisation, they laughed, sang and danced as before.

“The worst is behind us,” was said once more.

A crackling cold lay already over the land, where the first northern lights announced the dark, long winter. Provisions were hardly stored, when the season’s first blizzard assailed them. While it blew and howled outside, men remained in their rooms, whereas Huskies curled deeper in the snow.

After the storm a cold broke out which froze the tears before they reached the ground. The great, white silence spread over the boundless land, which was only interrupted by the singsong of wolves.

The Inuit endured the cold with equanimity; they did not bat an eyelash in raging storms or depressing darkness. Only Napatuk worried them.

“How is it with Napatuk?” inquiries were made of Mukpa, his wife.

“He is himself,” came the reply.

The good news rushed from igloo to igloo, travelled from mouth to mouth, it engendered high spirits all around. There was gossip, laughter and unconstrained visiting. Life was worth living, the bellies were full, igloos warm, besides Napatuk remained peaceful.

Tassagut the old one started to narrate. About his father Echaluk, who ran faster then the wind, furthermore could overtake the caribou at full run. Oi, was he strong. Could he not overpower a polar bear with his bare hands? Besides, he pulled the walrus out of the water like a seal. And persistent he was, persevering like a hungry wolf on the prowl. He was an Inuit like themselves, the mightiest hunters on earth, who without grumbling drink from the bitter cup of a strenuous life. Who roam over the endless tundra with wolves and bears, where, on the eternal hunt for food, they expose themselves to terrible loneliness and devastating storms.

Composed, almost cheerful they face the howling winds, which race unhindered over the limitless wasteland, driving snow and ice ahead of them. Suddenly a beating heart steps into their path. Like in a senseless rage the wind now aims its fury, snarling with threefold force at the little dark spot. But this mote on the horizon does not yield, no, to the contrary, it turns and snarls laughingly back. They are Inuits, who neither wail nor moan, when the oppressive silence and darkness stretches its clammy tentacles to weave a pitiless net around them.

As the others nodded, Tassagut went on. Of course they were Inuits, Inuks, unweakened by romanticism, unbowed by the yoke of ambition. They drew closer together to feel the warmth of identical convictions, to hear the pulsation of similar thoughts.

"More Tassagut, more," he was spurred on from all sides.

They wanted to hear it again, till each word became indelibly anchored in their minds.

But suddenly Kapik, the shaman, pricked his ears. At the same time Tassagut grew silent.

"What is it Kapik?" they wanted to know.

He shook his head.

"Nothing," he answered.

Then it grew deathly silent around them, they suspected the worst.

"Napatuk!"

The name leaped at them like a bowel wounded grizzly.

"Napatuk, Napatuk," they whispered with bloodless lips. Saddened, Tassagut hung his head.

"He is raving again," he gasped.

Abruptly the mood changed throughout the settlement. The clamour increased till dogs whimpered with fear.

Mukpa sat benumbed beside her husband. Mean was his scowl, poisonous the tooth of his rage. When Napatuk began stabbing blindly through the furs, Mukpa crept unnoticed towards the exit, where she disappeared with one bold leap.

He did not expect this, it added grist to his mill. With murderous threats and bloodcurdling curses he plunged after her. The whole settlement fell now into an uproar. Children wailed, dogs howled, frightened voices called incoherently from all sides, a terrible disarray ensued.

Suddenly a change occurred. The Huskies noticed it first, women then perceived it. They nodded, smiled at their little ones and touched them with their noses.

"It is over," they whispered.

Napatuk sat already in his igloo again, with a demeanour as if nothing had happened. Mukpa came also back. She lit the lamp as well as the cooking stove and brewed fresh tea. Napatuk showed himself lively and enterprising.

"Ho, ho Mukpa, get ready, we are going hunting," he sang out.

Outside the good news travelled from lips to lips.

"It is over, Napatuk is himself again."

They laid fear and weapons aside, after which they turned to more important things. It was a pity, but what could be done about it? Tomorrow everything will be better.

However, the younger men, supported by the shaman, where unwilling to endure it any longer. Napatuk was a thorn in their flesh which had to be removed. They decided to offer him banishment after his return. Banishment or death, said the unwritten law of their ancestors. It can only be prevented by immediate relatives, who in all cases must be a male, an Inuk. He must assume full responsibility for the condemned.

Okituk, the son, stepped forward, promising to be his father's surety.

"You know what it means?" inquired Kapik, the shaman.

"I know it," came the answer.

Because should the condemned become recidivous, the surety must then execute the verdict.

Shortly after Napatuk and Mukpa returned. They were tired but happy, because the hunt had proved successful. The nearer they came to the settlement, the more Mukpa muffled herself up.

"Napatuk, I have a strange feeling," she lamented.

"Be quiet," he chided, though he too felt a weight on his mind.

When he was apprised of the community's decision, he could not contain a smile.

Their plight with Napatuk was soon supplanted by a bigger event; a peculiar prickle lay in the air. Strained eyes of men observed the southern heavens, while dogs with pricked ears raised muzzles towards the horizon. Inspired by a great expectation, men and beasts forgot the hunger in their bellies, and the cold on their skins.

Then the time approached. One day the flame of life showed its face again; the sun came back. An unquenchable joy raced through every igloo, kindled every heart; but regrettably their happiness was short lived, it received a rude damper. Napatuk raved again, this time with the force of a rested volcano. All eyes turned now to Okituk, the son, because he alone bore responsibility for the father. With one single effort he stretched himself, whereupon he proceeded towards his parents igloo.

"All will go well," promised the shaman.

"Okituk knows his duty," others concurred.

Soon Okituk stood opposite his father; embarrassed and wordless, because he lacked the means to build a bridge over his father's silence. In the land of opulent revels and gnawing privation, reserve is valued above everything else.

"All going well with you, Okituk?" came the inquiry.

The ice was broken, a dialogue could commence.

"Was your hunting successful?" he wanted to know.

"Successful? Ha, seals crawled on the ice when I called, bears jostled into my line of fire, while polar foxes fought with wolverines over my traps."

Meat stewed in the pot, tea simmered in the kettle. All three knew the significance of this hour, but to the father belonged the first words.

Then an extended silence settled over the room. They waited. Mukpa stirred absentmindedly in the pots, whereas Okituk stared uncomfortable at the furs.

Finally the oppressive silence was interrupted by Napatuk.

"You have something on your mind, Okituk?"

"Yes," came a reluctant answer.

"Has a decision been made?"

"It has," answered the son distressed.

His father's glance strayed around the floor, while his mother avoided his eyes intentionally.

"What do you suggest?" Napatuk asked.

Okituk looked uneasy around, in the course of which his fluttering glances centred on his mother. The depressing responsibility made his blood rush, he would have preferred to talk alone with his father, but since his mother made no preparations to retreat, he finally burst out:

"Your death."

Mukpa winced like under the lashes of a whip. Even his father paled somewhat under his weather-beaten skin. He nodded quietly; it was the end.

"How?" he inquired.

"By my hands," announced Okituk.

A satisfied smile stole around his father's lips.

"That is well."

Mukpa looked closer at the men, as if she wanted to raise an objection. Only her husband's reproving stare forced her to swallow her words. Was it not agreeable, his countenance expressed, to be sent on the last journey by one's beloved son?

What could she really say, she thought. Her unfailing, all embracing instinct recognised the harsh reality. Napatuk was a good man, an able hunter, but he simply could not tame that demon irascibility. Wisdom, born of the need for self-preservation, spoke loud and clear. One must go, to bring peace to many. Life was too precious to be trifled with, or to be tormented by eternal, selfsame thoughts. Their destiny was intractable, no whimsical words could appease it.

"Let us begin," Napatuk said.

"I am ready," Okituk answered.

Napatuk did not disappoint the tribe, he accepted the proffered cup of bittersweet drops without wincing. He was willing to drain it to the bottom. His face betrayed precious little; the innermost emotions, when in distress, must be concealed from the outside world, they only belonged to him. Joy, sadness may not cross the threshold of his soul, they must remain forever imprisoned. Life, the wild partner extended its hands for the last time. But not as before to break into a whirl of pleasure, no, the laughing, kissing romp bid him farewell.

With one single movement he linked arms with destiny. Without regrets, free of self-pity he prepared himself. All will go well, he thought, the tribe acted properly, there was no other way. The two edged sword remained in its scabbard, unsullied by the blood of innocents.

He only felt sorry for Okituk. He fervently hoped the imposed duty left no scars behind. But was he not an Inuit, a son of his ancestors, besides young like the tundra in July?

The men looked at each other intensely, whereas Mukpa sat forlorn and half paralysed in a corner. Outside the northern lights danced and flickered over the sky, ghostly, like a message from another world.

Hardly had Napatuk turned around, when a shot tore through the silence, which raced Mukpa through every limb, but threw Okituk into the abyss of despair.

Outside there was great relief. A heavy burden had been removed, a poisonous thorn was torn from their breasts. Although this relief, boundless in extent which made them glad and lighthearted, was not expressed in their feelings, nor even hinted at with their demeanour. The gypsies of the north, barbarous on the surface, had a noble mind.

Afterwards the deathwatch began. For three days Napatuk's deeds were praised in songs and words. On the fourth's day he was laid on a sled.

His burial ground lay about three miles from the settlement, a short distance that could be covered in less than an hour. The last walk belonged to father and son, no one else's presence was allowed. Upon arrival Okituk laid his father gently on a selected spot. Immediately after he encircled the corps four times. Then an opening was cut in the thick fur. So, that was done. The soul, his name could now escape unhindered at the first call.

Without a word he turned around, his eyes were fixed undecided at the village.

Suddenly the dogs raised their muzzles and began to howl piteously. Okituk was taken aback, but not for long, before he too threw his head back and sent long-drawn mournful cries into the awakening day. Moved by a deep sorrow, his bitter exclamations resounded over the endless plain. Startled, the Huskies fell silent, they listened, awed by the heartrending dirge, which ended as unexpected as it had begun.

Okituk then tightened the reins with one single tug, while his whip whizzed around the ears of the lead dog, till the whole pack raced towards the village. He knew his father was in good care, then although he killed all his life with a strong hand, the souls of the animals were always respected.

As they came nearer to the village, a golden, yellowish shimmer began caressing the earth. Soon, he thought, the warm breath of the midnight sun will swallow snow and ice. Before his inner eye appeared the tundra with its flaming carpet, and a thousand boisterous voices.

May the eyes of the envious burn out, he was happy, because the worst lay behind them; tomorrow everything would be better.

# Misunderstanding

Jakob Lahai awoke from wild dreams. Greedy hands with ice-cold fingers seemed to be tearing at his inside. With terror in his eyes he tried to sit up, but in vain. The mere thought of it caused unspeakable pain. He felt paralysed, from head to toes beset with numbness. But the greatest plague was his thirst.

"All over," flashed the certain realisation of the wilderness through his mind. His number was called, the hand of destiny reached for the staff of his life.

Gradual silence reigned again outside. The terrible storm, source of his plight, was passing over the mighty mountains. The great silence of the Northwest settled over the land again. Even the ravens on the roof, attracted by the smell of doom, remained silent in expectation. The feeble winter sun pushed slowly over the summits of the Mackenzies. A new day had begun, rays of hope smiled encouragingly at the land.

But the old man in his lonely hut received little comfort from that peaceful picture, because other thoughts tormented him. The inexorable hand of fate was about to drag him to the gates of eternal darkness. All bitter reproaches were meaningless; he was doomed. To worsen his misfortune he tormented himself with remonstrances. How could anyone be so clumsy? A man like him, over forty years exposed to the treacherousness of the Nahanni, fumbled like a greenhorn into the most obvious trap. Of course the sight was hindered, veiled from the whirled up snow, driven by a howling wind. But to be deceived appeared to him incomprehensible.

It was not the first time that he was surprised by the scourge of the north, that sudden, vehement snowstorm which shakes the rocks and builds tamped pathways over gullies. Lahai stepped with both feet on such a deceptive bridge. It was the most fatal step of his life. Half unconscious, more in a dream than reality, he clawed himself out of that icy grave. How he reached his cabin stiff with cold remained a mystery to him. Mind and words could not explain it, only the habit of long years to battle the perils of the Nahanni drove him on.

The Nahanni was his homeland. From the roaring waterfalls to its expansive mouth he considered all his own. Inhospitable could this region be called, even dangerous, but he liked it more than all the cultivated meadows and forests of Europe. He would not have traded with El Dorado or Pope Benedict, in spite of the unearthly silence in the winter, interrupted only by his own heartbeat; despite the summer heat that brings to life the bloodsucking insects, which fight over every pore of the skin. He was free, free like the eagle high over the cliffs, footloose as the wolves on the plateau.

His condition got noticeably worse. Razor sharp teeth seemed to wrangle for his marrow and bones. The worst torment, however, was thirst. Assistance from outside was unthinkable, therefore he depended solely on himself. Only through the means of his own power could he be freed from a hopeless situation. But how? For the first time in his life he cursed his complete isolation. A sip of water, a little warmth, was all he desired from the world. But who should provide it? Only he, no one else. First he must reach the stove, no matter what, because the icy buckles of frost began to encircle his body inexorably.

Only to whom the unshakeable will of the free man is known, can imagine the pains with which Jakob Lahai went to work. His situation was serious, but not hopeless. After all it was not the first time that a disaster stared him in the eye. Take the incident when he lay on his bunk with a splintered neck, where he waited patiently for improvement. Only the drops from icicles on the window kept him alive, not to forget his unwavering belief for better times.

One thing he knew: his strength could bear no more than one attempt. Whatever he undertook must be successful at the first run. Three steps separated him from the stove. A short distance, yet worlds away. The iron giver of warmth stood in the corner, as always ready to be kindled, a precaution unfailingly taken whenever he left the cabin. Perhaps this solicitude could now save his life.

First of course he must reach the stove. To rise from the bunk was out of the question, but to roll off and push himself slowly towards it should be possible. With iron determination and last bit of strength, he started to make preparations. Every fibre of his being was strained. The command came, muscles and sinews got ready, but nothing happened. He could not move a limb.

With the sweat of desperation on his forehead, and the look of terror in his eyes, he accepted defeat after a few attempts. Resigned like a man on his journey to the beyond, Lahai prepared for the end. It could not last long anymore, because the paralysing cold crawled irresistibly towards the seat of life.

He took leave, half awake, half dreaming, from an incomparable existence on the legendary river. He was king of all that the eye perceived, sovereign of everything the mind could grasp.

'Nahanni or Bust' was inscribed on the side of his canoe, as was written in his heart. His mind wandered back, far back to the time when as a young man he followed the call of the Nahanni.

"Gold!" came the resounding cry from the mountains. "Gold!" murmured the riffles at every bend. "Gold! Gold!" roared the mighty Victoria Falls. An echo hundredfold reverberated from the headwaters to the mouth of the river. He heeded the call which he never regretted. To be sure, other adventurers followed him, fairly intoxicated by the scent of the Northwest, lone wolves imbued with hope to find their luck on the fabled river.

They came from all quarters, but most returned at the sight of the first grizzly. A few, however, with coarser shells pushed onward to the lower valleys. Driven by dreams of immense fortunes, they never heard the portentous rustling over cliffs, nor the whispers from gulches; they remained. Whether they ever unveiled the mysteries of the Nahanni is not known, because bleached bones tell no tales.

Jakob Lahai outlived them all. Tenacious like his forebears from the mountains of Tennessee, he roamed through the boundless land, forever with the fragrance of great discoveries in his nostrils. Promising nuggets were washed all over out of riverbeds. From the Columbia to the Klondike fabulous riches were recovered. Only the Nahanni with his hundred voices did not release his hoard. Nothing was bestowed upon Lahai except the malicious sniggers from the ravines and scornful laughter over cliffs. The Indians maintained that these sounds emanated from the faded skulls of failed adventurers.

Ha, once he was on the heels of that wretched treasure. It happened in the transition period when every creature waited, yearning for the first signs of spring. He began jubilantly to gather the smiling nuggets, which were stuffed one after the other into his spacious pockets. After the last pebble was either retrieved or safeguarded, he looked contemplatively around, till the whole terrain became indelibly imprinted in his mind. Later, when the discovery revealed itself as pyrites, he could have howled with the wolves in the uplands. It stuck to his memory as if it had happened yesterday.

He came no further in his reveries, because voices reached his ears. The realisation rushed through him like a flash of lightning. Then he listened sceptically into the silence outside. Nothing could be heard, not even a squeak. Why should there be a sound? remonstrated his reason. Who indeed should wander around in this godforsaken region, in the winter to boot?

There, again! His ears now perceived unmistakable a muffled murmur. His attitude changed in a flash, rays of hope melted his previous resignation. While he strained his senses with rising blood and pounding temples, he wavered a while between the talons of doubt, and the caressing hands of expectation.

Kraa, kraa, screamed the ravens on the roof, while fleeing to the tops of the pine trees. He could hardly believe it, but the voices proved to be real. They were now clearly audible, even shuffling steps could be perceived.

He was saved, because someone approached the cabin. Although the senses balked to admit it, increasing sounds spoke louder than reason. While he listened with burning eyes and feverish anticipation, enticing pictures fluttered already around him. Before his mind's eye he could see the little settlement at the river's mouth, that refuge of the stranded. A week in cosy surroundings, cared for by the shopkeeper's wife, should soon bring him around.

But what kept them, he asked impatiently, because strange enough steps and voices disappeared again. Faster, faster he would have liked to shout, if not to roar. Alone his vocal cords regrettably denied their services. Heavens, how he pined for warmth. This uncertainty gnawed cruelly at him. Are they nearing, withdrawing, or do they not even exist, did he merely suffer from hallucinations? Thank God, life returned again at the outside, voices could now clearly be heard. There were two men who approached the cabin, no doubt about it.

His joy received nevertheless a damper at the next moment. Assuming they did not see his hut, or paid no attention to it? The thought struck him like a blow. Impossible, he consoled himself, nobody could be so obtuse or negligent. Who knows, perhaps they themselves were in distress, maybe in search of warmth, sustenance and shelter. All could be found here with two tolerably robust arms and legs.

His misgivings dispersed in the next instance like bubbles in the wind. His cabin had been detected; voices, which almost tumbled over each other in surprise, gave evidence of it.

"Tell me Jan, am I dreaming, a hut in this place?"

"Surprising but true," came a reply.

"Even in liveable condition still."

"What do you think Jan, does somebody live here?"

"Living! Frank where are your senses, don't you know where we are?"

"Oh well, we could at least investigate, one never knows," retorted Frank Romer.

He was from day one somewhat bolder than his hunting friend Jan Solta.

Jakob Lahai gave a sigh of relief, the fear of before fell heavily from his mind.

"Is somebody in there?" inquired both repeatedly.

Since no answer was heard Romer added:

"We are hunters from the south with friendly intentions."

Both then started to knock at the door. First hesitantly, then steadily louder, till finally a regular din arose. No answer came from inside. Lahai attempted with all his might to give a sign of his presence. He simply did not succeed. A terrible dryness in his throat suffocated all sound. In addition the pitiless cold paralysed every joint in his body.

A desperate rage arose within him. His life hung by a thread, every minute was precious, if not crucial, while those outside bantered about. Such bungling behaviour, bordering on negligence, he thought quite puzzling. Resentment arose within him, which increasingly intensified to hatred.

There! finally something happened, judging by the rattling. An instant later the old man was seized by a ghastly realisation which raced through his bones. The door was barred at the inside! To be protected from the raging storm he had bolted it with his last bit of strength.

Of course there was still the window, whose shutters could be pulled off with one vigorous tug. Even the biggest dolt must then comprehend his plight. He now cursed his exaggerated carefulness for which only his distress could bear responsibility. As a rule he left everything unlocked, whether absent or present. His worst fears were soon fulfilled.

"Nothing doing Jan, not even an earthquake could move this door," Frank Romer called out, all the while belabouring the planks.

"Try the window," encouraged his companion.

Lahai listened spellbound for every sound. In the meantime his concentrated fury unloaded itself upon those two pussyfoots. Guessing by their voices they seemed still young, but judging by their actions they had to be as old as the hills, and infirm to boot. To be sure, the shutters were latched on the inside, but what of it? One hefty blow would splinter the boards in a hundred pieces.

Unbelievable, if not uncanny deemed Lahai such helpless puttering out there. A blind man would have noticed his presence by the traces all around him. From the peculiar behaviour of the ravens to accumulated snow around his tracks, all pointed to the proximity of humans. Locked doors, latched windows? Bah, every Indian knows that in violent storms a man feels the penchant to barricade himself as much as possible.

Suddenly there was a change outside. Lahai noticed it with that sure feeling of one threatened by disaster. The ravens grew restless, they hopped from branch to branch while increasing their ghostly croaking. Gradually they returned one by one back to the roof. He knew what that meant, he feared the worst. His hunch was almost instantly confirmed; they were about to give up. The ravens with the smell of death in their noses came nearer to the set table.

"The window too is barred from the inside," shouted Jan Solta, whereby he rattled at the boards with a feeble effort.

Frank Romer, his companion, had seen and heard enough. He waved his colleague closer, while he made signs to keep quiet. The whole thing appeared to him eerier by degrees. He could not shake off a creeping feeling that sinister forces were at work here. To describe it more accurately, he suspected a trap. Why? For two reasons. First he recalled reading a report about the north, which averred that a trapper's cabin remains always unlocked, even during extended absences. Second, an overpowering suspicion gripped him that someone was hiding in there.

He seemed to have heard repeated suppressed breathing. What was going on? They were hiding from them; somebody, possibly sought by the police, entrenched themselves in there. Did they plan a surprise attack? After all, their outfit alone possessed considerable value. How could they be so blind and deaf. The presence of ravens for instance was a sure sign of human proximity, to say nothing of the well cared for cabin.

They are being spied upon, that much was sure, wherefore they must reckon with an attack every moment.

Jan Solta stepped surprised from the window; as if thunderstruck he looked at his companion.

"Frank, what got into you?" he wanted to know.

"Why should I remain quiet," he added, as Romer endeavoured by means of signs and hissing sounds to silence him.

"There is something wrong here Jan, someone is hiding in there, and I suspect not for reasons to exchange pleasantries."

He explained his observations in a suppressed voice. Jan Solta was easily persuaded, he had little inclination to expose himself to unnecessary dangers. True, his conscience bothered him a bit, but nevertheless he departed with Romer.

What went on in the meantime within Lahai, no pen can describe. Somewhere deep down of his being, heart rending voices prayed for deliverance. He was ignominiously forsaken, meanly and cowardly left behind, for reasons he could not understand. Fortuna had briefly, oh, so briefly, lifted her skirt, but not high enough. The monster despair emerged again with the key to the bottomless pit in its foaming mouth.

He reflected feverishly what should be done. Those two outside were on their way, that seemed obvious. Alone the behaviour of the ravens said more than a thousand words, not to mention the receding, almost stealthy steps in the snow.

Cold and thirst were forgotten, driven to the background by thoughts of his rescue. He had to draw attention to himself, somehow it had to be done. With all his might he tried once again to loosen his furred tongue. Poor old man, he could have stopped wasting his strength. It stuck so fast that no other power but three drops of water could have freed it. Consequently he had to try once more rolling off his bunk, in the hope to create enough noise, whereby even these two deaf and blind stumblers must hear something. Because they still remained within earshot; but not for long.

With gritted teeth he started out, with pounding temples he gave up. It was lamentable, but he could not stir.

"Don't give up, do not give up!" demanded his inner voice.

"Think hard, think harder!" requested the inexorable instinct of life, which oddly enough had flared up again. There was surely a way out, it just must be found. How could he draw attention to himself, how – how?

"The stare of the basilisk! Good mercy, why did I not think of it before!"

Was it too late to be effective? Hardly, those creepers out there could probably still be found in the vicinity, they might even loiter about nearby, now as before, undecided what to do.

Now, the stare of the basilisk possesses a quality which borders on magic. The Indians employ it at times, conceding it can be crowned with occasional success. With enough willpower, persistent belief, supported by concentrated attention so they claim, one's will can be imposed on almost anyone. Every means will do when in distress, thought Lahai as he began to bundle nerve upon nerve to a dense ball in his eyes. This concentrated force he hurled like flashes of lightning after them. They contained a clear command.

"Come back! tear the door and the window out of their frames, come back and rescue me from the claws of death!"

Although he felt the breath of unconsciousness, and the effort drove his eyes almost from their sockets, he did not relent. This was the last and ultimate way out. Either he succeeded to convey his will to them, be it with doubtful, yes even sacrilegious means, or sliding towards ruin was inevitable.

With failing strength and strained ears he then listened. Nothing stirred except the ravens on the roof, and steps which slowly grew distant. A deep leaden despondency overpowered him now.

'Nahanni or Bust,' the inscription on his boat was about to be fulfilled. The legacy of the inexorable river had spoken; its will must come to pass. Tears of melancholy welled in his eyes. His thoughts turned to spring, which before long will send its harbinger, the wind with its hot breath, on a journey. Chinook, Indians call these warm winds that suddenly arise. They blow constantly till ice and snow melt from the rocks.

Close on their heels follow the buffalo, their long excursions over the uplands would commence; and, oh, the loon, that eccentric with a voice of the beyond. Nothing he wished more than to hear once again the unearthly call of that bird. Its cry awakens the world and stimulates man and beast to higher achievement. Messenger of calamities, the Indians call that irrepressible fowl; but Lahai knew it was the soul of the north.

The ravens became gradually as quiet as a mouse. Lahai recognised the sign; evening was approaching. As always around this time, shortly before the sun crept behind the mountains, a rapt silence hovered over the land. Only a fading, ever fainter growing crunch in the snow interrupted the oppressive calm. Every dying step gave his hope a stab. Then utter silence followed; his bitter end had come.

"No!" he wanted to shout, because a sudden thought seized him. The rifle! As always it lay at his side, ready to be fired. God in heavens! fate smiled once again. An indescribable excitement gripped him, which grew by degrees, driving his numb condition into the background. With infinite pain he forced his frostbitten fingers towards the rifle.

Spurred on by a new awakened will to live, his hand crawled along the barrel. Inch by inch it groped towards the guard, till finally his stiff fingers found the trigger. In the next instant a blasting shot rent the agonizing silence. Then a second, third, till the chamber was empty. A pungent fume filled the small room, while outside a concerted echo resounded through forests and over mountains. A lovelier roundelay Lahai had never heard in his life.

"Saved – saved – saved!" it reverberated over summits and valleys.

The ravens fluttered startled into the air. With a murderous clamour they flew away, because they all knew that sound.

The terrible exertion took its toll; the old man from the Nahanni fell into a deep swoon.

At the sound of the first shot both hunters turned around dismayed.

"Take cover!" shouted Frank Romer, as he nimbly scurried behind a tree.

Jan Solta needed no second urging, in a flash he was on his companion's heels.

"Did I not tell you someone is lurking around," Romer uttered through his teeth with a hushed voice, so as not to betray their location to the marksman.

"By God Frank, you were right," admitted Solta, while both scampered carefully from tree to tree.

When after a while no more shots were heard, they proceeded hastily to their camp.

"That was close," meant Frank Romer.

"Closer than I appreciate," agreed Jan Solta.

# Rekindling Passion

Willy Rusk was a small man, in stature that is, albeit not in heart and mind. Meek he could not be called, just peace loving and tolerant. He abhorred violence with a passion, his propensity leaned towards reasoning and debate. Sharp-witted discussions were more to his liking than importune arguments. Any form of physical intimidation were anathema to him. Then how did such a peaceable man end up in front of a jury, charged with endangering the life of others with a lethal weapon? He was lucky to be out on bail, which was ascribable to an absence of a criminal record, as much as having had no previous charges against him. By the statutes the maximum sentence, if found guilty, was five years penitentiary.

Rusk held an important position down at the sawmill, not far from his home. His wife Anna, a fiery Serbian woman, found him too yielding and timid, which did not entirely correspond with reality. Albeit detesting showy or vehement behaviour, he nevertheless possessed rigid principles, which no amount of persuasion was able to negate. He certainly could not be called a funk, though without flinching a man resenting any form of boisterous encounters.

Such aversions contrasted with his wife's inclinations, who hesitated seldom to rush into any fray with flashing eyes. Unlike him, who gave conflicts a wide berth, she thrived on them. Their relation, particularly on account of such divergencies in character, enjoyed little marital bliss; they endured each other rather than feeling respect or love.

Rusk had no enemies in the world, men as much as women liked him almost universally. Men because of his small size, women for his courtesy and considerate demeanour. With them he showed himself ready to acquiesce even in the face of spurious assertions and untenable views. Disputatious he was not, dogmatic even less.

His wife Anna, in contrast, was well endowed with such attributes. She seemed to be forever entangled in some kind of friction with neighbours. They were not overt quarrels, mind you, but rather consistent grumblings meant for his ears. These raised objections created a source of vexation in the house, for he felt called upon to remedy unpleasant conditions, roused to life by his wife's fertile imagination. Not that any of their neighbours conducted themselves boisterously, yet Mrs Rusk, a woman with mischief in her veins and sparks of unrest in both eyes, found reasons for complaints anyway. Perhaps just to rouse her complacent spouse, whose unmanliness in her eyes deserved nothing but scorn.

It all started on account of a dog, which hitherto behaved rather well, but had lately turned aggressive, meaning he barked, and sometimes even snarled. Anna objected to such behaviour, she found it unseemly, and above all exacting to her finely tuned ears.

"Willy, that dog over there is getting out of hand," she announced one rainy morning.

He flinched visibly, fearing her wonted string of grievances being heaped on his frail shoulders, thus spoiling his whole day. He usually left the house before his wife was fully awake. Lingering on the way to work in this rainy weather – he always walked – had no allure for him. He loved these strolls through the lonely wilderness park, along the shore of the mighty Fraser; they elevated his spirit in the morning and fortified his mind on the way back in the afternoon.

"You mean Zurn's next door?" he feigned unawareness.

"Of course, who else's? Something must be done about it, you ought to give Heinz a talking to, tell him to keep his mutt inside."

He felt disinclined to do so, although the dog's barking, increasingly more insistent, annoyed him too. First, Zurn had a volatile temper, second, he was married to a vixenish woman. True, his wife hardly played second fiddle in the art of offensive retorts, but he felt abhorred by the idea of unleashing a contest of vituperate tongues.

The other side of the coin was that denying Anna's wishes raised impenetrable barriers between them, and extinguished the sparks of love which barely smouldered at the best of times. Conjugal relations his sensuous wife had increasingly attuned to his compliance, meaning submitting to her subtle tyranny. Therein lay his quandary. Unlike his wife, he was unable to sublimate instinctual drives, which of course she knew quite well. She enjoyed her advantage to the full, as would happen again he realised, should he fail to succumb to her wishes.

No doubt, Anna was still attractive, moreover seductive like Ahab's wife Jezebel. His desire for her engendered conflicting feelings of joy and anguish in his breast. How he abhorred these intervals of punishing withdrawals, words could not express. They seemed to have grown in length and numbers. It always took him aback, seeing otherwise lively features turning suddenly into a mask of stony inanimateness.

Wrapped in layers of grievances, growing pale from thoughts of having been wronged, she then displayed signs of an avenging angel. Suffering silently like a modern Griselda, she nevertheless paid him back in full measures. Her demeanour then brimmed with a desire to hurt, her eyes radiated a will to harm. Having no desire to invite one of these pilgrimages to the realm of bitterness, he remarked:

"Very well my dear, I will talk to them."

"Talking will do no good. Inconsiderate people like that need stronger medicine. Either he muzzles that cur, I say, or else."

"Yes, yes, Anna, but now I must be on my way, I'm late already, you know."

Matters developed rapidly from thereon, which came as no surprise considering the situation. Ingredients conducive to trouble were present, they were easy to recognise. A tame, love-starved husband hitched to a sensuous, albeit increasingly unyielding woman, were sure indications of approaching predicaments. Like donkey and rider they prayed to different gods; he to Cupid, beseeching him to prick his wife with leaden arrows; she to Quirinus, the god of war, imploring him to imbue her husband with manly virtues.

Rusk knew that strife lay ahead of him, a contest impossible to circumvent. Confronting Zurn filled him with trepidation, the man was too aggressive for his liking, besides being endowed with brawn, which he flaunted at every opportunity. To tell the truth, he was afraid of Zurn.

Rusk lingered on his way back from work, making repeated stops at clearances that afforded an unobstructed view of the river. Standing at the shore, he could not help but compare fate with the ever changing flow of that historic stream. Up and down its water went, the same as his own life. Now he was on the way down, undeniably sliding towards a bog, from which to extricate himself might prove difficult.

Anna, his seductive wife, who in the bloom of maturity exercised an irresistible power over him, would undeniably make him suffer should her request not be met. But challenging Zurn might be the greater of two evils. Neither option appeared attractive. Anna's sulkiness, accompanied by an inevitable denial of her favours, he dreaded, but more so the idea of challenging that irascible Zurn with the Heraclean built.

He had passed the age of fifty, when the sap of life dries up rapidly in men who worship what they fear and hate, yet depend upon it. His wife knew the ropes; she had learned quickly the mores of the new world, where women are deemed queens, not as in her homeland because of beauty and character, but merely because they were females. Although she exploited this weakness, she nevertheless pined for men of her childhood and youth, who were wild and free inside, but gentle on the outside, and ever ready to tackle women.

Rusk became absorbed in reflections. Destiny had betrayed him, he mused, it led him through one maze after another, and finally into the arms of Anna Miclas, a true daughter of Venus. There he found love and passion, hitherto only imagined, but never experienced. Her display of emotions, shocking and exciting, would have been unthinkable within his prudish circle. Although ten years his junior, her experience of life, as much as instincts, uncorrupted in an environment of free spirits, were far more profound than his. She possessed an unfettered character, that was frank in speech without being abusive or unseemly, moreover she showed boldness, yet never approached depravity. She had inspired him to deeds that till then he dared not talk about. An adventurous young woman she was, filled with zest for life, who enriched his mind and encouraged him in times of failures.

That happened a long time ago, it all petered out within a few years after their marriage. But now he recognised his chance to rekindle the old flame, be it only for a little while. Surging excitement gripped him at the thought of Anna's amorous surrender, spontaneous and sensual, given with an abandon, foreign as much as contemptuous to women around him. Spurred on by concepts of ardent embraces, he hastened homeward.

First of course Zurn had to be straightened out. Shooing off reason and attempting to cast caution to the wind, he persuaded himself to act. That dog would be silenced, come what may. Poison leapt up, but he dismissed that notion immediately. Anna would think it a cowardly deed, which surely would not ignite the fire of stagnant passion in her veins. Only confrontation could achieve that, steadfast demands coupled with threats of consequences.

Hardly did he warm up to the idea, when Zurn's hulking figure rose up before his inner eye. The man was a ruffian, no amount of pretence at gentility could hide that fact. He managed a nightclub down at the New Westminster wharf, where he was forced to deal regularly with boisterous customers. When Rusk was told about it, he remarked:

"I suppose you need to employ bouncers?"

Long after he recalled Zurn's amused look prior to saying:

"What for? I have two sturdy arms, have I not? Here I will show you how it is done. First I admonish loudmouthed revellers quietly. Should he, or she for that matter, pay no heed, then watch."

Before Rusk knew what was up, he felt himself in mid-air and carried around the yard. Setting him down, Zurn chuckled:

"You see Willy, I need no bouncers. So far I have met no one that I could not handle. Three, four steps and out they go. Whether vertically or horizontally is up to them."

Yes, Rusk remembered well, even more so Zurn's closing remark:

"Ha, not too long ago two toughs were going to show me. Do you know where they ended up?"

When Rusk shook his head, Zurn said between bursts of laughter:

"In the hospital Willy, where they are still praying for better times."

That is were I am going, Rusk mused, unless – unless; yes, unless I manage to intimidate this high-flown muscleman somehow, prior to an approach, but how? Racking his brain all the way to the edge of the park, a great sigh of relief escaped his breast. He had an idea.

"Well my dear, how was your day?" he inquired of his wife, who stood outside the fence.

"Miserable, that confounded hound snarls and barks every time I step out of the house," she complained.

"Don't worry Anna, I will take care of it," he promised.

"You – you will?" she remarked with rounded eyes and a tone sounding more disbelieving than appreciative.

"Yes darling, just give me a few days to work out a plan."

That she found odd, yet typically Willy. To her mind walking over to the fence and calling Zurn to have a man to man discussion, needed no prior stratagems. However, she said nothing, but her pouting lips spoke volumes. Knitting his brow, Rusk remarked somewhat puzzled:

"Isn't it peculiar that a dog behaving well for years, suddenly acts up?"

"What does it matter, I'm not a psychoanalyst, just a woman trying to stand on her right to peace and quiet."

It was a reasonable request, he decided. After all, neighbours must be considerate. Should they forget, well, a gentle reminder could do no harm. Yet he had a presentiment of ungentle consequences.

There were two things Rusk was unaware of. One was his wife's recent high words with Hilde Zurn, who accused her squarely with seeking a dalliance with her husband. The other, that Anna intentionally provoked the dog. His ability to observe was marred by images of Anna's soft embraces and heavenly promises. He sorely needed love and appreciation, considering his sinking self-confidence, as much as rising rivalry at his place of work. Younger men were nipping at his seat of power.

The next day he visited one of the gun shops downtown. The eager vendor, blessed with a discerning eye, sensed immediately a profitable sale. A well-dressed gentleman, displaying a refined deportment, usually presented no difficulties. They had money, besides being well regarded in the community, therefore precluding complications with permits.

"A pistol you say, sir, what kind?"

A sheepish look skimmed over Rusk's countenance, he was not prepared for such inquiries. To scare someone, he was about to say, however, he bit his lips on time. The vendor, a reliable judge of personalities immediately took on the demeanour of a mentor.

"Is it meant to practice shooting, protection, or to start a collection?" he asked.

That was a routine question, hardly a probing one. The police would want to know in any case before considering the issuance of a permit. But the man across the counter appeared to be in a quandary; he hemmed and hawed as if his well-being depended on that simple answer.

Just naturally shy and irresolute, the vendor decided more amused than apprehensive. In his line of work one met all sorts, from paradoxical to felonious characters.

"For protection," Rusk blurted out.

He could not very well tell the truth, the law would not condone intimidation in any case. The salesman's face lit up. With one movement, so it appeared, he laid three formidable looking weapons on the counter. Rusk shrunk back visibly, whether on account of the noisy clank, or the sight of items he abhorred, was not evident. He chose the biggest one for reasons only known to him. The vendor advised:

"Of course a permit is required, which in your case I reckon, will be issued as a matter of course."

Saying so he produced an application form and handed Rusk a pen.

"How about ammunition Mr Rusk, will a box of one hundred do for now?"

Taken aback, Rusk nodded ascent.

A few days later, after successful conclusion of formalities, gun and ammunition lay in his hands.

"What is that for?" Anna wanted to know, surprised by his sudden change of heart, for she was well aware of his loathing for firearms.

"Oh, just – just in case," he muttered with a suggestive air, implying that their peaceful neighbourhood is changing to the worse.

Anna said nothing more, but a sardonic smile transformed her face into a mask of scorn.

Rusk took care to receive Zurn's attention while handling the newly acquired weapon, which was not long in coming. Zurn's booming intrusive voice in no time resounded across the fence:

"What's up Willy, playing solitaire?"

Rusk, pretending to be engrossed with something on the lawn, raised his hand, the one holding the pistol, and waved.

"What are you trying to do, scare the snails?"

Receiving no answer, thus feeling a bit peeved, he roared:

"Want to be hired on as a body guard? ha, ha, ha. Be careful now, the thing might be loaded," he admonished, not exactly solicitous.

These facetious remarks, not really taunts, nevertheless pricked Rusk's sensitive skin. Of course Zurn, being a persistent fellow, gave no peace till he received an explanation.

"I have joined a gun club, learning to shoot is the objective," he advised, while sending allusive glances towards Zurn's dog.

Noticing these purposeful gazes, Zurn swallowed the words that lay on his tongue. He looked quizzically from Rusk to the dog. Nodding as if comprehending, a smile, more of a smirk appeared on his lips. Stretching out his hand he said peremptorily:

"Here, let me see what you have."

Rusk shook his head decisively.

"No Heinz, can't do it," he replied firmly.

Taken aback, Zurn bellowed at him:

"Come off it Willy, don't be childish. I have handled more guns than you could imagine. There now, hand it to me."

Rusk stood his ground; for the first time since their acquaintance he refused to comply with Zurn's request. An innocent one certainly, but irksome to a man trying to assert himself in front of his wife. Because Anna witnessed all, she was standing in the upper balcony where Rusk espied her the moment she stepped outside. Her presence stirred him on.

As he gripped the pistol tighter, he felt an exhilarating force surging through his veins. Something unthinkable happened; he no longer stood in awe of his overbearing neighbour. Zurn's imperious manners failed to intimidate him for the first time since their acquaintance. This surprised and worried him at the same time, albeit not for long, because a rising elation gripped him like a sudden fever. Undoubtedly it was kindled by a vision of intoxicating rewards, surely coming his way after trimming Zurn to size.

She will revive her love, he thought, with the wild abandon of their early months of marriage, once convinced that small he might be, but still a man. Anticipation drove him on, innate caution tried to hold him back. Nevertheless he approached Zurn scowling fiercely and mocking loudly:

"Give it to me this instant, the great man says. Ha, ha and ha again! Your old tricks will not fly this time, nor ever after. Your clodhopping days are over, I tell you."

At the first instant Zurn was stunned, at the second he decided to put a good face on his neighbour's quirky behaviour. Raising both hands he said:

"Whoa Willy, take it easy."

Then as anger rose within him, Zurn raised his voice and bellowed:

"Are you drunk, or just straight crazy? Put that pistol away and start talking sensible."

Meanwhile the dog beside his master started barking furiously. That poured oil on Rusk's fire. Raising his arms and pointing the gun at the dog, he yelled:

"Tell that mutt to be quiet, or else."

"Or else, what?"

"He gets a slug right between his beady eyes," Rusk screamed loud enough to rouse the whole neighbourhood.

Turning to Zurn, who by now doubted his neighbour's sanity, Rusk threatened:

"As for you overgrown blowhard, you keep that cur quiet, if you know what's good for you."

To emphasize his warning Rusk started to wave the pistol violently in front of Zurn's face. At least that was the intent. But it never came to it, for Zurn, convinced that he dealt with a maniac, had taken to his heels shouting:

"Police, police, somebody call the police."

He ran for cover. His cries, however, where drowned out by the frantic yelps of his dog, who followed him into the house.

When Rusk realised what had happened, he visibly shrunk in body and soul. All life seemed to drain from him, transforming the fire-eater of a moment ago into a picture of misery. The pragmatic businessman, rather deliberate than rash, found his footing again. Moaning audibly, he dropped the gun and clapped both hands over his face. Amatory trysts, as much as Anna's alluring figure were pushed aside by the return of reality. His sober mind, proudly vaunted, recognised a sequel with all its unpleasant trimmings.

The law would take its course, governed however by proof that could be tailored. That much he had learned from business dealings; facts at times are secondary, what counts is presentation and believable witnesses. They were two, Zurn was alone, thus at a disadvantage. Raising his eyes he looked for Anna, whom he was unable to see. Had she witnessed all, he wondered, and if so, what would she say? The police would be here shortly, no doubt about it.

"Anna, Anna," he called just loud enough for her ears.

Receiving no answer, he proceeded towards the house. Then a thought struck him that raised his hopes. Maybe, just maybe Zurn might be seized by a fit of magnanimity and forget the incident after he tendered his apologies. Yet hardly had the notion entered his mind, when he cast it vigorously to the wind. Sooner would hell freeze over, he decided, before that imitation of a braggadocio could be so high-minded.

His wife could nowhere be found, which seemed curious, since he saw her a moment ago up on the balcony. Calling her name repeatedly, he searched through the house. Suddenly he remembered the pistol left behind. Prior to proceeding to the spot, he looked outside. True enough the police were on their way. Lights flashing, two cars stopped in front of Zurn's property. Soon they would show up at his house, for which reason it was imperative that he spoke to Anna prior to their arrival. Just as he collected the discarded gun, Anna called to him from the balcony. Waiving at her he announced:

"There you are Anna, the police are on their way. Can you come down for a moment."

When they met, Anna was shocked by her husband's paleness, reversely he was startled by a strange glow all over her face. But such was her nature, he remembered. Never to worry, live for the day, and the devil fetch the hindmost had been his wife's attitude since they met.

"You saw what happened?" he commented.

"Not really; I went down to answer a knock at the front door. But why do you ask?" she wanted to know more amused than concerned.

"The police will be here any moment, they will want your statement," he advised.

She chuckled.

"I might decide not to give one."

He shook his head.

"No Anna, that would look suspicious, besides Zurn, like myself, might have seen you on the balcony."

"What do you suggest, Willy?"

"To tell the truth."

"That would not look good," she interrupted.

"But not the whole truth," he finished by a knowing smile and a few nods.

"I will say that I heard voices in the backyard that roused my curiosity. You and Zurn were having words, which I assumed concerned the yapping dog. Just as I prepared to come down and enter the fray, the bell sounded, followed by repeated knocks. It was a youngster attempting to sell magazines, which I declined decidedly. When I later stepped outside through the back door, all was quiet again. The rest you know."

"Unfortunately so does Zurn," he almost blurted out.

The gun was not mentioned, whether intentionally because of an oversight, or out of unawareness, he neither knew nor attempted to find out. There was no time anyway, since the bell rang, announcing the arrival of the police. Two cruisers had pulled up, four grim looking officers in uniform stood at the threshold. Suspicion was written all over their faces, they seemed unsure whether to barge right in or to behave in a more civilised way. Perhaps Rusk's staid appearance, as much as his mature years, exerted some influence to show decorum.

"We come to investigate a complaint," said one of the policemen, a sergeant as it turned out.

"You know what it is about," stated a serious looking constable.

"More or less," admitted Rusk, acting surprised.

What a commotion over a trifle, his countenance seemed to express. He was in control of himself again, albeit still regretful of the recent lapse.

"Come in," he invited more amused than concerned.

He was not overly worried, nothing more terrible could happen beyond embarrassment with neighbours. Anna's deposition, while not exonerating him completely – it would not have been prudent to go that route – nevertheless was not particularly incriminating. Having heard noises had made her curious, thus stepping outside to investigate. Although surprised to see her husband engaged in an argument with their neighbour, it did not alarm her. True, she would have liked to hear what it was about, but the bell rang, accompanied by knocks at the entrance door. After she had dealt with the salesman outside, she hurried back upstairs to the balcony. Silence reigned, husband and neighbour, including his dog were gone. The police questioned her in detail.

"Did your husband aim a gun at Mr Zurn or his dog?"

"I saw nothing of the sort."

"Did he have a gun in his hand?"

"Not that I could tell."

That should be the extent of her testimony. Knowing his wife's obstinate Slavic mind, Rusk felt assured of her unyielding stand. Neither cajolery nor attempts at intimidation would change it. As mentioned, Rusk was a man of circumspection, not easily influenced by illusory concepts or dreamy suppositions. He recognised the possibility that someone else might have observed the altercation. Not in detail, since high hedges obstructed the view, but enough could have been seen that would render total denials more incriminating than exonerating. He and Anna understood each other, certain things could not be denied, it might promote the evidence rather than obscure it.

An ambience of distrust marked the police's investigation, manifesting itself by the officer's miens and gestures, not mentioning chuckles and snorts. His explanations, sounding contrived in view of the policemen's impressions, fuelled their suspicion rather than allaying it. It seemed improbable that an intrepid man, robust from head to toe, would show the white feather when confronted by a notoriously mild mannered, confirmed pacifist, almost half his size. No, Zurn probably sought the safety of his house amid a serious threat, which Rusk, a sedate, small man could not have caused unless armed.

Rusk's misgivings, never running deep, began to evaporate completely. The whole affair, unfortunate to be sure, might peter out. At least as far as the law was concerned. Of course making up with the Zurn's could well prove trickier. First, however, the police must be convinced, he realised. Indeed, he sensed their scepticism, a reluctance to believe his version, which ran counter to logic as much as their speculations.

However, it would be difficult to build a bridge from supposition to evidence, unless corroboration existed, or circumstances supported such assumptions. At the end his word might have to be weighed only against Zurn's testimony, thus precluding a tilt of the scales.

Little could be construed from the fact that this overgrown blusterer of a neighbour flew from the scene, with his yelping hound at his heels. The pistol? Well, that could be explained. First it was not loaded, ruling out intent to harm anyone. Zurn said he aimed it at the dog and him. That was but a figment of his imagination. Thus averred Rusk at the start of the interview, and now towards the conclusion his avowals did not change.

"You said, to begin with, the pistol was not loaded, inferring there is a sequel," remarked the sergeant, who evidently possessed more acumen than his subordinates.

"Quite so, sergeant. I meant to add that the gun, which I had taken out for cleaning, remained inadvertently in my hand when I hastened outside to investigate an unusual din."

"Din, what do you mean by that?" burst out the rookie.

Rusk cast a bemused glance in his direction, prior to continuing:

"A dog, heedless of his master's attempts, boisterous efforts I should add at appeasement, barked as if gone insane. Hurrying outside, I neglected to leave the gun behind."

"What happened then?" the sergeant inquired.

"I have told you twice already," Rusk replied with a tinge of reproach.

"Could you tell us once more?"

"When I approached Zurn, to find out the reason for the uproar, he bolted, followed by his yapping dog."

That appeared to be the end of the interview, from thereon all would be clear sailing. He could see the police report on the well-worn path to the archives. True, they were obliged to knock at all the neighbour's doors, taking their statements with waning enthusiasm, for some would no doubt be nothing but repetitions of rumours, originated and fanned by the Zurn's. It should be noted that the Zurn's were not exactly popular in the area. She was considered a vixen, as already mentioned, and he a chest pounding showman throwing his weight around.

Rusk chuckled quietly to himself, that file would be closed quick and irrevocably. He was barely able to suppress a complacent smile. They had conducted themselves well, he and his wife. They managed to finagle a potentially ticklish situation into a bagatelle. Indeed, how could the authorities wangle an indictment out of an incident lacking even a whiff of malicious intent, nor a single trace of harm done.

The pistol was not loaded, a fact duly noted in the policemen's little books. Let them try to fault him, because that burly, fang bearing fire-eater showed the white feather. The pistol in his hand? What of it. Zurn had known him for many years as absolutely peaceable and considerate. The district attorney would simply shake his head and put the report out of sight.

Such thoughts occupied Rusk as he accompanied the officers on their way out. For unknown reasons the rookie, a strapping young fellow, tarried behind the others. He seemed reluctant to leave. Turning his head repeatedly, he fell farther behind. A strange sensation gripped Rusk, he hardly dared to admit it; that young Lothario was ogling his wife. Knowing Anna, he was not surprised to notice her receptiveness. That Serbian blood of her's never rested. Did she wink, point, or just inadvertently raise a hand? He could not say, though in time he pondered considerably about it.

Without preamble the young policeman turned fully towards him and remarked with feigned unconcern:

"Mr Rusk, you said the pistol was not loaded."

"No, and I repeat, no."

"Is it loaded now?"

"Of course not," came a reply dripping with condescension.

At that moment Rusk's fate took a proverbial salto-mortale, meaning a leap backward. The sergeant, already beyond the threshold, stopped in his tracks. First a puzzled expression, as if trying to remember, darkened his face. Then all of a sudden he turned around and made his way back into the house. Anger creased his brow, shades of embarrassment hovered over his florid countenance.

"The gun, the gun," he mumbled while glancing approvingly at his subordinate.

He knew about its status of course, a mandatory check was made instantly after receipt of the complaint.

"Can we examine the gun?" he asked curtly.

Rusk, taken aback by this belated, moreover inappropriate request, hesitated, then just nodded his head. One of the constables had taken matters in hand already, because he too, like his chief, realised that they had been inexcusably negligent.

Opening the chamber, his face lit up, he gazed partly triumphantly, but also sheepishly at Rusk, and then at his fellow officers. Tilting the pistol, a bullet fell clanking on the table. Turning the drum slowly, five more followed. Every time one of the live bullets clattered on the table, the constable mocked:

"No, the gun is not loaded."

Rusk winced whenever a bullet dropped, while shrinking visibly into himself. Disbelief was written all over his face, the satisfied glow from before gradually changed to a mask of vexation and fear. He realised, without being told, the significance of this discovery.

"Impossible, it can not be," he muttered, while gazing distracted from one to the other.

"I don't understand, I don't understand," he moaned.

"Sergeant, I swear to it, that gun was never loaded since I bought it. You must believe me officers, I do not even know how it is done."

"What, the loading?" asked the rookie.

"Yes. The salesman wanted to make a demonstration, but I declined, pretending to be an old hand in matters of firearms."

His protestations led nowhere, they could not alter the fact that the pistol, contrary to his avowals, was fully loaded. Whether intentional or through an oversight, lay not in their precinct to decide. The sergeant said as much:

"We are only investigators, what we believe matters little, much less than what we see and hear. Our report will be submitted to the district attorney's office, who decides the next steps, if any."

"But – but…" Rusk tried again to remonstrate, however, the sergeant's raised hand silenced him.

Outside, when they were out of earshot, the sergeant turned towards the young constable:

"I'm sure glad you drew our attention to the pistol. It would have been deeply embarrassing had you not done so," he praised his subordinate.

"You thought of it in the nick of time, I will remember that, Tom," he added benevolently.

"What gave you the idea?" one of the other constables wanted to know.

"She did."

"You mean Mrs Rusk?" asked his superior.

"Chief, I don't know how to put it, the lady kept on looking at me in a most revealing way. To tell the truth, I thought she was giving me the eye."

"Well, that would not surprise me, my boy, after all you are good looking, besides some women get easily enamoured by men in uniforms," the sergeant chuckled.

The rookie's normal ruddy face turned crimson, averting his colleagues amused glances he said more:

"It was not that at all, as I soon found out. The lady endeavoured to arouse our interest in some object in the room. She repeatedly motioned her head towards the table, surreptitiously, mind you, but unmistakable so. When she finally made a sign of holding a gun, who's trigger she pretended to pull again and again, it dawned on me what she meant."

"I be darned," the sergeant uttered.

"Very interesting, Mrs Rusk, very interesting," he added.

Inside the house reigned complete consternation. Stung to the soul, Rusk paced the floor like a man chased by evil ghosts. Around the table he strode, stopping occasionally and clapping his hands over his face, which he removed not abruptly but gradually, while turning his head towards the pistol on the table. Seeing his hopes shattered, for the six bullets were now as then present, he started to wail anew:

"That gun was not loaded, Anna, I tell you, it could and can not be. Is fate playing a trick on me, or have I lost my mind?"

Off he went again, stomping around the table, lamenting more vehemently than before:

"Anna, tell me, am I a victim of rampant anxiety that induces grotesque visions? Say it Anna, please tell me it's all a mistake, a weird dream. That box of ammunition, practically obtruded on me, had never been opened. I will prove it in a moment."

Saying so he rumbled upstairs, where she soon heard him cursing and rummaging all in a lather. When he came rushing down, more tumbling than walking, he triumphantly held the bullet box in his outstretched hands:

"Here, take a look, the box has never been opened. See for yourself, the wrapping is still intact."

So it was. However, his wife only gave it a half-hearted glance. She no longer felt at ease in his presence, for she noticed that the husband of many years underwent a remarkable metamorphosis. Since their first kiss she had never seen him so out of joint. She always knew him as a man well composed, who deliberated prior to proceeding. Exuberance, her own for instance, he simply smiled at, or roundly condemned in others. Yet look at him now, she mused, he was turned into a regular stormy petrel.

To be sure, grounds for petulance were on hand, he needed no augur to foretell coming events. The loaded pistol, combined with his vehement denial that it was so, changed the entire aspect of the incident. But who put those bullets in the chamber?

Racking his brains about it led nowhere, suspecting his wife Anna confounded more than it enlightened. Alone the thought, fleeting as it were, made him wince as if lashed with a whip. First it was senseless, second he doubted that she ever handled firearms. She would not know how to place bullets into an empty chamber. Besides, who would give them to her without proper authorization.

So it went for days. Weary of his unceasing litany about sinister machinations, bearing all signs of an inflamed, if not disturbed mind, she avoided his company as much as possible. His mordant expostulations, at times aimed at everyone, including himself, drove her out of the house. He found no peace during daytime, nor rest at night.

Laying in bed, desperately seeking sleep, the ever recurring question assailed him: Who inserted those bullets, and why was it done? It certainly was not him, that conclusion he had reached some days ago at a rare lucid interval. The box containing the hundred bullets remained untouched, no doubt about it. Besides not a single one was missing, he determined after counting them three times.

He also distinctly remembered inspecting the chamber, as advised by the dealer, and in accordance with the licence's tenet, prior to taking the pistol with him. It was empty, no doubt about it. Therefore the bullets got in there between the time when the gun fell to the ground and when he picked it up again, after a lapse of less than five minutes.

But there was no one in the yard beside himself. Anna, perish the thought of even suspecting her, never stepped out of the house during that entire period. He appeared to be faced by an unsolvable mystery, an uncanny, yet momentous occurrence portending grief, and more grief.

The proverbial sword fell upon him three weeks later when two policemen announced themselves, armed with a warrant. The charge: Endangering the life of others with a lethal weapon. An arrest was not deemed necessary in view of his respected standing in the community, supported by long and noteworthy participation in the world of business. A preliminary inquiry was set for a Monday, three months hence.

After the police had departed Rusk staggered towards a chair, where he slumped down. Burying his face in both hands, he groaned:

"Now we are in a fix, our happy days are numbered."

His wife gave no immediate reply; when she did however, his head came up in surprise.

"It could have been worse," she consoled.

"What do you mean?" he burst out.

"Well, you could have pulled the trigger, thereby killing or maiming Zurn."

He looked at her fully, confused, then quizzical. He did not want to trust his eyes at first. Was he seeing a spectre, some strange apparition never encountered before? Her face, customarily well-meaning and open, had acquired an expression utterly strange, if not frightening.

He blinked several times, endeavouring to remove possible motes from his eyes, which blurred his vision. But no, there she stood, the wife of two decades, familiar in body, yet alien in intellect. Like a woman scorned, it flashed through his mind, vexed by shattered hopes, disappointed and frustrated beyond control.

However, it could not be. His imagination, distorted by worries and fear, must be playing him false, he determined. Anna had faults, but deviousness counted not among them. He shook his head vigorously from side to side, in an effort to rid himself of fancies conjured up by a harassed soul. It was just as well, for Anna took on immediately her wonted guileless air again, including that ever seductive smile.

"How could I injure someone with…" an empty gun, he meant to say, but recalling the police's findings, he fell silent.

Something else, however, induced him to swallow his words; his wife's demeanour. Granted, he was in a state of confused agitation, that could easily obfuscate a man's judgement. But just the same, the sting of suspicion had entered his heart.

The firm's lawyers, Hurton and Meach, undertook his defence. Mr Borge, an associate versed in criminal law handled the case. He possessed a sharp wit, topped by an acerbic tongue, which he was ever ready to bring to bear. Shilly-shallying he abhorred, taking the steer by the horns was more to his liking.

"Now, Mr Rusk, let us understand each other from the word go. Tell me all, little or less, but don't attempt to bamboozle me. Whether I believe it is immaterial. I will ask you questions that the prosecutor will surely confront you with to the point of nausea. Those you must answer, therefore you might as well get used to them. I know two things: the law and court procedure. What I am not privy to is what happened. So start telling me."

That was stated right after the initial handshake. At the first meeting they got along fine, taking as it were each other's pulse, treading lightly while smiling extensively. The second time around, however, wrinkles of annoyance darkened Mr Borge's brow, he was no longer pleased.

"Let's recapitulate," he requested with a tinge of irritation.

"The gun was not loaded you say, from the moment you took it to the yard till it dropped out of your hand."

"That is so."

"Why did you take it with you?"

"I – I could not say."

That was when clouds started to accumulate, announcing the attorney's displeasure. He looked at his client without moving a muscle, however, his eyes said it all. Shrugging his shoulders he went on:

"When the police checked the pistol, about two hours later, six live bullets were found in the chamber, is that correct?"

"Yes, but I do not understand how they got in there."

"Somebody inserted them," the lawyer announced.

"Maybe so, but who?"

"You, your wife, or persons unknown," Mr Borge intimated laconically.

Noticing Rusk's bewildered stare, he added:

"It was not you. According to your statement no one else visited the yard nor the house, therefore your wife loaded the gun. There you have it in a nutshell."

Rusk started as if stung:

"To say that is preposterous," he exclaimed.

Hardly had these words been uttered when he was reminded:

"Yet you are saying it."

Chuckling, Rusk admitted:

"I can see your point."

"Have no worries, no one will believe it anyway," he was advised.

Next time they met, Rusk immediately sensed signs of misgivings etched on the lawyer's countenance. He came to the point:

"I have received adverse news," Mr Borge said.

"What kind?"

"They have a witness who saw and heard everything, so they claim."

Rusk's face turned several shades paler.

"Who is it," he wanted to know.

"They have not told me, any guesses?"

"Hm, not really. Probably some pesky neighbour set on mischief," Rusk offered, then continued to say:

"No reason to fret, our yard is pretty well hidden from view. Some busybody most likely is vying for centre stage, his allegations will crumble under examination."

"It is a she, I am advised."

"A petticoat? So much the better."

Mr Borge looked worried, he evidently did not share his client's optimism. Sitting there motionless, his probing eyes seemed focused at intangible dangers lurking behind layers of portentous vapours. He was a prudent man, not readily swayed by impalpable evidence, and even less by hope. His keen mind, honed by years of experience balked at confidence conjured up by nothing more than anticipation, which in his profession could evaporate quicker than gossamer in the morning sun. He felt neither regret nor joy in destroying his client's expectations, reality must be faced.

"The witness apparently corroborates Zurn's allegations in most parts."

Rusk started:

"In what way?"

"That you were in a frenzy; that you pointed a gun first at the dog and then at Zurn, who turned and fled."

"She is lying," burst out Rusk.

Mr Borge had a knack of expressing disapproval by means of facial movements, which said more than a hundred words. He noticed Rusk's sudden pallor, as much as his overzealous utterance and fidgety demeanour, hardly befitting a staid businessman. He asked once more:

"You have no idea who this witness might be?"

Shaking his head several times, Rusk replied:

"Maybe Mrs Zurn, or some other prying neighbour."

Mr Borge was not pleased, observing his client closer, he remarked:

"It is not Mrs Zurn, nor any of the women living nearby. I checked them out. Incidentally I can inform you that you are universally liked, certainly by the womenfolk."

Mr Borge felt tempted to add that this could not be averred in the case of his wife. But he refrained, being aware of Rusk's Achilles heel in matters concerning his wife.

On the way home more than one thought raced through Rusk's mind. Ideas tumbled over suppositions; some he hurled in the direction of no return, others he merely waved aside for later use. Who loaded the gun, when was it done, and why? Why indeed! As Anna said, he should thank his stars for not pulling the trigger. What a calamity that would have been. He could see himself sitting behind bars the rest of his life.

Mulling over his wife's comforting words, something suddenly struck him. It was this: He had left the room after ascertaining that the chamber was empty. Merely a minute, mind you, but still the gun remained out of sight for that period. But what of it, only his wife was in the house during that time, precluding any tampering with the gun on the table.

As mentioned, Mr Rusk was a pragmatic man, circumspect and imbued with sound reasoning, and the gift of keen observation. Normally that is, but not of late, as remarked previously. His wife's allure instilled desires that increasingly remained unfulfilled, therefore blunting his sagacity as much as blurring his judgement. In his eyes she could do no wrong. As his ardent feelings grew, critical observation waned. Even remotely thinking of Anna's involvement in this affair, he considered sacrilegious. Besides, he felt assured she was incapable of handling any firearms, not mentioning the procurement of bullets.

True, she was the only person around while the pistol lay unguarded on the table, yet drawing any conclusion from that deemed him absurd. Even more so when searching for a motive. None existed of course, the mere notion deserved a good laugh and two sound kicks. Who in the world would think of such an eccentric idea that could sling a noose around his neck, yet benefit no one. For revenge? hardly, because enemies he had none. For gain perhaps, or prestige, or just following a whim of the moment? Hang it, the more he pondered, the less he understood; least of all the veritable Houdini feat of entering their house unseen, finding and loading the pistol, then leaving the house again unseen. All within one minute, presupposing of course that he knew the gun's calibre.

Neither rhyme nor reason existed for such obtuse theories, he emphatically murmured to himself. By the same token he derided the assumption that someone had tampered with the pistol left on the ground. Yet that gun was found fully loaded by the police who inspected it. No doubt the prosecution would construe some sort of intent, not friendly to be sure.

His wife was at home when he arrived. The door flew open before his shadow touched the threshold.

"How did it go?" she asked eagerly.

"Not too good," he answered glumly.

She glanced at him in her inimitable fashion, with one eye encouraging, and the other twitting.

"Well, sit down and tell me all about it," she said in a reassuring tone.

He walked to a chair where he sunk down heavily.

"What is amiss, darling?"

Raising his head he was going to say: "They have a witness who saw and heard everything." But seeing his wife's peculiar gaze, he gave an evasive explanation:

"They, the prosecution that is, claim to have an airtight case. However, Mr Borge, the lawyer, thinks they are blowing their own horn."

It cost him considerable effort to refrain from fixing his eyes on Anna, for a palpable transformation darkened her usual bright countenance, which fascinated and repelled him at the same time. A sardonic expression, tempered with regret, whisked across her strained face, leaving behind shadows he had never seen there before.

Bewildered he rose and turned away. Feeling a twinge of guilt because of the prevarication, he nevertheless obeyed a voice from within, timid yet oracular, exhorting to be cautious. Anna was not herself, she appeared to be in the grip of mysterious forces.

His head was in a spin, he felt the need to be alone, remote from his wife, down at the shores of his beloved river. She was a good companion to him, a trusted partner, supportive and plucky. True, love had fluttered away, carrying passion on its wings far beyond the broad Fraser. But friendship had endured, at least so he thought until now.

What went on behind that brave, defiant front erected by Anna Miclas, his wife of twenty years? Her ever present, seductive smile had grown forced and twisted. Her eyes, till recently enlivened by a host of dancing imps, were taking on a dull, veiled look, as if to conceal a sprouting uncertainty.

Of late she daubed herself with kohl and make-up, which in his eyes made her appear like a woman in need of attention. Albeit not his, although it was offered in abundance. She was still an attractive woman, enticing enough to turn any man's head. No, Anna was no longer herself, that refreshing ingenuousness seemed gradually to fade, giving way to a surprising and alarming brashness.

Indeed, Anna was no longer herself. She seemed buffeted by doubts, assailed by the winds of uncertainty that forced her hitherto undaunted spirit to seek refuge between the walls of deceit. She was never like that, meaning devious, morose and evasive. He decided to have a heart to heart talk with her, clean the slate as it were, since he felt responsible for her uneasiness. Most likely nothing serious burdened her mind, beyond anxiety over his approaching fate. His normally keen insight had obviously forsaken him, or at least had been curtailed.

Unrequited love, as much as desires unappeased, marred his judgement. Otherwise he would have realised that Anna's personality began to change over six months ago. True, he noticed her sudden fondness for finery, accompanied by an untoward penchant to doll herself up. However, what his eyes saw, his mind refused to acknowledge.

"Anna, what is troubling you?" he asked.

Startled she raised her head abruptly. For an instant she looked vulnerable, he noticed a flicker of uncertainty emanating from that robust exterior. But only for an instant, almost at once her eyes, dark and shining, were all daggers and arrows again.

"What do you mean?" she demanded to know in a bellicose tone, softened by traces of remorse.

She looked ill at ease, as if caught in some shameful act. The realisation made him bolder, reckless really beyond his wonted discretion. He could not free himself from the impression that she had something to reveal, if prompted the right way. All was not well with her, nor between them.

"Are you worried about the upcoming inquiry?"

He remained standing while wavering between an urge to say more and the desire to be tactful. She looked at him with eyes as never before, mournful yet illuminated by a manifestation of genuine relief.

"Sit down Willy, it is time to make a clean sweep," she said in a voice neither defiant nor rueful, however, leaving no doubt that something momentous was going to follow.

Astonished he took a chair and waited for her to continue. How desirable she still is, he thought, while glancing almost shyly at her. A strange glow spread over her face, emanating from the depth of an anguished, genuine soul.

"I will tell you all Willy; be shocked, detest me, divorce me, do what ever gives you relief, I deserve the worst."

"Anna, what are you alluding to?"

"Treachery Willy, infamous deceit."

He shook his head in disbelief, which soon changed from astonishment to repugnance, and finally to sheer horror. His perception of Anna's character received a resounding blow.

"Your lawyer must have advised you that the prosecution has a material witness besides Zurn."

"Yes, he did, but in my estimation that is nothing but scaremongering."

She gave him one of her quizzical smiles.

"The witness is I," she announced.

"But – but…"

"I know, I know, my testimony given to the police in your presence should cause no concern. But I made a mistake, the last one I hope. To explain it strains the imagination in retrospect, I can't do it. Perhaps out of contrariness, confusion, or momentary mental aberration, I told Martha Stanix everything."

“The neighbour across the street?”

“Yes. You know what an awful gossip that woman is. In no time the news, surely a morsel to Mrs Stanix, travelled around till the police got wind of it. They contacted me to make a statement, which I did after a few promptings.”

“Did you sign it?”

“Yes,” she said, nodding her head.

“What did you tell them exactly?

“The truth.”

Burying his face in his hands he moaned:

“You sealed my fate.”

Then he added in a voice dripping with disappointment: ”You stabbed me in the back, I can’t believe it.”

“More than that, I stabbed you through the heart,” she confessed.

“I don’t follow you.”

“For one thing I loaded your pistol,” she said so deliberate that he felt stung to the quick.

Jumping from his chair he cried:

“Humbug, you are talking nonsense. I know how you loath firearms, even the sight of a pellet gun makes you bristle. I bet you never had one in your hands.”

“Bet on, Willy, bet on, but let me tell you that you are going to loose.”

And so he did, as subsequent developments proved. She continued:

“Devious thoughts teach quickly. Let me tell you, I soon learned to insert and remove bullets in a jiffy. The pistol was at my disposal for days during your absences at work. Therefore ample time existed to practice.”

Rusk threw up his arms in exasperation:

“But you had no bullets. Remember the box has never been opened, the intact wrapping attests to that. Come, Anna, give it a rest. You are distraught no doubt, which is not surprising in view of recent occurrences. Your judgement is skewed to the point where imagination and reality become blurred. True, the bullets were in there, how it was managed, or who perpetrated it, I can not even guess. One thing, however, is certain: not even a magician could have charged that pistol practically under my nose, besides in less than a minute."

His wife could not help smiling. What she heard was vintage Willy, loyal and trusting to the end. It made her uncomfortable to cause an upright, albeit priggish man so much grief. However, she vindicated her treachery with a sting of self-serving explanations.

To begin with, he was not the right mate for her. As time ticked on, this realisation became the proverbial worm that never stops turning. His flaunted tolerance, condescending and false in her perception, vexed more than it enhanced. The most crushing burden, however, she found to be the ambience of primness. Natural feelings were suppressed, thus creating a fertile field for prurience.

What the girl from far away Serbia accepted blithely, the mature woman perceived as a passing bell to her spirit. An atmosphere laden with hypocrisy, heavy with pretentious virtues, had confused and hardened her. After a while she saw her husband as nothing but a mechanical man, devoid of passion, mortally afraid of nonconformity. He neither made her blood rise anymore, nor her heart quiver. No, they were not meant for each other. The tree of life, her being as a woman, had wilted under that stern gaze of a strait-laced man. She said more:

"Procuring bullets was easy. There are dozens of illicit places along Hasting Street that sell them with no questions asked. Willy, I set you up, and now I will tell you how and why."

She continued after a moment's pause, while her gaze wandered across the park, down the embankment to the restless river below. Often she sat there, lost in thoughts, pretending to be among explorers who nearly two centuries ago paddled on the fabled stream. But not today, maybe never again.

Rusk, by now thoroughly confused and annoyed, wanted to leave the room. He felt an urge to run away from his wife, who so dastardly had betrayed him. He sat down again instead, waiting for her next words.

“When I noticed you walking around the yard, wielding the pistol in a revealing fashion, I was struck by an idea; I saw my chance.”

“I am not following you,” her husband interrupted.

“You will soon. There was an opportunity to see my wish fulfilled. You see Willy, I wanted Zurn dead.”

“You are insane. Just because of a barking dog? That is beyond me.”

“I’m not insane, just a scorned woman intent to get even. I had an affair with him which he ended abruptly in a most humiliating fashion. Perhaps now you will understand why I put these bullets in the gun. I hoped you would shoot him.”

“Which I almost did,” Rusk moaned aghast.

Then he lost his composure. The proud descendant of stiff upper lip Anglophones collapsed on the table and wailed:

“What a mess I’m in, how could you do that to me!”

He broke out into a regular jeremiad, thereby sealing his fate. In his absence at the lawyer’s, Anna had reached a decision. She would not only make a confession to her husband, but repeat everything at the court inquiry. True, this would incriminate herself, but Willy might be saddled with nothing more than a suspended sentence. The danger of a lengthy jail term for herself looked real enough, but what of it. First, she deserved it, second, her husband might retain his freedom.

But such noble and atoning sentiments subsided quickly, they were drowned out by Willy’s sobs. As he lamented abjectly, her sympathy changed to annoyance, then gloating, and finally to outright abhorrence. A moment ago she wanted to beg for his forgiveness, but not anymore. Now she was prepared to let him have his punishment, whether just or not.

For something curious happened to Anna Rusk, conventional wife, conformist down to the frozen smile and coy behaviour. She became once more Anna Miclas, the wide-eyed wench from the spurs of the Carpathians. The man sitting there, crumbled up, railing against perfidious hussies, a foreigner whom he so graciously had taken under his wings, appeared terribly strange to her.

The notion that he could have been her husband, with whom once she was intimate, made her chuckle derisively. He was not a man to be compared with the ones in her memory, who tilled the ancestral fields in the shadow of the wild mountains. How different they were. Although they ploughed and hoed till their muscles ached, they still laughed uproariously while dallying with every female between the ages of fourteen and ninety.

At break times they invited each other to tussles, crowing lustily after each victory. They brawled, drank and sang. Yes, they cried, but never whimpered. Their reckless foolishness earned them many a blow, which was taken on the chin uncomplainingly. When at sixes and sevens they squeezed their troubles between callous hands and shook them to the roots. True, sadness came easy, as much as crying out in sorrow. Yet they never snivelled.

These reminiscences were cut short by a more pressing matter; the realisation that she stood at the crossroads of life. A decision had to be made; to prolong present conditions was unthinkable.

In a flash she knew what had to be done, she must return to the place of her youth. Her heart grew cold at the thought of such a momentous leap, but oddly enough her spirit rose. A sudden excitement gripped her, a rising elation as once at the sight of her first love. Walking beside Laszlo Marek made her heart leap to her throat while the ground swayed under her feet. Thrilled to the core she felt then, inspired to giddiness she was now.

Without deigning to look at her husband, whom she had meanwhile eliminated from her future, she walked out. He could rot in jail for all she cared, she would find someone else. A man this time, who would not shrink from a woman with blood in her veins and the mark of boldness imprinted on her brow. He always found her too earthy, despite her efforts to be the prissy damsel in distress of his concept. Let them send a hundred subpoenas, she vowed, her evidence would never grace their transcripts. Serbia was far away, Anna Miclas would be difficult to find.

Life in the house grew unbearable. Her nature being what it was, quickly stung to the soul, but even quicker to reach out again, she made several attempts to have a heart to heart talk with her husband.

"Willy, I have something to say to you," she announced.

When he turned on his heels and walked away, she was about to flare up, but thought better of it.

So it went for a whole week. Anna, now as before determined to divorce herself from him, nevertheless felt the need to sort things out, if only to soothe her troubled conscience. Not being available as a witness would certainly be advantageous to him, as much as to herself.

Had Willy reported to the police what she had divulged in a burst of sentimentality? Hardly, she decided, because it would expose him to ridicule, besides tarnishing his manly pride. Moreover, who would believe it, especially after checking with Zurn who most certainly could be relied on to deny it; the affair that is. Because she had not told the whole truth for obscure reasons, which she now welcomed.

There was no affair, just an embarrassing rebuff which, though opening the sluice gates of her wrath, did not ignite the wish to see him dead. His tattling to his wife managed that, who of course spread it around the neighbourhood. They all had a good laugh no doubt, but she almost had the last giggle.

Suddenly Rusk's attitude changed, he showed himself amenable to reconciliation. One morning after greeting her most cordially, he said contritely:

"Forgive me Anna for being so beastly lately, I was in shock, that is the only excuse I can offer. But now I am out of it and ready to thrash things out as you suggested several times already."

Unable to disguise her satisfaction, she consented.

"How about this afternoon when I return from work?" he proposed.

"That would suit me fine," she answered.

They met as arranged in the living room. After a string of small talk, seemingly unending to Anna, he steered towards the vital points. Not however, before he went to open the patio door leading to a veritable thicket of roses and lilacs. Returning he chuckled as if disconcerted over his obtuseness.

"I brooded and ruminated for over a week now without reaching a conclusion. While I can not accept the fact that you had an affair with Heinz Zurn, I can understand and believe it. After all, he is handsome in a sort of roguish way. Wishing him harm after being jilted, well, that is hardly surprising. But Anna, I am still unable to swallow the fable that you loaded the pistol, under a minute to boot. Now as before I'm willing to wager my bottom dollar that you do not know how."

Stung to where it hurts, Anna jumped up.

"You bet, will you? Well, I shall prove it right now," she cried.

"Give me that gun and don't forget the ammunition. By golly, I shall show you."

She did not notice the smile on her husband's face, nor did she pay any attention to the astounding alacrity with which weapon and bullets were produced. No, Anna was all afire for being called in doubt. She grabbed the pistol with both hands, opened the chamber and inserted six bullets, all in less than a minute.

"There," she cried jubilantly, "do you now believe me?"

Indeed he did, as much as Mr Borge who crouched nearby behind the shrub. He had heard and seen everything.

Next day two policemen took her in custody. She had won the bet, but lost a dream.

# The Warrant

Harry Rupert was still young, which might have accounted for his readiness to go with Roald Rudin to the bush to lay out an area on behalf of the government. Gold had been discovered in the Selkirk Mountains, in the middle of nowhere. He did not like the older man from the moment he laid eyes on him. Asking why, would have been futile, for young men usually possess far more intuition than psychological vocabularies. He probably would have shrugged his shoulders, saying:

"I don't know, but he gives me the shudders."

In any case he needed the work, besides being of an adventures bent, he liked roughing it in unchartered terrain.

A keener, older observer would in all likelihood have noticed something odd about Rudin. His eyes were not synchronised for one. The left drooped as if ashamed of the right's expression of rampant trickery. It made him look like a satyr. The other disconcerting impression conveyed could be termed greed, it practically oozed out of every pore of his body. It was not in his power to conceal this vice for long, sooner or later one gained the impression that both his hands were forever stretched out and grasping.

Rudin was an excellent surveyor, but regrettably hardly anyone liked to work with him. Now, of what value is the best surveyor without a reliable rodman. Out east he had made the rounds, as the saying goes, his firm's difficulty to supply him with help increased to a point where he had to be laid off.

However, they hesitated not a moment when he asked for a written recommendation; it was issued in the twinkle of an eye. With that paper in his pocket, plus his gear securely tied, he wandered westward. He did not stop till he felt the burning prairie sun on his back. No reputation he figured, good or bad, could follow him so far. Obtaining work proved to be easy, keeping rodmen, however, turned out to be more difficult.

He drifted right across the immeasurable plains of Manitoba and Saskatchewan, till he arrived at the oil fields of Alberta. In between he did a stint, just for money, up in Churchill one summer. He was happy to see winter approaching, which signalled the end of his contract. He neither liked the migrating polar bears, nor the needle sharp winds that came howling down Hudson Bay. He finally ended up in Revelstoke, British Columbia.

He could have fallen on his knees when one fine morning he stepped out of the train. So much beauty amid an air of innocence was almost painful to take in at one glance. True, the Rockies were majestic, an impressive sight to see, their allure is instantaneous. Soon however, they appear cold and distant compared to the Columbias, which inveigle rather than challenge.

Finding work as always set no hurdles. Wages were surprisingly high in the less developed west, though working conditions were harsh. The gold commissioner introduced four young men to him, all of sturdy build and equable disposition. He chose Harry Rupert, which he soon regretted.

Their gear, pack animals plus themselves were transported by road up to a halfway point between Revelstoke and Mica, about fifty miles north. From there it went eastward, almost in the shadow of the sombre Argonaut Mountains. Gold had been discovered some ways up at the Goldstream River, therefore land needed to be delineated for mining use. Roads in those days did not exist in the region, just a footpath of sorts led to the foothills of ice fields. Trouble lay in the air from thereon. Not in any physical or even visible way, but nevertheless seething underneath diminishing layers of social pretence.

From the moment they were alone with their donkeys, Harry's resentment grew, which, however, he made an attempt to disguise. It was not easy to suppress an innate confiding and gregarious nature. One side of him was forever ready to show his hail fellow well met disposition, but the other, unable to divest itself from hereditary prejudices, held him back. Had reason been allowed to prevail, life would have been more amenable for both. Nothing detrimental could be imputed to Rudin, he showed himself fair, honest and companionable. The only stroke against him was his appearance, an irritant to Harry Rupert's sense of ethics.

Rudin was not always so harmoniously disposed; far from it, but he had learned to keep his vile emotions in check. He knew that he was no beauty, but even more so did he realise that looks can deceive. To be considered ugly, very well, a man sustains little disadvantage from it; but being thought treacherous and evil was an entirely different matter. It took a long time to accept the fact that his unsavoury reputation stemmed solely from a self-consciousness, because of his appearance. Deeming himself unsightly of course rendered him so. A look in his direction unleashed the demons of insecurity. Feeling scorned and judged adversely, he became defensive and belligerent. But as mentioned he succeeded in great part to overcome these impulses. Somehow however, young Rupert tested his resolution sorely.

Their first row took place on the third day, rather evening, while setting up camp for the night. Rudin was seething inwardly the whole day already. Overt reasons for it did not exist; his helper gave no grounds for displeasure, he showed himself tractable and uncomplaining. But his antipathy towards his boss was evident, no amount of good will could deny its presence. Rudin felt hurt and grew defensive, which in turn made him morose and prone to nit-pick. Of course Rupert was not loath to parry with defiance and recalcitrance.

An outburst appeared unavoidable, and it did come. True, Rupert was not exactly gentle when handling gear and outfit, but no matter, his boss by that time would have found fault with the very way he walked, whistled, or looked at the mountains. Alone his rebuking glances and withering stares annoyed Rupert more than the most scathing criticism uttered. It made him rebellious, which might have explained his clumsiness when unloading their gear from the donkeys' backs. He dropped one of the bags. Rudin started as if attacked.

"Kindly be a bit more careful," he practically bellowed at him.

Rupert just laughed, because really there was no cause to become upset. Bags containing tents and blankets were never treated gingerly. In fact he was astonished at the rough and tumble way with which his boss handled them.

"Not to worry chief, there is nothing fragile in there," he said casually.

"Fragile or not, I absolutely forbid you to roughhouse what is mine."

His agitation increased with every word.

"Since I'm at it, let me tell you something else," he cried.

"Oh, what is that?"

"It is this: From day one you have been a strain on my nerves. Inimical to the bones you are, refractory beyond endurance; I have a good mind to send you back," he threatened.

Of course it was but a bold front, and well he knew it. Out in the bush different values prevail than amidst civilisation. Authority meant very little unless bolstered by physical strength, determination and gumption. Rupert possessed all three of these attributes, Rudin none. Not yet old, but prematurely worn out by brooding and the heavy chips on his shoulders, he hankered for an easier time. He wanted so much to change his life around, to end his flight from the long shadows of an unpleasant past.

But once again his hopes were dashed, frustrated by a man he actually liked. Whose beaming countenance, so in contrast to his own moroseness, he thought would act as a guiding light to a brighter future, perhaps even lead to an amiable fellowship. Reality, however, went its own way; he found himself, as dozen times before, on the path of never ending dissension. His fondest wish, an all consuming desire to be liked and respected, lay shattered at the column of his helper's resentment, which bristled with challenging mockery. Any doubts were dispelled by Rupert's next words, rather a diatribe.

"Ha, ha, ha, you promise what you can't deliver. Sending me back, will you? Shoo me away like a disobedient poodle. Ho, ho, ho, you and which army. I could pick you up with one hand and toss you halfway across the river."

Indeed, such boasting was not so far-fetched, the younger man's physical prowess could not be easily matched.

Hostility now took its course. Both, however, tried to smother it with a new found courtesy. For a while Rudin seriously played with the idea of turning back. But on second thought he realised, while revenge on Rupert might be sweet, consequences for himself would certainly be sour. Rupert's outburst had cut him to the quick, for deep down he was a sensitive man, easily aggrieved, hankering for acceptance and praise. However, going back without completing his task was unthinkable, in particular because of such flimflam as an incompatible rodman.

His name from thereon would give cause to slam many doors before his nose. At his age and sullied fame, by now probably approaching the foothills of the Rockies, it would be worse than a Pyrrhic victory. Just the same, he could neither forget nor forgive his assistant's slight. Time would come to pay him back without harm to himself.

Rupert sensed his chief's intentions, but also his indecision. Nevertheless it made him more careful, for he needed this job more than could be imagined. Not only was he down to his last dollar, but also in dire need to be far away from civilisation, for reasons which he would have been averse to blazon abroad. His skeleton in the closet could now rest for a while without being rattled. He too fled from a tortured past, as much as from the cities of Eastern Canada.

Here, west of the Great Divide he felt reasonably secure from harassment and persecution. A few years respite would do wonders for his ego; by then, time should have healed the wounds of injustice. His mood became conciliatory, his behaviour compliant, for he harboured no wish to goad his superior.

Two days later they arrived at the main camp, which consisted of a sturdy cabin sitting above the Goldstream River. As mentioned, Rupert took great care not to offend his chief, whom he now found shrouded in clouds of animosity. No, Rudin was unable to forgive, but powerless to set in motion what his heart desired. With just a few thousand dollars to his name he would have quit the very day of Rupert's display of impertinence. The thought of inflicting punishment on him looked enticing, but turning his back on years of misery he deemed even more alluring. He yearned for a change, away from here, perhaps moving to Mexico where life was more benign and less expensive.

Despite an atmosphere of gloom and tension, work progressed without a hitch till the day when an accident happened. Rupert fell down a cliff and hurt himself badly. When Rudin heard his outcry, followed by loud moaning, his first impulse was relief; a sense of euphoria took hold of him. He hesitated a while, unsure what should be done. An urge to run off, somewhere at least out of earshot, almost overcame him. But an ingrained sense of duty, a reflex borne out of habit, gained the upper hand.

He looked for a spot where rocks offered a foothold and climbed down. It was no easy feat, but much less of an effort than bringing Rupert up to his cot. When after a cursory examination, Rudin discovered no outward injuries, he wavered between pangs of disappointment and flushes of satisfaction.

"Are you hurt badly Harry?" he asked his moaning assistant.

"I am afraid so," came a reluctant answer.

"Well, let's look at you closer."

They found no visible wounds that would give rise to alarm. Abrasions yes, contusions for sure, but no gaping cuts. However, Rupert, no sniveler by any measure, groaned incessantly.

"I'm sure every bone in my body is fractured or broken," he lamented repeatedly.

His chief said nothing, he just raised his head and seemed to study the huge fir trees outside. Despite Rupert's obvious pain which made him squirm and nearly double up, a creeping suspicion forced his attention towards the man at the window. What he read in his face he could not determine offhand, but he sensed that it bode no happy message for him. He knew he was in his power, as much as that he hated him.

"You have to get me to a doctor," Rupert almost croaked.

"Yes, yes," came a response of little conviction.

"Let's start out now," entreated Rupert in a quivering voice.

"Hm, hm," muttered his boss while stepping outside.

Obeying emotions not completely understood, he walked upstream till the cabin disappeared from sight. He stopped and let his thoughts run freely, which raced through his mind like little imps no longer controllable. – This is your chance to get even – whispered one. – He deserves to die – lisped another.

Momentarily shocked by such insinuations, he attempted to suppress these unworthy suggestions. After all he was a man of feeling, he told himself, perhaps temporarily a bit confused, but certainly not wicked. Nevertheless he set up his tent a good stretch away from the cabin. Why? asked that secret monitor within himself, called conscience. In order not to disturb the injured man, answered the ever ready voice of vindication.

Inside the cabin Rupert understood his predicament. He was in dire need of a doctor's attention, which could only be obtained through the assistance of his boss, who showed precious little inclination to take him anywhere. What was he waiting for? Where did he keep himself? Rupert felt still strong, albeit crippled, despair had not yet crossed his threshold, despite a creeping premonition, unnameable, but nevertheless present.

When he saw Rudin taking out camping gear, he sighed contentedly, for he perceived it as a sign of progress towards their return to town. But that happened at least three hours ago; since then he neither saw a sign nor heard a sound of him. By nightfall Rupert grew alarmed. His chief had earlier in the day looked in a few times, but nothing further came to pass. When he asked:

"Are we leaving soon?" the answer every time was:

"Yes, yes."

But his only hope for a continuing existence disappeared as quickly as it had shown up. Harry Rupert's premonition took on airs of reality, it seemed no longer to be mere fancy. True, giving this presentiment a name lay now as before not in his power. Knowing his chief's dislike for him could not by itself explain the man's mysterious behaviour, bordering on irrationality. A wholesome mind like his was simply unable to conceive the path, a road to infamy, that Rudin had entered upon. Hate, nourished by brooding, fanned by a guilty conscience had corroded the shields of the chief's decency and reason. While he lay on his lonely cot, writhing in pain, but still propped by hope, Rudin had already resolved to let him die.

Night passed and morning neared. Rupert crept closer towards the edge of despair, chants of doom filled his ears, shadows of a grim fate darkened his eyes. Between stabs of pain, occurring in ever shorter intervals, he gradually realised that he was to be abandoned. This lonely hut above the never resting river, surrounded by towering ice fields, would be his grave. He thought of Rudin, whom he never trusted, yet at the same time considered incapable of such a dastardly deed.

As sometimes happens in the face of inescapable distress, courage rises, the heart grows truer and scales fall from the eyes. What hitherto would have been unthinkable, now unfolded on its own. He not only knew his destiny, but also realised why it was about to engulf him. A dismal end beckoned, because he did not, nay, could not cosy up to a man who repelled him.

Although he attempted to suppress his antipathy, Rudin, sensitive to slight, real or imagined, could not forgive such instinctive feelings, triggered by a countenance deemed treacherous and rapacious. Indeed, Rupert could never look at his boss without flinching, shrinking back as if abhorred by a face that exuded avarice and discontent from every pore.

"Greed, discontent, greed, discontent," he murmured.

Why, he could not have said, but these attributes seemed to get stuck in his mind. Again and again, despite his terrible plight, he thought of his boss' countenance wrought with avarice and dissatisfaction. He could almost hear his lamentations over a lot so undeserved, could perceive his hankering for an easier life, which only the paucity of money rendered unattainable. Money, money, was deemed a universal cure by his chief.

Suddenly Rupert saw the light, he knew how to escape the clutches of death. When early next morning Rudin sidled to the cabin, not a sound could be heard inside. Slowly, stealthily, he opened the door and peeked in. Rupert lay doubled up on his bed, he appeared to be in a coma. Seeing this, Rudin stepped inside and approached gingerly. At first glance he noticed the mess on the floor. Papers were strewn all over, indicating that Rupert had frantically searched for something before he swooned.

Then he saw the paper, a poster with Rupert's picture. His eyes popped when he picked it up and took a closer look.

Reward – Fifteen Thousand Dollars – for information leading to this man's arrest. The following description fit his assistant's particulars in every respect. The wanted poster was issued three months ago in Toronto. However, every police station within the country would attend to the details, it said.

With hands shaking from excitement, he pocketed the poster and tiptoed outside. He walked away quickly, on legs that almost wobbled. His head was astir with turbulent thoughts that nearly made him dizzy. Unable to believe his luck, still doubting his good fortune, he stopped and pulled the poster from his pocket. No question about it, everything tallied, it was his assistant who was wanted by the authorities.

He wiped his eyes and rubbed them dry, after which he read every word again from top to bottom. Fifteen thousand dollars were offered for information leading to his arrest. By all saints, he could do better than that, he promised under his breath; namely deliver the culprit almost on a platter. Ha, what an opportunity to kill two birds with one stone. Punish a man hated with all heartstrings, and get paid for it at the same time. The idea of Mexico had lost its utopian aspect. Fifteen thousand dollars would endow him with an existence in that warm and friendly land.

Fifteen minutes later he went back to the hut, though noisily this time.

"Wake up Harry, breakfast is on the way," he hollered from afar.

"Hurry, hurry, my boy, get to it quickly, we are going to the hospital," he encouraged his still supine assistant.

Rupert stirred and groaned at the same time, he appeared to have difficulties gaining consciousness, yet managed to nod repeatedly.

"Don't worry son, we will have you up and running in no time," he promised in a tremulous voice.

Rupert from thereon never felt so coddled since the day he learned to wipe his own nose. His boss, handy as ever, quickly assembled a sort of sedan chair, which fastened on the back of Rupert's donkey. Padded with sleeping bags and soft blankets, it served quite well as a conveyance. Of course the ride to the main road proved rocky and cumbersome, but after two days they reached open land, and at last a semblance of civilisation. Once on the main road, transport to the hospital proved easy and quick.

After Rudin delivered his assistant at the hospital, he raced over to the police station. Spreading out the wanted poster before an astonished desk sergeant, he advised that their man lay fairly helpless over at the special care unit, where he had just left him.

"You should apprehend him immediately, injured or not, this man is tricky, I can attest to the fact that he possesses a constitution of iron. He might find a way to give you the slip," he added.

When the police officer made no move to follow his urging, Rudin became emphatic.

"I tell you, this fellow has tricks up his sleeves, someone should be sent over without delay," he insisted somewhat piqued because of the sergeant's shown nonchalance.

Indeed, the officer seemed in no hurry to go anywhere. He took out a form and started to ask questions.

"Your name please."

"Roald Rudin. But – but…" he almost sputtered.

"Now tell me what happened. You took Mr Rupert to the hospital."

"Yes, yes, but man alive, what are you up to, won't you go and arrest him?"

"There will be no arrest," the sergeant informed him.

"Also no reward," he added with a grin that made Rudin's blood rise.

"No arrest, no reward," he repeated aghast.

"This is what I said; now to my report."

"I don't understand, officer," Rudin almost stammered, by this time utterly bewildered.

The police officer eyed him closer. With a brow knitted indignantly, and a set countenance, he demanded to know:

"Where did you find this poster?"

Rudin resented this line of questioning. Instead of being showered with gratitude, the officer, obviously inept and remiss in his duties, treated him like a suspect. Before he could protest however, he was apprised of an amazing fact. It took a while to sink in, to digest what the officer disclosed.

"The man at the hospital is not wanted."

"But here is his picture," Rudin objected vigorously, while thumping the poster with his fist.

"That's not him."

"Who then?"

"His twin brother."

Rudin gaped at the sergeant like a man paralysed, he was too stunned to mutter a word. While still staring disbelievingly ahead, evidently comprehending nothing, the officer explained the facts. It turned out that the man depicted on the poster was not his assistant, but an identical twin by the name of Kevin Harry Rupert. Charged with a criminal offence, he was apprehended two months ago. All posters were forthwith removed and destroyed upon Harry Rupert's request. It was considered a reasonable demand in view of their identical features.

At first Rudin had difficulties to take it all in. But slowly, under the withering glance of the policeman, the truth, a shattering realisation, came home. He had been outwitted.

# The Vow

The lure of British Columbia is legendary. Rumour has it that men and women are willing to crawl on hands and knees to set their eyes once more on sights beyond description. Expatriates would give all to walk along the Pacific Rim, feeling high winds on raw November days tugging angrily at one's clothes. They dream of waves whipped into billows by furious storms that break thunderously on rocks and roar unobstructed over the wide, endless beaches. They are unable to forget the charm of the Okanagan Valley in spring, when the blossoming fruit trees, mixed with sounds of an exuberant nature, bring smiles to the most melancholy spirits.

But nothing equals the allure of the Kootenais in autumn. Camping and wandering under endless blue skies amid a wondrous silence, interrupted only by the ripple of rivers, will instil an irresistible compulsion to return.

Such sentiments were shared by Derek DeWitt and Edgar Moider, two of three hikers on their way to the 'Lake of the Hanging Glacier'. They met every year in that lonely region where black bears and grizzlies roam freely, and eagles circle overhead. The third man, Claude Carrol, had joined them in Radium, where they met at the Hot Springs.

DeWitt and Moider, both of Anglo-Saxon stock, were serious looking fellows, rather quiet and bent on portraying figures of manly deliberation, consistent with unwritten rules of the West. They both learned in a society totally dominated by women, to keep their thoughts to themselves.

Not so Claude Carrol, the man from Quebec; he neither feared women nor was beset by feelings of male inadequacy. His sparkling personality and refreshing unaffectedness simultaneously attracted and repelled the two friends. Their maxim, never announced to be sure, was that showing emotions is a sign of weakness. Carrol had no inkling of such inclinations, his sentiments were displayed freely. In any case he simply ignored their unwonted primness.

"Why fret over customs alien to me," he said to himself, "it must be the way of the West," a region he never before set foot onto. Besides he appreciated the invitation, since undertaking such a sojourn alone would have been foolhardy. His fellow hikers' peculiar starchiness probably discomforted them more than himself.

Thinking no more about it he looked up. Not a cloud marred the wide open sky, neither did a breeze stir the half-wilted leaves. Snow covered the higher summits, glittering playfully in the bright sunshine, beckoning the wanderers to come closer. The heat of summer was gone, leaving behind a sweet melancholy. A sigh lay over the land filled with regret and anticipation. Jubilation had left, but the profound calm conferred upon the whole countryside a magic of its own, which enamoured Carrol immensely.

He was tempted to halt at every unusual sight, to marvel and express astonishment. However, his companions showed no inclination to tarry, for they intended to reach the waterfalls before darkness. Even at a good clip that was still five hours distant.

"You don't have mountains like this in Quebec, Claude," DeWitt teased, although he was not quite sure, since he never stepped beyond the Great Divide of east and west, which to him was the Saskatchewan River.

Carrol whistled appreciatively:

"No, that we don't have," he admitted, then added:

"Were you gents ever in Quebec?"

An amused smile appeared on DeWitt's face, while Moider turned up his nose as if sniffing the air, prior to suggesting:

“Isn’t that a foreign country?”

“Ha, ha, ha, you have scored a hit my friend,” Carrol lauded good-natured, at the same time looking sideways first at DeWitt, then at Moider.

How should that be construed, his glances seemed to say, but their inscrutable countenances betrayed little. They surely would not let on that Quebec was an anomaly to them, a province not quite belonging. After all, its inhabitants hardly spoke English, furthermore they possessed a deportment considered un-Canadian, meaning of course un-American.

“The answer is ‘no’ on my part. Winnipeg is the most easterly city I have reached so far,” gave DeWitt to understand.

Turning to his friend, he inquired:

“How about you, Edgar?”

“Oh, let’s see.” The West Bank of the Saskatchewan is my limit,” he said in a voice of regret.

Carrol chuckled to himself, while thinking how paradoxical these men were, trying strenuously to be nice, attempting to be pleasant, yet diffusing an atmosphere of tension disquieting to him. How strange, that men will heed their words with such care, yet nourish biased feelings undesirable to others, as much as demeaning to themselves.

They were obviously decent men, he had to admit, but bottled up with unexpressed sentiments, that made him, a French Canadian, feel a bit uneasy. However, his exuberant nature suffered no setback, he talked unrestrainedly and even belted out joual songs. To tell the truth, DeWitt and Moider liked the Quebecois. From his droll way of talking to his stories, evidently a bit on the tall side, they found him entertaining. His openness was refreshing, although deemed somewhat indiscreet to their stolid minds.

They arrived just in time. The sun had disappeared behind the Selkirk Mountains, rendering the air surprisingly nippy. That however, did not disconcert the three men. Out came their axes, in a twinkle the solemn silence was interrupted by resounding blows, originating however only from one source. Three men were at work, but only one chopped, the others seemed to be entangled in a scuffle. Carrol swung his axe like a voyageur of bygone days. At every well-aimed stroke he expelled a loud 'han' before driving it deep below the bark. Beaming all over his dark countenance he twitted his companions:

"Ha, les anglais are tickling the wood, ho, ho, ho, don't hurt it, mes amis."

They took his teasing in good spirit, seeing how adept he was, indeed they marvelled at his strength and enthusiasm. A chore to them was obviously fun to him. Soon a roaring fire crackled in the twilight; it was high time to pitch their tents.

After a hearty meal they began to chat, or rather listened to Carrol's narrations, which in their opinion occasionally drew the long bow.

Gradually a queer sensation overcame DeWitt and Moider which they could not name, yet it touched them pleasantly. Surprisingly they found themselves talking more freely than ever before, even expressing ideas that hitherto did not cross the thresholds of their thoughts.

Now, that was peculiar, exhilarating and disquieting at the same time. They felt like being on a voyage to the unknown, exciting but also scary. Their maxim of keeping up their guard, not to discard reserve, took a poke in the ribs. Males in their society, meaning English North America, were taught before they could stand on their feet, that displaying emotions is synonymous with being womanish. Although DeWitt and Moider knew each other for more than ten years, despite considering themselves close friends, they never once confided in each other, nor eased their hearts unless well oiled by liquor.

How different Carrol, the man from Quebec, behaved. He related experiences freely, with little concern whether they enhanced or disparaged his image. His candour affected them strangely, they came close to pulling the cork from the bottle of their penned up feelings. Almost, but not quite, for while unmindful of Carrol, who soon would disappear from their lives anyway, they certainly eyed each other with less confidence. Admitting embarrassing weaknesses could easily lower one's prestige, therefore granting the other undesirable ascendance.

Nevertheless, they gradually drifted into a mood hardly ever felt before. Mental barricades fell by the minute, a relaxed state ensued, which allowed bridges to be built over hitherto daunting chasms. Carrol intrigued them, his droll expressions, coupled with an amusing accent elated their spirits. Neither DeWitt nor Moider could have explained the tingling sensation sneaking up on them. Surrounded by eerie shadows of the night, and the monotonous splash of the distant waterfall, moreover warmed by a blazing and crackling fire, they experienced a sense of inner freedom. A friendly feeling towards the world and themselves almost overwhelmed them.

"Claude, you mentioned that you are a bush pilot," DeWitt remarked.

"Yes my friend, I am."

"You must have hair-raising adventures at times."

"I sure do," Carrol admitted.

"Would you care telling us some of them?" asked Moider.

Carrol looked up. His face took on an arcane expression, as if to say, "I know you are not going to believe it, but I will tell you anyway." Pointing to his forehead he said:

"Do you see this ugly scar?"

When both nodded, he continued:

"This eyesore will always remind me of the most memorable experience I ever had. Do you want to hear it?"

"Most certainly," they said simultaneously.

Carrol cleared his throat prior to this amazing narrative.

"Believe it or not, but here it is. As a bush pilot my main routes are in northern Quebec. Beyond Shefferville neither roads nor trains exist. I have flown over terrain and landed in places that no magnifying glass can find on any map. The region is called Nouveau Quebec, it stretches from Hudson Bay in the west to the great drainage divide eastward, which also happens to be the border between Labrador and Quebec."

"Isn't that border in dispute?" interrupted Moider.

"It might be, but battling howling winds and drifting snow nine months of the year, moreover fighting off bloodsucking insects the remaining three, leaves little time for heeding lines on a chart. Anyway to continue my story.

"One early morning in spring I took off from Shefferville, pointing the nose of my little plane northward to Fort Chimo on the Koksoak River, a run of about two hundred and fifty kilometres. It was a clear, crisp day, a joy to one's bosom to be up in the air. True, the land lay still under a blanket of snow further north, lakes and rivers were covered with ice, but the sun was tickling my nose and laughing down at me, making my heart beat quicker. Singing songs of my childhood and youth occupied me to such a degree that it distracted my thoughts from the weather.

"Turning my head away from the sun, I should have recognised the signs of an approaching menace. However, I paid no heed. After all the sun, quite high now, shone with undiminished brightness. In any case I should have been no more than twenty miles from my destiny.

"Suddenly the settlement of Fort-Chimo disappeared before my eyes. That was not all, far from it. Minutes later I saw what looked like a bank of clouds pushing towards me, no doubt originating over the shores of the dreaded Hudson Bay. I knew that sign well, no mistake about it."

"You got into a storm?" inquired Moider.

"Let me tell you, it could hardly have been worse. That ominous wall of visible vapour seemed to be poised at my little plane, as if singling me out for punishment. As expected, the wind needed no special invitation, I soon felt buffeted about like a nutshell in choppy water. Then came the snow, which hardly surprised me, for, as mentioned, I knew the indications.

"Soon swirling flakes danced around me like a million sneering white devils of Wallachia set to do mischief. There remained only one thing to do; that is diving and landing. Now, you gents probably are aware of the first tenet of a bush pilot."

Both shook their heads while saying:

"No, what is it?"

"When in trouble, look, see and land. Don't ever climb onto the wings of hope that you think might carry you to greener pastures, it seldom happens. Tip the nose of your plane, say a short prayer and down you go. That is what I did. Luck was on my side, I detected a wind-blown swath on the frozen Koksaok. It seemed almost bare of snow. Flying practically into the eye of the storm made an approach relatively safe, albeit not the landing."

"Oh, what happened?" interjected Moider.

"I hit a few moguls."

"What are they?" asked DeWitt?

"Little wind tamped mounds of snow as hard as ice. I tell you fellows, I crashed right into them."

"That is how you sustained your head wound, I suppose," speculated DeWitt.

"Yes, although I can't recall any details, since I passed out after the first few jolts. When I woke up it was pitch dark. Trying to rise from my seat proved impossible, I felt like having been run over by a Juggernaut, and not only once. Meanwhile a full blown blizzard howled outside; inside cowered a moaning pilot beseeching all saints of La Belle Province to save him. Every bone in my body seemed to be fractured, if not broken. I was in a dither, but I survived."

"As can be seen," remarked DeWitt.

Carroll eyed him visibly pleased, for he liked a wag.

"Now to the story, which even today after many years at times deems me a psychedelic experience. Though barely able to move, I was in a position to reach my rations and blankets. To my chagrin I soon became aware of a disconcerting fact: Communicating with anyone seemed fruitless. All frantic and repeated Mayday transmissions remained unanswered. But there luck approached again. As we say on the Barren where caribou graze and wolves howl: No matter how old a man is, if he possesses charm, dame Fortuna will always raise her skirt. Well, she did.

"On the morning of the next day the storm abated as quickly as it had arisen. A few hours later I heard scraping feet and loud voices nearing. Soon a man and a woman pried the door open. It proved not easy, however, they finally managed it. Not long after, I lay muffled on a sled which my rescuers were soon pulling towards a nearby house, standing high above the river's bank.

'I am professor Karl Zinner, and this is my wife Klara,' they had introduced themselves at first contact. Both seemed to be in their sixties, though their physical bearing implied a younger age. Did I tell you I was lucky? of course I did. There the good lady Fortuna now showed me more than just her knees."

"What do you mean?" Moider asked laughingly, tickled by Carrol's quaint description.

"The professor was a medical doctor who spoke French fluently, albeit with a German accent that somehow accentuated the beauty of the French language. To put it succinctly, I was in good hands."

"Is that the end of your story?" Moider wanted to know.

Carrol looked at him half amused and half reproachful.

"No my friends, it is the beginning. They were a strange pair, obviously highly cultured, fluent in at least three languages, well read and of equable disposition. As a man of feeling I thanked my guiding angel to have delivered me into the care of such high-minded people. High-minded and refined, but strange."

"What is strange about being cultured?" asked DeWitt.

Carrol contemplated his companions closer, as if in doubt what to say next. Knitting his brow and pursing his lips, he displayed the typical expression of a French Canadian in doubt.

"It is difficult for me to explain in English, however, I will try. Arriving at the house, built entirely of logs in a style reminiscent of Tyrol, they bedded me down in a charming room. The doctor gave me a strong sedative, which immediately rendered me semiconscious. I hardly felt the professor's hands busying themselves all over my body. He tugged at and twisted my aching bones, and kneaded my sore muscles. How long I do not know, since a pronounced lethargy overpowered me gradually, leading to a stuporous sleep.

"When I woke up after fourteen hours, I had a distinct feeling of being observed. Forcing my eyes to open fully, I perceived a figure scurrying away from my bed and disappearing through the open doorway. Even in my drowsy state, despite the fact of having seen the shape but a fleeting moment from behind, I could have sworn it was Mrs Zinner, the professor's wife."

"Aha Claude, she was probably attracted by your handsome face," kidded Moider.

Carrol shook his head.

"Nothing doing, I must have looked uglier than the famed philosopher Khorassan who walked around forever veiled. I'm not exactly a beauty at best of times, therefore considering my bruised and battered face, unkempt head and overgrown beard, no woman of any age would have given me a second look."

"Perhaps your plight awakened her womanly pity," suggested DeWitt.

"Then why did she practically flee at the moment I woke up?"

"What happened after?" Moider inquired, sensing a ticklish development.

"I tell you, Mrs Zinner showered me with attention, but always furtively. It perplexed and embarrassed me at the same time. Soon I became reluctant to raise my head in her presence, yet was unable to resist an urge to do so. Her surreptitious glances, never obtrusive, rather contemplative, accelerated my pulse, moreover disquieted my conscience. What could this woman, attractive no doubt despite her age, possibly want from or see in me? More than one thought raced through my head, some unworthy I have to admit, others too bizarre to repeat. Remember that was ten years ago, when I was still a young man, vain as a coxcomb and equally brash."

They were now listening with increasing attention, spurring him on silently with appealing glances and suggestive gestures. Carrol needed no invitation, for he had much more to tell.

"Professor Zinner sure knew his trade; though not inclined to pamper his patient, namely me, he had a delicate but firm touch. Wincing or crying out deterred him not in the least, he just continued his vigorous treatment. I remarked after one of his examinations:

'Thanks to you professor I will soon be on my feet again and continue my journey.'

'Not so soon, Mr Carrol, perhaps in ten days or two weeks,' he advised in his quaint French, rolling the 'r' like only a German can. Although I knew the answer I asked him anyhow, just to make conversation you will understand.

'How far from Fort-Chimo are we?'

'Almost ten kilometres down river,' I was told.

'I suppose my plane has seen its day,' I stated more than asking.

'It looks a wreck to me, but wait till you are mobile again and convince yourself.'

"May was approaching, consequently the ice should soon break up. My plane would most likely sink, or float down river. There was not much to be done now, because surprisingly enough my hosts were not in any way connected with the outside world, possessing not even a wireless. Walking, or by boat was their only means to communicate with others. What happens will happen, I thought, the matter would soon be in the hands of an insurance agent in any case.

"The sun rose higher every day, daylight had extended to seventeen hours at least. Nature was stirring, one could feel the breath of the pleasant season. The sweet song of snow buntings, sure harbingers of spring, turned my head. Listening to their joyous warble fanned my desire to be outside among them."

"Did you ever find out why the professor's wife stole glances at you, or was this just a figment of your imagination?" asked Moider when Carrol paused to catch his breath.

Carrol's next words were preceded by characteristic heaving of shoulders and head tilting.

"How I wished you were right, but ultimate developments proved my suspicions warranted."

"You mean she was still giving you the once-over?"

"More than that, she definitely had me under scrutiny, covertly to be sure, but undeniably so. Let me continue, even though it does appear long-winded what you hear, it is necessary to appreciate the outcome.

"In the house reigned an atmosphere of peace, they both went their ways quietly and performed their work in harmonious contentment. The ever prevailing tranquillity engendered confidence in me, an optimism so conducive to convalescence. Their exchanges of words, not too voluble, moreover unintelligible to me, nevertheless embodied an air of well-meaning and mutual solicitude. True, since I was unable to move around my judgement had to be taken with a grain of salt.

"However, enmity between them, as manifested usually by bickering or the silent treatment, I could have sworn did not exist. In any case they were two delightful people, that was my conviction then, and still is today, despite later occurrences that turned me topsy-turvy. They both seemed occupied from sunrise to sunset. The professor, retired now, conducted scientific experiments, whose findings were published in many medical journals.

'My laboratory would be the envy of more than one university,' he announced proudly. His wife, besides doing artistic work, assisted him with all her strength and ability. They evidently kept rancour at bay. I say this advisedly considering later revelations. There reigned an atmosphere of intellectual stimulation in that solitary house, mixed with an aura of contentment, which deeply effected me."

"In other words they were happy," interjected DeWitt.

Carrol stoked the fire before he answered:

"No, they were not."

"But Claude, you just painted a picture of sublime bliss," remonstrated Moider.

"Well, let me retouch it then. They lived in harmony, in easy circumstances which often bestows contentment, but happy they were not. Soon I should find out why. You see, they shared a secret that tormented them, they were plagued by a past incident which poisoned the presence. It quickly quenched the spark of joy, the flames of anticipation, without which happiness is but an elusive experience. They evidently lived in dread of a phenomenon, unpleasant for sure, that could assail them at any moment. Well, I saw no such spectre, but soon I heard something untoward."

"What do you mean?" they called out in unison.

"One evening, about ten o'clock, I was awakened by an exchange of words, muffled, mind you, but nevertheless unusual. Rising on my elbows I listened. The professor and his wife were arguing, not virulently, but certainly with unmistakable insistence. It quickly dawned on me that they kept their voices down for only one reason."

"Because of you," suggested Moider.

"No mistake about it. I am loath to tell you I pricked my ears fully, but of course they spoke in German, rendering comprehension impossible. Nevertheless, I quickly took the pulse of their utterances, it was an altercation, and none to friendly to boot. Hearing Mrs Zinner mentioning my name several times let me believe that they were discussing me.

"Next morning the professor entered my room rather officiously. Contrary to his habits he dispensed with preliminaries, he produced two crutches which he leaned against the wall.

'Mr Carrol, these are for you, they should accelerate your recuperation,' he said while looking me straight in the eyes.

"I instinctively knew what it meant, words did not fail me to describe the allusion. 'I have done my part' his action intimated, 'now the onus is on you,' in other words, 'be on your way.' He departed as abruptly as he had arrived. Let me tell you I felt the nudge distinctly."

"You figured he wished you gone," Moider remarked.

"I did."

"Because something was brewing between him and his wife?" DeWitt wanted to know.

"Obviously yes, although another week passed before I found out what it was."

"Well, tell us," urged DeWitt.

Carrol surveyed his listeners closer, whereby he chuckled satisfied, because their attention was riveted. That was hardly surprising considering his reputation as a raconteur. Raising a hand he said:

"Don't be hasty my friends, the evening is still young."

"By the way Claude, I meant to ask before whether someone was looking for you."

"Of course. After I failed to show up in Fort-Chimo as anticipated, the wireless started humming. However, the unsettled weather, followed by dense fog hindered their effort to find me. When a rescue party finally discovered my whereabouts, I was well on the way to recuperation, besides by that time I felt obliged to unravel the mystery of that house. In hindsight I wished I had departed with them."

Looking up wistfully at the moonlit contours of the mountains, he repeated:

"Yes, I should have left that house then and there, it would have saved me many a haunting memory. Anyway, here it goes.

"The next day I forced myself to walk around a bit, actually hobbling on crutches with legs dangling down like superfluous appurtenances. My astonishment turned to amazement upon seeing more of the house. Picture to yourselves a lonely stretch of no man's land at the edge of the Great Barren, almost a thousand kilometres from civilization, yet the ambience of that house gave the impression of being in the middle of Montreal. My hosts, two peculiar people without a doubt, had managed to create a veritable Eden amid the wilds of Northern Quebec. That many books I had seen previously only in libraries, not to mention priceless artefacts, carvings and statues."

"Yet you say they were unhappy," reminded Moider.

"Decidedly so, especially as evening approached. All day their behaviour towards each other was admirable, but as soon as the sun dipped towards Hudson Bay in the west, lo and behold, their attitude changed. A tangible nervous anxiety gripped them both, creating a tension that made me feel uncomfortable. They became more courteous, albeit less cordial with each other, at the same time practically ignoring me. From the first evening among them, meaning being on my feet outside of my room, I clearly recognised the harmful element in their relations."

"And what would that have been?" DeWitt asked.

"Lack of ease in each other's company, caused by a feeling of guilt, I presumed then, and found later confirmed."

"You mentioned their increased discomfort after sunset. Did one or the other perhaps suffer from nyctophobia?"

"What is nyctophobia?" demanded Carrol to know.

"A morbid fear of night or darkness," he was told.

Carrol shook his head emphatically:

"No, no, they were plagued by demons of their own creation; that is guilt fanned by isolation and kept alive by pride. An incident in their past united and separated their lives simultaneously."

"Did you ever find out what it was?" Moider asked.

"I'm coming to it. As soon as the mistress saw me limping around, she took me in tow. With a decorum befitting a hostess of Europe's great estates, she showed me the house. Opening all doors, I was given a view of every room except one at the end of a wide corridor."

"Aha," DeWitt ejaculated.

"Yes, that one she completely avoided, pretending it did not exist."

"Your suspicions surely must have been strengthened then," DeWitt interjected.

"No doubt about it. Instinctively the thought hit me that behind that door lay the source of their discontent. Another three days saw me walking without crutches. Not venturing outside for the moment, I kept to the house. Climbing the stairs to the professor's workroom and laboratory turned out to be a chore without crutches. But I managed to do it. Driven by a desire to have a word with Dr Zinner, I crawled more than walked up the steep rise.

'Professor, I should be on my way soon, latest Friday,' I announced when I met him. He did not protest, neither had I expected it. Today was Monday, I figured by Wednesday to be in fairly good shape. Friday would see me on the road. Snow was melting fast. The ground, however, remained frozen solid, rendering a short walk to the settlement quite feasible.

"Wednesday arrived, with it an opportunity to satisfy my curiosity, which meanwhile had grown into fixation."

"You mean you found out what was behind that door?" interposed Moider.

"Attempted to, my friend, attempted to. They were both outside, I could hear them talking some ways off. You should have seen me move, compadres. Despite my somewhat handicapped condition I stood at that door in a flash. Trying to open it, however, proved futile. It was locked solid, no amount of pushing and rattling moved it. I found that significant, since all other doors were either left ajar or wide open. Moving away quickly again, just in time as it turned out, I noticed Mrs Zinner standing in the entrance doorway. She smiled enigmatically, it was more of a self-satisfied grin, expressing approval. Just as her lips moved to say something, the professor appeared, causing her to remain silent."

Carrol made one of his reflective pauses, trying to gauge the impression the narrative was making. His next words confounded his companions more than before.

"I could have sworn that the professor's wife winked at me. Not visibly, mind you, nevertheless her facial expression indicated awareness of what I was up to. Not only did she know what I thought, but encouraged me silently to continue my endeavours.

"While walking around outside, still a bit clumsily, searching for a hill to view the town site, that room, purposely locked, refused to vanish from my thoughts. Climbing a nearby hill, the settlement lay before my eyes.

"Seeing signs of human habitation lent reassurance to my bewildered mind. For I had to admit the house, or rather its occupants made me feel uncomfortable. One side of me wanted to remain till the mystery is unravelled, whereas another side awakened a desire to flee. The behaviour of the mistress frayed on my nerves, she treated me increasingly like a collaborator of a scheme I was unable to divine."

"Did she intimate her intentions at all?" DeWitt inquired.

"Never in words, though she evidently had me singled out to render a service somehow connected with that room. Standing on the hill I almost forgot my dilemma. That small, unsightly town never before looked so friendly; I could not refrain from waving and shouting: 'Ho, ho, ho, Rene, start uncorking the bottle old boy, I will see you on Friday.' Rene Chunnard was the airport manager whom I knew very well.

"Walking back to the house, reluctantly I must admit, I met the Zinners. We stopped to talk. The professor inquired in his calm, persuasive manner how things were.

'Mr Carrol, how is progress?'

'Thanks to you, professor, I am almost myself again,' I answered.

'Are you still leaving on Friday?' his wife asked.

'As much as I regret it, yes,' I lied.

"The professor cast a reproving glance towards his wife, while saying:

‘The weather is favourable, the patient appears hale and strong, moreover a short hike will stimulate his mind and body, so don’t try to hold him back.’

“Before proceeding on our separate ways, Mrs Zinner’s face started twitching in an unmistakable fashion.”

“Aha, she was emitting signals again,” remarked Moider.

“Almost imperceptibly, yet at once understood by me. The door is now open, her demeanour revealed.”

“Did you try again?”

“I did, however with few signs of enthusiasm. I found myself in a peculiar state of mind, listening to two contradictory voices, as it were. One urged me on, while the other whispered to slow down. My desire to learn about the room’s contents was stifled by a baffling reluctance to do so. I practically had to force myself to go on.

“As suspected the door was unlocked. Twisting the handle I hesitated for a moment before pushing it open. I sincerely wish I would have turned around there and then.”

When Carrol ceased talking, his listeners cried out:

“What was in there, Claude? come on tell us.”

Their curiosity was bursting at the seams, especially when they noticed that Carrol’s countenance, lit and warmed by the fire, took on an expression of disgust and terror.

“What was in there? nothing except a figure more gruesome than I had ever encountered. For a moment I took it as an apparition from Madame Toussaud’s chambres of horror. This, this spectre stood in the middle of the room, grinning and leering at me, neither moving nor emitting a sound.”

Chuckling to himself, therefore relieving built up tension, he explained:

“All for a good reason, because it was a skeleton, a human shape once, but now nothing but bones, hollow eye sockets and bared teeth grimacing idiotically.”

“My goodness Claude, you must have been surprised,” commiserated DeWitt.

Smirking satisfied, nodding repeatedly, Carrol went on:

“I assure you my friends, a miracle happened.”

“How do you mean?” asked DeWitt.

"With me I mean. I was cured quicker than anyone before in human history. You should have seen me jump backward, then turning in a flash and racing to my room."

"I don't blame you," condoled Moider.

"Arriving in my room, bewildered as never before, I remembered having left the door open. So back I went, with pounding temples I'm not ashamed to say, to shut it. However, not until I had looked closer at that apparition, grimacing now more derisively than before. At least so it seemed to me. It just stood there, propped up somehow, arms dangling grotesquely over bleached rips and bony limbs, ugly and menacing, a herald from the realms of the nether world. No doubt this weird bone structure had once been a human being, an adult judging by its size, possibly a man."

"It could have served the professor's research," conjectured DeWitt.

"Yes, that thought entered my mind also, but it was quickly rejected. Why lock that otherwise empty room, when even the laboratory remained accessible during my stay. Added to it Mrs Zinner's outlandish behaviour convinced me otherwise. That skeleton, locked away from sight, served a more sinister purpose."

"But you had no inkling what it could have been," remarked Moider.

"Not even a hint. Soon, however, the enigma unfolded before my eyes. Its revelation drove me from that place in the middle of the night, without a parting word, with nothing but the clothes on my back."

"What did they do to you?" DeWitt cried.

"Nothing physically. But let me tell you, what I learned next day made my hair stand on end, it strengthened my suspicion to be a guest and patient in a house of bedlam. Listen to the conclusion.

"When the Zinners returned from their outing, no doubt instigated by the missus, I pretended to be asleep. Racking my brains to the point of exhaustion brought me not an iota closer to an explanation. Wild speculations raced through my head, ideas both bizarre and witless entered my mind. None however, stood up to the tenets of reason. Nevertheless I realised that these refined people, both highly educated, were involved in some weird, how should I put it, possibly sordid machinations. Recalling their suppressed squabbles after dark, implied some kind of villainy.

"Later on, rising from my bed I mingled among them. Mrs Zinner's sideways glances were a source of embarrassment to me. I was certain that she tried to attract my attention, but I ignored her completely. Not so her husband, however; him I followed hot on his heels. Was that erudite man astonished on account of my sudden chummy behaviour? Did my freshly awakened thirst for knowledge raise his eyebrows? You bet it did, although his good breeding forbade to mention it.

'You were a lecturing professor at the Universite de Montreal, Dr Zinner,' I remarked with forced nonchalance.

'Yes, Mr Carrol, for over twenty years.'

'Your field of activity was anatomy, human anatomy, was it not?'

"His head jerked up. Giving me a sharp look, accompanied by a sardonic smile, he declared:

'Not at all sir, my sphere of knowledge has been and still is pathology.'

"There it was, as I had suspected, that skeleton bore no relevance to the professor's work, its presence augured a more sinister significance. The next day the professor made one of his excursions down to the river. The moment Mrs Zinner saw her husband's back, she turned to me murmuring:

'You have seen it.'

'Yes,' I admitted, at the same time pretending to leave the house.

'You must help me, Mr Carrol,' she called out behind me in a beseeching voice. Turning around, I said:

'Help you, in what way madam?'

'Take that skeleton away,' she announced.

"Now, that was a peculiar request. I hesitated, unsure whether to laugh or show anger.

'I don't understand, Mrs Zinner, I am a guest here, surely not authorized to remove someone else's belongings,' I remonstrated.

'It does not belong to anybody,' she hastened to tell me.

“I can’t remember exactly what my reaction was, but no doubt I was dumbfounded.

‘But – but, whose is it, or rather who was it?’

‘My lover.’

“Believe me fellows, by now I wished myself to be anywhere except in that house, or even nearby. Immensely bewildered I turned away. Through a window the professor could be seen walking away from the house, a fact not unnoticed by his wife, whose company I had not the least desire to share any longer. She told me more.

‘My husband killed him, being a scientist rendered it easy for him, as much as turning the corpse into a skeleton.’

“My head was reeling, my legs, not the strongest yet in any way, began to wobble. I had to sit down.

‘But that is murder, did nobody report it?’ I rasped rather than spoke.

‘No, and neither did I. What could it have earned me but further grief, plus pity and derision. Imagine for a moment, a man of my husband’s stature, esteemed from coast to coast, celebrated in many influential circles, trusted and loved, decried by an adulteress. In any case, who would have thought him capable of such a dastardly deed?’

“I could not put my finger on it, yet her communication struck me as being odd. Something was left out, a vital element was missing. An absence of animosity between them for instance, so peculiar under these circumstances. For indeed they honoured and cherished each other.

‘Mrs Zinner, you asked for my help a moment ago, what do you wish me to do?’

‘Steal the skeleton,’ she answered.

“Being more baffled than before, I suggested a bit petulantly, I am afraid:

‘Why don’t you do it yourself, or for that matter just destroy it?’

“You should have seen the look she hurled at me. Aghast, with eyes distended, staggering backwards, she stammered:

‘I can do no such thing, for you see, I made a vow.’

“The short of it was this: Her husband had discovered their liaison, but never let on that he knew. Her lover just disappeared suddenly. Four weeks later the skeleton showed up. Ostensibly for the professor's research. Her suspicion, rampant in any case, received confirmation. One fine morning he led her to that frightful shape, where he made an announcement that chilled her to the bones.

'Klara, I know all about your treacherous affair with Herbert Schal. Prove can be produced in court at a moment's notice. As a convicted Jezebel your rights are curtailed, a divorce would be granted me readily. However, there is a way out for you.'

'What is it Karl?'

'You must take a vow,' she was advised.

'A vow, Karl?' she asked relieved that disgrace might be averted.

'You make a solemn promise to God, a pledge of atonement, to embrace and kiss this skeleton every night before retiring. If you do that, our lives will go on amicably to the end of our days.'

'Whose skeleton is it?' she asked him, feigning ignorance.

'I do not know,' he answered curtly.

"There that woman stood, with wide open eyes, wringing her hands imploringly, while moaning:

'Don't you understand sir, if you steal the skeleton, or destroy it, I am released from my vow, life can be normal again for me and my husband.'

"As I said before, something appeared to be amiss here. To begin with, their relations were not only normal but congenial, if not affectionate. Yet I said nothing more, my mind was only occupied with flight. Turning my back on this house with its strange occupants dominated my thoughts. I felt no inclination to be drawn into an orbit of strife caused by dark secrets, or mysterious practices.

"To my relief the professor returned, rather he approached the house in his measured stride. Pointing it out to Mrs Zinner I hurried to my room which I did not leave all evening. Yet repose I could find none. Assailed by a longing to be among down to earth people again, my patience was sorely tested. I came within a hair's breath to walk away there and then. But reason prevailed, rather bashfulness regained the upper hand, since I felt loath to storm out in front of my surely perplexed hosts.

"However, I resolved to be on my feet as soon as they had retired, which I did. It was dark and quiet in the house when I sneaked out unnoticed. By all the saint's, fellows, standing outside in the crisp air of the night, a sigh of relief escaped my breast, loud enough to evoke fears of waking them up. After I had pushed the door's latch in place, I went on my way. To see me scurry through the starlit night would have been worth something. Finding direction was easy, given the river on my right, and the lit up settlement ahead.

"Prior to reaching the airport, the sun started to push over the Torngat Mountains. The spectacle of fiery colours spreading gradually across the eastern sky and illuminating the ghostly taiga is an experience not easily forgotten. It gives the soul a lift and eases the mind. Even the most timid grow courageous when the warming rays of a northern sun tickle their skin, and the wide open country all around them beckons to be explored.

"I found Rene Chunnard at his desk, poring over some schedules. His surprise to see me was only excelled by joy written all over his face.

'Salutations old man, come let me embrace you,' he shouted in his booming voice.

'Is it too early to hoist one?' he added laughing with such gusto that his heavy frame shook.

"He needed no answer. With one movement of the hand he held up a bottle, while the other reached for glasses.

'Make that a double, old gander, and leave the bottle on the desk. I have much to drown,' I declared.

'How so, mon ami?'

"I related my recent experience. Not in detail, just the part about the skeleton. Chunnard listened, however, neither with anticipated attention, nor did he display expected astonishment. To my chagrin he tried to interrupt a few times. Scepticism as much as amusement was written all over his large face. His head swayed left and right, while every muscle of his countenance twitched as if in competition with each other. He evidently had a difficult time to refrain from laughing. Several times he turned his head away to hide a merriment which irritated me.

"Hardly had I finished when he broke out in a veritable hee-haw. Seeing him thus, slapping his thighs repeatedly, put my back up. I felt offended, injured actually, since commiseration seemed more appropriate than derision. After all what I had just gone through could have smitten a weaker man.

'What are you laughing about?' I shouted thoroughly annoyed.

"Chunnard would not, perhaps could not stop this boisterous merriment. He broke out from one guffaw to the next. Finally he managed to collect himself sufficiently to speak:

'Tell me, Claude, did you examine this – this skeleton closer, touch it for instance?'

'Not on your life, it was an abhorrent shape of bleached ribs and bones, which I was disinclined to be even in the same room with,' I answered reproachfully.

'They are not bones my old one,' he advised.

'What do you mean, what do you mean?' I cried.

"Well, he told me what he meant. Here it is:

The professor and his wife turned out to be confirmed practical jokers, in other words, they liked intricate hoaxes. It enlivened their solitary days, so dearly loved yet with equal fondness spiced by occasional diversions. I served them well towards that end, a more gullible victim would have been difficult to find. I furnished them reasons for many a giggle and titter, as much as rousing entertainment for the more uncouth denizens of the northern plains. Within a week, I reckoned, the news of my dupery would travel faster across the Barrens than equinoctial winds."

Carrol chuckled good-naturedly.

"What a simpleton I was for not seeing the signs."

"You mean indications existed pointing to their penchant for trickery?" remarked DeWitt.

"Yes. A little more erudition would have helped. Take that sign for instance, prominently placed over the entrance.

'Welcome to the House of Ochus Bochus' was written on it in astounding calligraphy. But of course a habitant from way back would hardly have heard of 'Ochus Bochus,' the famous magician invoked by jugglers and jesters alike. But back to Chunnard. I asked him:

'You imply that all was staged?'

'Most certainly. The Zinners' pranks, as much as their victims are known throughout Nunavik. I'm surprised you have never heard of them.'

"I remonstrated: 'But Rene, that skeleton was there.'

'A painting my son, a clever portrait, nothing else. Claude, old cuckoo, you should have stolen it, ha, ha, ha. We could have set it up outside as an inukshuk, ho, ho, ho."

In a way DeWitt and Moider were disappointed over the anticlimax, they had expected a more dramatic ending. Yet they nodded towards each other expressing admiration for an extraordinary tale, told by a gifted raconteur.

# A Conversion

To see Frank Montour fawn around Tim Bonner was not a pretty sight. It intrigued some beholders, but mostly it engendered an aversion culminating in loathing. Montour and Bonner seemed ensnared by a classic relation of interdependence, that is, of master and servant. Each needed the other, but both were resentful of the fact. To see such lording and subservience in Canada seemed totally out of place, at least a hundred years outmoded. How such unaccustomed toad-eating developed was not easy to ascertain, it just seemed to exist from the instant they met.

Trying to understand it led nowhere, analysing it would have proved impossible. Was it a game they played for their own amusement and that of others, merely an acquired habit, or just coincidence? None of it; their behaviour obeyed an innate necessity, that is, a need to be venerated on Bonner's part, equalled by a desire to be subservient on the part of Montour. Of course this latent craving to idolise was governed by certain principles. A scrawny lightweight, or someone poor could have never triggered it into action. Physical stature, accompanied by a pertinent deportment were necessary, along with a burning desire to be adored.

Tim Bonner was not built like other men. Huge in body, he resembled an ageing prince Siddharta, also known as Buddha. He owned an up-and-coming company, which Montour managed. He had a habit of smacking his lips, which drove many an acquaintance to distraction. Montour claimed to be a Mohawk Indian, which made Mohawks cringe and Whites break out in guffaws. He spoke not a word of Mohawk, besides bore no resemblance to any Indian tribe. Actually he was a quarter-blood, who nevertheless possessed a band number.

All went well till Pat Horne obtained a position with Bonner's company, no doubt supported by Montour's recommendation. The two knew each other for many years, both belonged to the country club in St.Lambert. They were on good terms, which however should soon change.

Horne disliked Bonner from day one, but not as much as he resented Montour's puzzling bowing and scraping, or Bonner's infuriating gracious nodding. Of course it was not actually done physically, but the intent was indubitable there.

"Rick, it gives me goose pimples to watch that performance of genuflection and benediction, metaphorically speaking of course," Horne told his friend Ralston all in a dither, which seemed out of place in a man known as a cool reckoner.

"What is it Pat that bothers you?" Ralston asked, being hardly able to suppress a yawn.

They were sitting in the Chambly Inn, their favourite haunt, so warm and cosy, while outside wind driven rain pattered against the window panes.

"Their behaviour is disgusting, I tell you. You have heard about courtiers and king's jesters, no doubt."

When his friend nodded, he continued, growing angrier by degrees:

"Well, their shenanigans surpasses all, hands down that is."

"Oh well, you just have to live with it, or stay away," his friend advised.

That was just vintage old Rick Ralston, forever acquiescent, never mutinous, always leaving well enough alone, just wandering happy-go-lucky on the path of least resistance. Quite unlike himself, who almost thrived on controversies. Drawbacks hardly fazed him once a need arose to act, like helping a friend for instance. True, they were not overly intimate, he and Montour, but close enough to extend a hand in a predicament resembling the present one.

"By the by, are you still leasing that cabin up at Kempt Lake?" Horne asked out of the blue.

"Yes, for another year," came Ralston's answer, somewhat surprised over the sudden change in subject.

"But why do you ask?"

"Oh, I just thought to rent it perhaps for a week or two this summer."

"Settled, just let me know when, and not another word about rental, if you value our friendship."

When Horne made this inquiry, it served no purpose, it was just done on impulse. But after several more encounters with Bonner and Montour, Ralston's cabin acquired a more purposeful aspect. Their nerve racking behaviour with each other robbed him of his equanimity. Whether it was Montour's kowtowing that grated more on his sensibility, or Bonner's lip smacking acknowledgement, he could not say. However, one thing was sure; it was an abomination that had to be stopped. But how?

First Montour needed a heart to heart talk, which no doubt required a good measure of tact. Allusions to such personal quirks, if not aberrations, should not be made unceremoniously, under no circumstances in a tense, businesslike environment. An informal atmosphere would be more conducive to broach such sensitive topics. One had to be relaxed, be at ease with oneself and the world. Ralston's camp, far away from it all would be most suitable.

Gentle nudging amid the soothing laps of water, and the loon's eerie, but reassuring cries, should achieve the desired result. Just the two of them up in that unique spot, among rustling leaves and sighing pines, should mellow his companion sufficiently to make him receptive to a conversion; that is a change as it were, from a jellyfish to a man with backbone. Surrounded by serenity, playfully interrupted by the lap of water and gentle wind, he surely would come to his senses.

But to get him up there was another matter, for despite Montour's professed identity with Indians, who ostensibly prefer solitude to crowds, he was not known to stray far away from the bustle of modern society. He discussed his intentions with Ralston and Flint, his golfing friends. Although both were unable to understand this preoccupation to wean their comrade of a peculiarity, or even affliction according to Horne, they recognised a certain novelty in it.

"How to lure him up there is not so difficult," Flint said.

"How?" Horne inquired.

"Shame him into it," came the answer.

After a short discussion it seemed reasonable enough, so consequently it was agreed to put their plan in motion.

A week later the four met at the Cavendish Bar. They sat at a table surrounded by mostly regulars, who more or less knew each other. Montour slipped into high gears. True to form when tippling, he began to extol the virtues of Native Indians, to whom he referred as my race. Despite surreptitious, but recognizable signals by the others with him, some could not suppress a snigger, while others haw-hawed under their breath. Mind you, not because of the panegyrics aimed at Canada's First Nation, but solely on account of his inclusion in that race. In their opinion he was about as Indian as any of them.

A twinkle now crept into Horne's eyes, which all seemed to notice except Montour, who meanwhile showered Natives with a veritable crescendo of praise, and at the same time denigrating Europeans. Normally this would have been greeted with catcalls and good-natured advise to be quiet. Not tonight, however, because everyone close enough to hear sensed that something was up. Horne bent forward with a smile on his face:

"Now Frank, you Indians love solitude, don't you?"

He had to kick Ralston and Flint under the table, who in spite of their briefing started to chuckle.

"Particular in the middle of nowhere," Horne added, loud enough for all interested parties to hear.

"Of course we do, even more so if there are no white men within a hundred miles," Montour growled, while casting defiant glances from table to table.

A flicker of hate crossed his face, mingled with uncertainty, sending a contradictory message of challenge and a desire to be accepted. His confused countenance, riven by conflicting feelings, worn down by the search of a friendly fire, where every crackle means welcome and is not a threatening sound, was not a pleasant sight. It deserved pity rather than scorn.

"Did you know that Rick leases a cabin up at Kempt Lake, not far from the Manouane Reserve?"

"No, but why do you ask?"

"Well, since you love seclusion, we thought that you, or both of us could spend awhile there. It's yours for the asking, you know."

"Seclusion, wilderness? You know it's in my blood," he announced for all to hear.

"It's settled then, I will take you up there myself," promised Ralston with enthusiasm.

It was late spring when this arrangement was made, but it took awhile to carry it out. Montour's enthusiasm, so vociferously expressed that evening, began to wane drastically. He seemed forever occupied, scurrying from place to place, never at ease to discuss further details. Even worse, he appeared to suffer from loss of memory, any reference to Kempt Lake elicited but a vacant stare from him. Moreover, he now shunned the Cavendish Bar like the devil avoids holy water. But Horne finally buttonholed him, or rather Bonner did, whom they had apprised of their plan. He showed immediate interest, in view of Montour's visible edginess lately.

"Frank, you need a holiday," he announced in his benign, but authoritative manner, when dealing with his manager.

"I hear it is all in the works already," he added in a tone of finality.

And so it happened. Ralston drove Montour and Horne to Manouane, a small Indian settlement on the western shores of a maze of lakes and rivers. There, as always, he rented a boat for the journey to his camp, a good two hours away. The cabin was well stocked with provisions as much as angling and hunting equipment.

Montour had scarcely said a word all the way up to Manouane. His face, normally quite pinched and cramped, took on an expression of utter despair. He continually cleared his throat and jerked up his heavy shoulders, as if to throw off an oppressive burden. Whether the others noticed it could not be determined. In any case they did not let on. After all he was noted for his high-strung behaviour.

More surprising was Horne's conduct. Reputed as a cool, pragmatic man, somewhat taciturn, he displayed quite contrary traits since they had left Montreal. His tongue seemed to be in constant motion, while trying to direct their attention to this and that. Be it a landscape, not spectacular by a far throw, moreover familiar to all, or grazing farm animals, or even clouds in the sky. Ralston let him talk, meanwhile smiling as if amused.

This smile, however, froze solid when he caught a glimpse of Montour just before they set out from the wharf. He visibly shrunk back at the sight of his friend's tormented appearance. Not only his face, his whole body expressed downright terror, as if pursued by Satan and all his helpers. The man seemed aghast over something, panic was written all over him. His eyes bore a haunted look; a silent appeal shone in them, while shifting from him to a group of Indians standing nearby.

Was it fear that distorted his features, or just a transitory indisposition? Fear, fright? Impossible, it flashed through his brain, as he recalled Montour's enthusiastic readiness to spend, as he put it, the rest of his life in seclusion. It must be excitement, just wild anticipation that manifested itself in a queer way, nothing further.

"I will see you in a week's time," Ralston called from the wharf, while waving good-by.

There was no need for him to accompany them, for Horne knew the place quite well.

A week later Ralston came to collect his friends. He immediately detected Horne standing amid a small party of Indians engaged in a lively discussion. Barely did he lay eyes on him, when a feeling obtruded itself that something was amiss. Horne seemed agitated, beyond his usual equable self bewildered. In spite of an effort to remain patient, he appeared to loose his composure while trying to explain something to several sceptical men. There was no sign of Montour.

"Hello Pat, what's up?" he called out.

Horne, visibly relieved, hailed his friend with an unwonted exuberance.

"Ah, there you are," he shouted and hurried towards him.

"Where is Frank?" Ralston asked.

"Still over at the camp."

"I see," was all Ralston said, waiting in the meantime for an explanation, which he expected and got.

"You might as well come with me, it's better than remaining behind all by yourself," Horne advised.

"I will tell you everything on the way over," he added, after both were on board.

"So, what happened?" demanded Ralston to know.

"Nothing earth shaking, but still vexing. Yesterday morning when I went out fishing, just after sunrise, things began to happen."

"You went alone, I take it."

Horne chuckled before continuing:

"You know Frank and his banking hours, he was still snoring when I left. Well, hardly did I push off when a wind came up. In no time the water turned into a choppy, angry sea. About a mile out the motor stopped. Try as I would, it did not start again. However, luck was on my side. Wind and waves pushed me slowly towards the shore. Remember, rowing this big, unwieldy boat is no child's play, particularly in churning water."

"What happened then?" Ralston asked, increasingly plagued by an inexplicable premonition.

Why, was beyond his guess, since both friends were evidently hale and sound.

"Just when I got within a stone's throw of the shore, the wind changed. No amount of inveighing or cursing altered the fact that I drifted far out onto the lake. So it went for the rest of the day, plus all night. Helpless I was, but also fortunate. Of course no actual danger existed, since this boat is seaworthy, besides the shore, not too distant, was always visible."

"Quite true, but Frank must be worried about you."

"Hardly, he knows the score I imagine, for he saw the boat at the mercy of wind and waves bobbing up and down. Moreover my sign language surely apprised him of my predicament; besides he knows me well enough to realise that a little mishap like that would not throw me off balance."

"Oh well, everything turned out fine in any case I see," admitted Ralston.

"So it did. As mentioned, luck was on my side."

"Just tell me the rest," demanded Ralston, more to hide his apprehension than out of interest.

"Early this morning I noticed to my joy that the boat was drifting towards Manouane. Soon I could see people standing on the wharf pointing in my direction. When I signalled a few times, three men came out in a boat to investigate."

"What was actually wrong with the motor?" Ralston asked somewhat perplexed, since he had been using this same craft many times, never experiencing the slightest breakdown.

"Not much it seemed. One of the men, evidently a mechanic of sorts, made a few deft hand motions, and there it went, purring as before."

They now neared the shore where a single cabin stood high above the water.

"Strange, that there should be no sign of Frank, he surely must have heard us by now," conjectured Ralston more anxious than ready to admit.

That nagging foreboding of before assailed him again, this time with a force that almost squeezed the air out of his lungs. Something is wrong, he thought, all the manifested nonchalance of his friend beside him was unable to conceal it.

"Ah, you know Frank, he always acts contrary to one's expectations," he comforted with an air of forced indifference.

"Hello Frank, ahoy there, I'm back," shouted Horne.

"Come on, quit horsing around and start packing," rebuked Ralston loud and a bit annoyed.

There was no reply, only the wind sighed in the tall pines, and the water lapped rhythmically over the shore down below.

An eerie silence reigned around the cabin, not a sound could be heard from inside. The window shutters proved to be tightly pulled and hooked. To their consternation they found the door barred from the inside.

Panic now gripped Ralston, even Horne, the cool reckoner, started to pound the door frantically. He admitted what already weighed heavily on Ralston's mind since this morning.

"Something happened Rick, we must get inside," he uttered in a hoarse voice.

It was easier said than done. Only after they procured some hefty tools from the boat were they able to jimmy the door open. What a sight awaited them, a view they would not forget the rest of their borne days.

"Oh my god," groaned Ralston.

"What on earth," cried Horne half dazed.

Frank Montour, their comrade of many years hung motionless suspended from the ceiling. A noose lay around his neck, whose other end was tied on a sturdy hook. Cutting him down seemed pointless, because stiffness of death was already evident, besides both were cognizant of the legal tenet not to move anything in cases of death.

"Don't touch anything," was all Horne said before he waved his friend outside.

He, as much as Ralston knew what to do, that is, notifying the police without delay. First of course everything from door to shutters had to be nailed fast. Afterwards they jumped in the boat and raced back with full throttles. Chased by sparks of excitement, as much as the growing shadows of approaching evening, they skimmed above the water as never before.

Contacting the police from that remote settlement proved not so easy, though ultimately they managed to do it. By the time the police arrived, darkness had set in. Consequently not much could be undertaken except interviewing Horne and Ralston. After strict instructions not to venture across again without their presence, the police left with the promise to return first thing in the morning.

The authorities, after an official examination, arrived at the verdict: 'Suicide by hanging'. Reasons could not be given, therefore a coroner's inquest was held, to which Horne and

Ralston were summoned. In no time there emerged an astounding revelation.

Frank Montour, the deceased, had suffered from a malady called autophobia, that is a morbid fear of being alone. Furthermore records brought the fact to light, that this aberration could be termed hereditary, stemming from the mother's side. One of his sisters, it was revealed, lost her reason after being left alone over night at their summer cottage on the lake, not remote by any stretch of the imagination.

A slight rebuke was issued by the coroner, mind you, off the record, to Ralston and Horne for even entertaining such an outlandish notion of taking anybody so far away for just a little talk, as Horne has termed it. But since both had avowed complete ignorance about their friend's disorder, it was left at that.

About six weeks later Ralston had a chance meeting with Ron Lahache at the Kahnawake Country Club. They had not seen each other for some time. Both were playing a game of golf when they sighted each other. A call and a wink expressed their mutual desire to meet at the clubhouse after their respective games, which they did.

"Too bad about Frank Montour," Lahache voiced his regret before they even sat down.

"I guess you knew him quite well," said Ralston.

"We grew up together on the reserve, and we stayed in contact pretty well up to his untimely end."

They started to talk about other things, but it soon became apparent that Ralston's attention was divided, he seemed ill at ease, looking here and there, but never directly at Lahache. After a short lull in their conversation he said:

"You know Ron, I feel a bit guilty about Frank's demise."

"Oh, how so?"

"Because I was a party to a scheme, mind you, well intended, but in all likelihood a factor in Frank's death."

"You are making me curious, what did you do?"

Ralston told him about Horne's idea of weaning Montour of his disconcerting habit playing up to Bonner.

"I must admit it was not a pretty sight to see a grown man bowing and scraping, speaking figuratively of course, to that overgrown, lip-smacking oaf. It sure grated on my nerves too, but Pat, who of course had to witness it almost regularly, simply could take no more. So, talking or shaming Frank out of it, seemed a natural, if not a noble thing to do. However, had we been aware of Frank's, how should I say, idiosyncrasy, taking him up there would never have entered our minds. As was revealed at the inquest, none of us knew that such maladies even exist."

As Ralston related, Lahache grew pensive by degrees, he seemed to be searching for a missing link. His countenance kept changing from astonishment to doubt, then finally to an expression of recognition. He knew Horne well, and as mentioned Montour even better. His furrowed brow, indicating disbelief if not dismay, remained not unnoticed by Ralston.

"Ron, I notice a look on your face that intrigues me, is there something you want to say?"

"You mentioned a moment ago that none of you were aware of Frank's morbid fear to be alone."

"No doubt about it."

"You are wrong; Pat knew, rather knows all about it."

Ralston almost knocked his glass over, in an attempt to protest.

"Impossible, he denied it under oath at the inquest," he almost cried.

Lahache's face puckered up, whether from annoyance or amusement would have been difficult to ascertain.

"He was putting you on, all of you, I can tell you. Listen what I have to say, then you be the judge."

"Go ahead," encouraged Ralston, although still dubious.

"I have known Pat Horne since his return from the United States, that is about fifteen years ago. As a matter of fact, it was I who introduced him to Frank Montour and his family. As can be imagined, he noticed the condition of Frank's sister Rena, and I satisfied his curiosity by relating the incident, which caused her unfortunate predicament."

"I be darned," Ralston could not resist saying.

"You must have noticed Frank's predilection for crowds, moreover his persistent search for a companion to go with him practically anywhere."

"I did, but paid scant attention to it."

"Well, so did Pat, and contrary to you he put more than a light construction on it, judging by his constant inquiries. One late evening at this same club, after a few drinks too many, I told him all about it."

"All about what?"

"Well the fact that not only Frank's mother and sister Rena suffered from autophobia, but Frank even more so."

"Therefore he knew about it, you are saying."

Lahache nodded several times, before he continued.

"I sure do. More than that, let me relate an experience three of us had some years back."

"What was that?"

"We were hunting off the back road on the reserve one day, when Frank almost befell the same fate as his sister Rena. Even today I get all in a dither at the thought of it."

"Now, you have really stirred up my interest, please go on," Ralston said eagerly.

"Somehow Frank became absorbed in a pond in the middle of nowhere. Without noticing it we walked on, when all of a sudden, not more than a minute or two later, we heard him hollering at the top of his voice. Being in a sportive mood, we figured to have some fun. In a flash we hid behind a cluster of bushes, where chuckling we watched Frank darting about, constantly calling our names.

"But I tell you we soon had second thoughts about our little amusement. In no time the situation took on a sinister aspect. Frank became frantic, rushing headlong from bushes to bushes, he called for us in an anguished tone. Before we recovered from our amazement, he suddenly plunged head over heels in a direction away from us. His cries now were those of a soul in terror, chilling us to the bones."

"But Ron, I know that area. True, it is all underwood, but hardly remote. A half hour's brisk walk, no matter from where, would get you to the village or onto a major road," Ralston could not refrain from pointing out.

Lahache nodded.

"Quite true, but let me continue. We were too stunned to act. By the time we found our composure Frank was out of sight. Totally confused, also concerned I must admit, we stared at each other. Was he putting us on, perhaps playing one of his immature pranks, or were we witnessing a drama beyond our comprehension?"

"He lost his nerve, I guess."

"More than that, he almost lost his reason. When we finally caught up with him he virtually collapsed, mentally as much as physically. I can hardly describe it, but he was raving, babbling and ranting about being abandoned, purposely left behind to die."

"How did it end?" asked Ralston.

Shaking his head and raising both hands as if to shoo away evil memories, Lahache continued:

"We ultimately calmed him down, believe me, it took awhile. And you know what? After finding his composure again, he seemed neither embarrassed nor regretful. One had the impression that he was unaware of his outlandish behaviour."

After a pause Ralston asked:

"You said Horne knows about this?"

"I sure did, he was one of the men with us."

Both now fell silent, pursuing their own thoughts, wondering, conjecturing, not quite understanding, or rather refusing to understand. Ralston was first to break the uneasy silence:

"You know something Ron?"

"No, what?"

"That boat had a new motor, besides being in excellent shape. I have used it absolutely trouble free for many years."

"What are you trying to say?"

"Something more. I talked to the mechanic who fixed it so easily and quickly. He said there was nothing wrong with the motor, just the gas line had slipped off, which could have been pushed back in place in a second."

"Hm, that sounds strange," murmured Lahache who began to understand.

"Very strange," said Ralston, who had understood already.

# Calls In The Night

A hellish racket," said Ralph Mara already for the third time, while looking anxiously out of the window. There was groaning in the trees and rattling around the little log house, in which three men waited for better times. However, it should not be. On the contrary, the din and clamour rather increased. One had the impression that outside a many-armed, irate giant stamped around the log walls and shook everything not nailed down. Ralph Mara felt an uneasy sensation creeping under his skin. He conjectured loud:

"I bet we shall soon sit here without a roof over our heads."

"Come on, Ralph," chided Conrad Hawkes, whose father had built the log home many years ago.

"Don't forget my old man not only built durably, but also to resist any kind of weather," he added with justified pride.

"That is true; with a claw hammer, an axe and handsaw, he would have costructed a castle fit for a king," concurred Real Renard, who knew the family well.

"Moreover, it would not have taken long. Have no fear my dear fellow, sooner I expect the rocks yonder to crumble, before anything goes out of joint here," confirmed Hawkes laughingly.

"Now to something more important, how about a hearty sip," offered Renard as he uncorked a bottle.

"Two would be better," said Hawkes, extending his empty glass.

When Renard approached Mara, he shook his head.

"Thanks, nothing for me," he refused sheepishly.

His friends looked first surprised at each other, then flabbergasted when he put his hand protectively over his glass. Did they hear correct and see right? said their glances. Ralph Mara, jokingly called the son of Bacchus, known as a jolly tippler, rejected something alcoholic? True, doing so, he hemmed embarrassed, but it could not alter the fact that his friends lost their composure to a degree that they shyly left their glasses untouched.

"I say Ralph, are you not well?" inquired Hawkes, half in jest, but also a bit worried over his pal's mysterious behaviour.

"Sure, sure, but at the moment I just don't feel like it," came an answer somewhat defiant but also indignant.

Nothing further was said about it, though Hawkes as much as Renard could hardly disguise their bewilderment.

Outside the wind blew itself into a regular storm, it bent the pine tops and whipped the river's water over its banks. Onslaught upon onslaught beset the hut, one more furious than the next. At times so fierce that the walls began to vibrate.

Mara grew visibly more restless. At every howling gust he winced as if frightened. Occasionally he jumped to his feet and rushed now to the window, then to the door, which he flung open, then slammed shut immediately again. Even in the midst of an animated conversation did he undertake these incomprehensible dashes.

What drove him to it none could have said, because reasons did not exist. Storms more vehement than the present one hardly counted as a rarity around this time of year. To become uneasy because of it was really not necessary, even though their planned outing to the ice fields had to be postponed.

An oppressive silence descended after each of Mara's abrupt jumps, which embarrassed his friends, who neither knew what to say or to do. Their former unconstrained, merry meetings was gradually encumbered with inhibitions to the point of ruining their reunion. Oddly enough not a word was said about it. For inexplicable reasons they shrunk from mentioning what almost caused their tongues to burn a hole in the roof of their mouth.

Mara's peculiar behaviour, so contrary to his hearty, exuberant nature, started to tug at their nerves. What could have possibly gotten into him, expressed their clandestine glances from one to another. They felt miles away from the purpose of their reunions. Instead of spending a pleasant week in congenial company, shades of irritation hovered before their eyes. They became annoyed, questions were put warily, answers given were testy. But above all, they started to observe Mara's every movement with suspicion.

When maybe for the tenth time he flung the door wide open and stood there like rooted to the spot, looking outside, listening for god knows what, Hawkes could take no more. He asked gruffly:

"Say Ralph, do you expect someone?"

Mara started like a sinner caught in the act, while he answered subdued:

"No, no, I just thought a tree had been uprooted."

He then pushed the door shut again.

"Your nerves seem to be quite frazzled," declared Renard in such an accusing manner, that their friend hung his head in shame.

"Is there anything we should know?" inquired Hawkes somewhat more relaxed.

Whether it was meant to be sympathetic or censorious remained uncertain. Mara shook his head while keeping silent. They were intimate friends, who for many years held sort of a yearly conference in this former hunting lodge, which of course also entailed pleasure. There they spend one or two weeks in cheerful company, far away from human bustle. Their arrival always coincided with the anniversary of Dionysus, patron saint of wine, to which all three were partial. There on the wall hung his token; a thyrsus whom all only too gladly honoured with full glasses.

But not today, far from it, the entire row of unopened bottles still stood on the shelf. Even the decanter on the table remained half full. However, Hawkes and Renard did empty their glasses, furtively to be sure, when Mara had turned his back.

This yearly vacation was of great importance to them, it meant the world to one and each. Their journey started in Spillimacheen, where the impetuous Bugaboo River flows into the mighty Columbia. On the backs of their roans, with a packhorse in trot, it went westward to the edge of the wild and isolated Bugaboo Park, a section of British Columbia's pristine wilderness.

Days passed quickly there; before they knew it the horses had to be saddled again, riding back could no longer be delayed. During daytime the activities consisted of fishing, outings afoot or on horseback, as well as rowing on the foaming river, or sitting in front of the log house just prattling time away.

After sundown the bottles received attention; indeed, they had a glorious time. Glasses tinkled, voices rose, moreover feelings ran high, though only in a playful way. Soon after their throats were sufficiently oiled, they delved into conversation. But not today, a barrier inhibited the flow of words. Grey veils of mistrust descended over their forced gaiety, Mara's strange conduct robbed all desire for idle talk.

At first these outings served solely a desire for hunting, but such occupation lost its attraction with time, which however none would admit at first. Because such sentiments, limp and effeminate, where deemed unseemly in a man of the Kootenais, the last bulwark of masculine virtues. Hunting in that rugged wild region was considered an essential part of manhood, a sport which only chicken-hearted sissies renounced. Still, it happened one evening, after many cheers, that all three confessed having lost a desire for it. From thereon their rifles remained unloaded in a corner.

The wind had suddenly abated, it began to snow, which enlivened their spirits noticeable. Even Mara showed traces of his customary scintillating mood. With a roguish mien he lifted his empty glass.

"Well boys, must I die of thirst, or how does it stand?" he called out laughingly.

In a jiffy his glass was filled. While Renard did so from a decanter, also not forgetting their own, a second cork popped already, which Hawkes had pulled out of the next bottle's neck with many words of encouragement.

Then it got hilarious, lively words gushed from their lips, their tongues had some catching up to do. Each attempted to add zest to their experiences. The ensuing silence outside was perceived as a benediction from heaven. Renard and Hawkes thanked their stars for their friend's regained equanimity, while Mara greeted the stillness outside for reasons of his own.

Hawkes related his past year's experiences first. Not much however was to announce, except that he and his kin remained healthy and vigorous, for which he thanked fate. Business befell neither reverses nor unexpected windfalls. It just marched on in the old trot. Renard's situation stood similar, although his company had been awarded a contract to work at an important site in Calgary.

"Everything goes well there, I hope?" inquired Mara solicitously.

"As expected," he was assured.

"How are things with you?" Mara was asked, after he showed not the least readiness to make known what was so anxiously awaited since his arrival.

Were they mistaken, or did Mara indeed pull a face as if annoyed? There is something amiss, it flashed through Renard, this innocent question obviously touched a sore point in their companion. Indeed, Mara hesitated to answer. He stood up, looked about as if harassed, walked twice around the table, after which he finally forced himself to say:

"It's going."

"Oho, that does not sound too convincing," protested Hawkes, before Renard could signal him to be quiet, since he saw the pained expression in their friend's face.

He noticed how Mara winced, as if an old, healed wound had opened again. He was plainly adversely affected by the direction of their conversation, he seemed keenly determined to avoid the topic. But why? wondered Renard who remembered well what happened a year ago when they parted.

All three stood outside in front of the hut, where Mara's roan was saddled and the packhorse laden. Below, the wild Bugaboo danced and cavorted lustily, the water leaping at the rocks in its path. Above, ice fields glimmered in the warm autumn sunshine. Not a cloud darkened the sky, not a single worry burdened their spirits.

Mara trembled then for joyous expectation, he could not force himself to spend more than a week with his friends. He felt drawn back to Labrador, where he was tolerable sure to land a contract. They were told a lot about it, nothing but optimistic reports were heard. Only agreeable news rolled over his tongue when talking about it.

An unconcealable confidence glowed on his brow at the slightest allusion to it, for seemingly justifiable reasons. For besides him only one other bidder came under consideration, who, however, could hardly be called serious competition. A decision should be made soon, both were invited to submit their final offers shortly. This pilot plant, itself a considerable undertaking, would pave no doubt the way to a bigger, more profitable opportunity.

"Boys, this will be my Eldorado," he had said at least ten times a day.

As mentioned, he did not fear his competitor, because to him he neither possessed means nor experience to carry out a project of such dimensions.

"My word, I can feel already the warmth of a contract in my pocket," he called back, before he disappeared behind a bend.

That was a year ago, since then a lot of water flowed down the Bugaboo. Till now nothing could be extracted from him except, yes, his company obtained the contract, yes, they worked at it with all hands. Further inquiries he met with a pronounced silence, besides with the mien of a man who already had divulged too much.

Mara's ill humour had manifested itself at the first handshake. They noticed by his husky voice that clouds not only hovered over the mountains, but also darkened his mind.

Vexation was written on his face, uncertainty hampered his every step. Oh well, they thought, after all this annual vacation is meant to revive our spirits.

But at the present everything seemed to be in full swing again. Mara grew noticeable merrier, but oddly enough also louder, at times almost uproarious. His face smoothened, wrinkles disappeared from his brow, while a flitting blush might well have expressed more than just vinous bliss. His growing confidence and gaiety pleased his friends in their hearts. Only his eyes, unconcealable windows to one's innermost being, betrayed a restlessness, contrasting sharply with his expansiveness. They wandered continually about, despite an obvious effort not to let them roam arbitrarily. They whisked from his friends clandestinely to the entrance, where they remained glued for awhile, then wandered as if accidentally past the window. What fascinated him there they did not know, but no questions were asked, although curiosity almost got the better of them.

However, they had not long to wait for a revelation, it came with a change in weather. All self-deception was of no avail, Mara slid again into the claws of anxiety. No amount of tactful silence helped to disguise the fact that he was snatched again by his former excitement. But why, the devil? conjectured Hawkes, whom an answer eluded as much as Renard.

How could a man transform himself so drastically. What power might affect such changes, turning a hitherto steadfast, plucky man into a dithering rabbit, and so suddenly to boot. Did a force exist which induced a true son of the West, a daredevil without fear and reproach, to jump at every bang and crack? It had to be an illusion, their imagination most likely played them a nasty trick.

They themselves actually liked the turbulence outside, but not their friend's behaviour, who reached a point of loosing all composure. This rattle and rustle seemed to bother him to no end, although no actual reasons to be apprehensive existed. Nothing could seriously endanger the hut, it had defied far more relentless storms. No palpable peril faced its occupants. Should this filthy weather persist, there was always the possibility to ride back tomorrow. Most likely that would not be necessary, for since remembrance no one got snowed in at this time of year. In any case, saddling horses takes but a jiffy, and the way back could be covered in less than half a day.

Mara's jumpiness in the meantime degenerated to senseless fear, which no logic could explain. Something dreadful must have happened to him since their last meeting, an incident that cast his customary staunchness into the churning sea of petulance. This was the more surprising since he was never moody before, and certainly not irritable. They knew each other since early youth, a purely chance encounter developed into intimate friendship. Besides being congenial, their similar professions acted as a uniting bond.

Night approached, the snowstorm grew to a full-fledged blizzard. While it moaned in the trees and tore at the roof, which made the walls creak, inside, silence reigned more and more. Every commenced conversation came to a standstill, a flow of speech could simply not be attained. First because of Mara's taciturnity, but no less since he showed a determined reluctance towards any kind of conversation. Talk, even about others, seemed to disturb his train of thought, moreover it diverted his attention from the noises outside, which seemed to completely captivate him. Frowning, as if obeying an inner urge, he hurried again and again to the door, opening it hesitatingly, looking every way, searching, listening as if expecting an important message or visitor.

There he stood for awhile in the whirling snow, holding the door open with both hands, looking for something that did not appear, straining his ears for sounds that could not be perceived, his facial expression altering between unholy terror and groaning relief.

His friends finally had enough, it took one glance to reach an understanding. Both rose in a body, they approached Mara resolutely. While Renard took hold of his shoulders with both hands, trying to lead him back to the table, Hawkes attempted to shut the door. Neither one succeeded, Mara resisted with such startling vehemence, which deterred his pals. He pushed Renard back with one hand, while the other held the door open.

Hawkes was overcome by red-hot anger, he roared unconstrained:

“Get away from that blasted door, you are letting cold air and snow in. Man, are you completely out of your mind!”

Somewhat calmer Renard added:

“Ralph, come to your senses, don’t you realise how worried we are about you? By golly, we know each other long enough to deserve mutual trust. Why don’t you tell us what this is all about?”

“Silence, be quiet! I say. How can I hear what is going on outside, if you make so much noise,” Mara snarled at him.

“What’s going on? We can hear it, the wind that is, and we can see the snow, but that is no reason to become unglued. It’s a bit of a storm, nothing more. Tomorrow all will be gone,” said Renard in a soothing tone.

“What do you actually mean,” Hawkes asked, still upset.

“Him I mean, Mark Kirkland outside, we must leave the door open, that he can find his way back. Listen, don’t you hear his cries, are you deaf? Let me go, I must get to him, he is calling, imploring to be let in.”

“He is gone mad,” whispered Hawkes in Renard’s ear.

“We must pacify him,” he added, while four hands led Mara back with force.

It was easier said than done, because Mara seemed to suffer from a notion that a certain Kirkland was roaming outside, seeking shelter desperately, which his friends wanted to deny him. Finally he calmed down somewhat, he offered only slight resistance while being led back. Without further hesitation Hawkes bolted the door, while Renard diverted Mara’s attention by encouraging him to empty a proffered glass. His attempt to fill it a second time was refused.

“Nothing for me, Rene, that confounded wine is responsible for the whole mess,” he asserted, at the same time casting sidelong glances at Hawkes near the door.

“Responsible for what?” insisted Renard to know.

Mara began to chuckle without taking his eyes of his friends.

“You think I have lost my mind, don’t you?”

When his comrades turned their heads, conscious of their guilt, he waved his hand in appreciation.

"Really, who could take it amiss in view of my outlandish behaviour. Memories buddies, nasty recollections plague me to no end. But don't worry, this transitory aberration has passed, I'm composed again. Nevertheless, you have a right to know what all this is about. The journey from Labrador was exhausting, I had a strange experience there, but now I am among friends once more, among my own."

As Mara began to make long-winded speeches, the howling wind was interrupted by a tremendous crash.

"Another tree gone," said Hawkes with forced equanimity, which neither he nor the others felt. Mara bounded from his chair. When his comrades prepared to calm him down, he assured them with a wave of a hand, followed by a mocking smile.

"Relax, relax, I just want to show you something," he chortled while rummaging in a bag that stood in a corner.

"Here, read it," he urged with an air of a man who knew ahead of time what was going to happen.

In front of them part of a newspaper was spread out, consisting at least of two pages. Immediately some pictures caught their eyes, it showed on one side Mara, on the other a stranger. Both knitted their brows when they noticed the caption – Regrettable incident at Wabush Lake. Mark Kirkland, a well-known contractor perished in a snowstorm.

Hawkes looked up surprised, Renard followed suit, both seemed startled by something. Mark Kirkland, was that not the man whom Mara expected, who ostensibly stumbled through the snowstorm outside? They said nothing, but surmised a lot. Four perplexed eyes were fastened on their friend, two bewildered minds sought feverish an explanation. But Mara remained mute, displaying a countenance varying between defiance and gloating, which sent a chill through their limbs.

How could a man expect someone, holding a door open invitingly for him, if ten month ago this same man found a bitter end in front of his own eyes? furthermore thousands of kilometres away. Were they dreaming, perhaps dead drunk, or had they become victims of phantoms arisen from their overwrought nerves?

They continued reading, but only with one eye, the other remained fixed on their friend, whose puzzling manner revealed little, it rather cast shadows than light on this paradox. Besides they began to realise that he revelled in their consternation.

"Astounding Ralph, really regrettable, but I don't see how it involves you," Renard consoled him, relieved because he had expected worse.

Why the article cast suspicion on their friend appeared strange to him.

"I fully agree," added Hawkes with emphasis. "Fools just write what bigger fools think or say. I hope you don't lose any sleep over it," he snorted.

Mara did not say a word, only his troubled eyes found no rest, they scurried all over, never staying in one place for the duration of a pulse-beat. The mysterious smile now hovering like frozen around his lips, gave his friends goose pimples.

He was plagued no doubt by twinges of conscience, harassed by pangs of guilt, although according to the report there existed little cause for it. How could their friend help it, that a more or less stranger, a guest in the same house, either lost his nerve or became a victim of his own wantonness? How could he prevent his senseless, if not dangerous pranks? Refuse him access to alcohol, or hold him on strings? It was clearly written in the paper that, notwithstanding Mara's well intended admonishments, this Kirkland, indeed well oiled but scantily clad, roamed outside on that blustery night. Mind you, in a hellish blizzard to be sure. Every half sensible man would have remained inside, were it was safe and warm, except of course this fellow Kirkland it seems.

Here it said that after every crashing sound he hurried outside. This despite a crippling cold, howling winds which whirled up the snow, creating an almost zero visibility. Clad in indoor clothing, this man felt a need for scouting. Well, once he either strayed too far, or he lost his way. Mara, it seems, only saw him again next morning, cowering against some stumps near the main camp, mute and stiff as a corpse should be. To burden one's mind and conscience on account of it deemed them silly, to say the least. To be sure, such an unfortunate occurrence could cast a gloom over one's mind, but surely not for a whole year. Kirkland's mishap, doubtless self-inflicted, should really have been long forgotten, especially in view of Mara's increasing preoccupation with the plant construction.

They needed to cheer him up, rid his head of foolish notions, shoo encroaching shadows from his mind. That is what friends are for, not just to while away time, but to be there when need comes knocking. Why even talk about need, they said to themselves, till they looked at their friend's inconsolable face.

Undeniable he was tormented by more than just uncomfortable thoughts. That was evidenced through his fidgety movements, twitching shoulders, jerky head motions, but chiefly his harried glances at the door. At every louder than usual rattle he bolted upright, ready to plunge forward. Only the glares of his friends held him back. After every start he fell back again with a sigh. His inexplicable, irksome jerkiness acted like a damper on their spirits. A leaden veil seemed to descend over them, which neither Renard nor the more robust Hawkes could push aside. Renard finally made an attempt to shed some light on the mystery.

"Ralph, it says here the police were remiss in their duty, what do they mean?"

At these words Mara's face acquired an even more crestfallen, pallid expression, he seemed to collapse downright.

"It's an insinuation, nothing more," he forced himself to say.

"Towards you?" Hawkes asked.

"It seems so," came a subdued answer.

"But how is that possible, what had you to do with it?" followed Renard's question, which he rued at the same instant.

Mara started to say something, but swallowed whatever it was. Hawkes came to his assistance.

"Rumours circulate easily Rene, don't forget, Ralph and Kirkland were the only guests in that house, consequently all sorts of deductions could understandably be made. More so by newspapers, whose bread and butter depends on pointing fingers."

Mara cast a thankful look at him, but soon his eyes strayed to the door again.

A profound silence set in once more, an oppressive stillness only interrupted by the bluster outside. The storm did not subside, it rather increased in the same way as did Mara's restlessness. He simply could not sit still. True, he now avoided rushing to the door, but not to the window. Hardly had he returned from there, when he virtually spun around and stood there again after three or four vigorous steps. His comrades remained quiet, for they recognised his inner battle, an attempt to gather enough nerve to say something. He now cleared his throat loud, then hemmed repeatedly, but not a word rolled over his lips, they remained stuck in his throat.

Finally the will to talk gained the upper hand, they received startling news.

"You think I am innocent of Kirkland's death."

"Of course you are," they answered in unison.

"Well, you are mistaken, I had lots to do with it."

Had the wind carried the roof away from over their heads, they would have been only half as much surprised as now.

"He really has lost his reason," announced Hawkes under his breath.

"Let him talk," said Renard with a wave of his hand, hoping to pacify him with mimed attention.

He will surely find his peace again, he thought, in any case it's bedtime soon. Tomorrow morning everything will look different. He was convinced, as much as Hawkes that the storm would blow itself out overnight. To be sure, an abnormal cold usually followed which, however, seldom lasted long. At the beginning of October snow rarely remained on the ground, not even in the wild Bugaboos. Keeping him in good humour should be today's slogan, at least until tomorrow.

"Do you want to know what happened?" Mara asked.

Even though they only nodded weakly, he continued:

"You of course remember the day a year ago, when I took leave from you, filled to the brim with expectations. I looked forth to a glorious future, nothing but joy and success awaited me up in Labrador. I needed to get there in a hurry to make essential preparations for my final offer at the end of the month."

"You mean the pilot smelter at Wabush Lake?" Renard asked, although they all knew about it.

"You probable still remember the fact that, apart from my company, there was only one other firm in question, from which however I had little to fear. With that assurance I arrived there. Accommodation was made available in a recently finished log house, rather hidden from the main camp, which served as guest house for important visitors. However, one had to look after oneself, no service existed. I was the only guest, but only for one night. Next day another patron showed up, namely my competitor Mark Kirkland."

Hearing this name, Hawkes and Renard pricked their ears.

"I must admit, the man made a good impression on me. Already his first words of greeting made him likeable.

'We are competitors dear sir, but not opponents,' he said in a refreshing manner.

"It agreed with me, for as you know, I shrink from tense encounters. When he added:

'Now, how about a little fun in this burg,' I shook his hand with unconcealed enthusiasm.

"One should not forget that in my judgement the contract tingled, so to speak, already in my pocket. As mentioned, Kirkland revealed himself as an amiable, sociable person, forever in a jesting mood, imbued with candour which touched me most favourable. To be sure, he also possessed a, well, how should I say it, shadowy side."

"He drank too much, the newspaper says," interrupted Hawkes, who could slowly see a light being kindled by his friend's announcements.

"I would not really say so, but rather that alcohol consumption affected him in a peculiar way," Mara explained.

"Oh, how so?" Renard interjected.

"Well, it made him reckless and excessively talkative, to the point of giving the show away. Already on the second evening, after a few cheers, I was told in his frank way:

'Ralph, you need a lot of luck to land this contract,' he said with eyes winking at me cunningly.

"Although these eyes had looked already deep into the glass, I still took notice.

'Oh, what do you mean?' I asked with feigned unconcern.

"He then clammed up like a quahog on approaching danger. Nothing more could be gotten out of him after that.

"The next day heavy clouds began to gather above us, which shortly before darkness acquired portentous proportions. Then a wind came up, so stiff, that the skin of fresh ice cracked on the lake, and the treetops bent suspiciously. Snow followed in its wake, dense as a veil, driven in all corners by the raging wind. Nobody except Kirkland and I occupied the house, really a comfortable home, standing alone in the woods at the shores of the now agitated lake. We sat at the open fireplace, where it crackled and blazed merrily, a few bottles of red wine before us, prepared to spend the evening in pleasant conversation."

"That demon curiosity soon had me in its grip, nameless imps began to stir within me. Yesterday Kirkland wanted to tell me something, obviously revealing, that he regrettably suppressed before it passed over his lips. Wine imbued me with an unwonted boldness, the isolation amid this raging storm engendered a feeling of intimacy, which I managed to use to my advantage. Diligently I kept pouring wine, in the hope it would loosen his tongue."

Saying this, he looked at his friends quizzically.

"Oh well, I don't see much wrong with this," concurred Renard.

Mara thanked him with appreciative glances, before he continued:

"That's exactly what I too thought, when I steered the conversation to that subject at every opportunity. Mind you, it was done as if by chance of course, in no way apparent or intrusive. Kirkland was not aware what I had in mind, his unaffectedness seemed to be boundless, it slowly drove a flush of anger in my face. Finally I overcame all reticence. With my conscience pushed to the background, I began to put leading questions to him.

'Yesterday you said something about needing luck to be chosen as contractor, what did you mean by it?'

"At first he was reluctant to speak, but after several evasive 'oh well' and 'who knows', he at last imparted to me an astounding fact. It was this: The contract was already in the bag, in his that is.

'But why all these meetings?' I wanted to know in disbelief.

'Pure formality, nothing further,' he said with an air expressing satisfaction as much as regret.

"I shook my head incredulously:

'Impossible, nobody would chase me half around the globe for nothing, I just don't believe it.'

"Kirkland seemed to feel guilty, despite an alcoholic fog that bothered his sense of propriety. At last he spoke up. What came to my ears not only reddened my earlobes, but stirred four of the seven cardinal sins from sleep; that is: Pride, anger, envy and greed.

"The man surely meant well, he related information which could neither have been contrived nor wangled, even though it was to his advantage. Apparently an agreement existed between the province of Newfoundland, on whose territory the ore body is, and Wabush Mines, the owners. It read in short that all contract work must be awarded to local firms as much as possible. As mentioned, Kirkland had my welfare in mind, but I no longer his. It turned out the governing minister, a family friend, had personally acted on his behalf. He came, Kirkland that is, to sign the contract tomorrow.

"Outside turmoil reigned, but no less was my mind astir. My dreams came to an abrupt end, the bubble had burst. My next of kin, like myself, bathed already in the notion that this smelter will help us to rise above the middle class, and push us at least to the gates of fame and riches. My pride was first to take a tumble, for how could I endure my family's scrutiny, when apprising them that their hero's mission had turned out to be a miserable failure. What would friends and acquaintances say, not to mention fellow travellers.

"Anger was not long to rise, it was directed at Mark Kirkland squarely, even if silently. I had been cheated, shamefully deceived, and he, Kirkland, bore all guilt for it.

Envy and greed joined my surging anger now, bringing resentment to fermentation and at the same time creating reasons for vindication."

Mara paused, his glance wandered from his friends to the window, where it remained fixed for a moment. But as if forced to obey an irresistible power it travelled to the door. An expression of dismay took hold of him, a groan rose from the depth of his being. Then alarm changed to an unholy terror, groans turned into a throaty rattle.

Motionless, like someone paralysed, his eyes remained glued at the entrance, where he obviously heard or saw something that remained hidden from his comrades. Extending a hand, he pointed thither, unintelligible words, resembling extended groans emanated from his throat. His friends saw and heard nothing except the rustling in the trees and the turmoil around the house.

Yet Mara appeared to see much, and hear even more, like something that paralysed his tongue but not his limbs. Before his friends could prevent it he jumped up. With veritable leaps he plunged towards the door, which he flung open with all his strength. Nothing could be seen, no one stood outside in the raging storm begging for admittance. Only the snarling wind and whirling snow rushed in.

Disappointed, yet somehow relieved he closed the heavy door. Afterwards he seated himself again opposite his comrades, a picture of despondency and disconsolate despair. Everything had happened so fast, that neither Hawkes, despite his presence of mind, nor Renard were able to stop him.

Ignoring their quizzical looks, Mara continued:

"What I had just been told first produced a chill in me, then anger arose, in whose wake followed vindictiveness. As the newspaper reported correctly, Kirkland was in the habit of running at every loud crash from the warm house to look around outside. Even though this rushing about tugged on my nerves, I said nothing.

"For me the evening crept slowly onward, I downright dragged myself from minute to minute. What for did I even want to be there, why continue this humbug, I thought. Indeed, there existed no reason to prolong a game of deception that would bring no benefit to me. I felt like the victim of a hoax, who by serving a purpose was at the same time ignominiously taken advantage of. Nothing but hypocritical thanks expected me tomorrow. A rankling self-pity seized me, which ever so gradually was bein displaced by a fermenting fury that cried unappeasably for revenge. But how, or on whom, my imagination could not immediately determine.

"Kirkland got increasingly on my nerves, he chattered like a kakapo, incessantly, at the same time of course not ignoring the wine. Only his guilelessness protected him from my rising anger. Temptation gripped me repeatedly to assault him with bare fists. But I always managed to curb that desire at the last moment.

"Nevertheless, he became repugnant to me, I saw him as a schemer who smiled behind my back. I neither wanted to see nor hear him. I felt like being in a prison, held captive by isolation as much as foul weather, and laughed at by insidious conspirators to boot. Kirkland increasingly struck me as a brainless prattler. True, not perfidious by nature, but in any case a barrier on my path to success. His twinkling eyes, set in a kindly natured countenance, deemed me now rather defiant, contemplative, like harbingers of an evil message."

While Mara talked, his demeanour changed. The former semblance of a man in distress, befallen by a great injustice, yielded to a Mephistophelean expression, cunning, lurking, capable of anything but regrets or sympathy.

His friends noticed this transformation with bewilderment. Their long-time comrade, righteous to a fault, exceedingly goodhearted, seemed to crawl into the skin of a relentless malefactor. His face distorted to such an extent, that the others turned their heads as if on a sudden command. The lurking, sneering expression displayed, utterly unwonted, so completely unexpected, engendered a creeping uneasiness in them. They would have liked to close their ears and veil their eyes.

Instinctively both had a premonition of an unpleasant sequel to his report, which in one way was anticipated with curiosity, in another repulsed with aversion. Gloomy memories seemed to plague their pal, which had followed him all the way from that immense land, lit by northern lights, across vast plains and wild mountains, from sea to sea, to the western wilderness.

No doubt he was haunted by remembrances, a nasty experience somehow connected with a snowstorm. Renard attempted to shoo away these dismal apparitions from his friend. He tried to cheer him up with merry words, force him to smile and laugh, if need be by means of buffoonery. Yet it was to no avail, Mara would not let himself be distracted, he just shook his head and said with a raised hand:

"Listen, I am not finished yet. When Kirkland once more jumped up and ran outside to investigate, I was hit by a lightning thought. Assuming, I mused, while he roams outside, the door suddenly slams shut, getting stuck in the frame, jamming up in a way that not even the strongest hands could free it again."

Mara looked significantly at his comrades, chuckling, then laughing gloatingly like a man having discovered a means to retaliate.

"I asked myself how long a scantily dressed human being could stay alive in such terrible weather. I tell you, it was bitter cold, frost glistened even on the thick logs inside. Outside hung a thermometer, which hours ago indicated thirty-nine degrees frost, which did not say all, since its column consisted of mercury, which by all knowledge solidifies at that point. In reality the frost could have been ten degrees higher.

"While these peculiar images forced themselves upon my brain, Kirkland came back unhurt. But did that man shiver from cold. His normally deep red face had taken on a shroud-like pallor. My wish that he should have stayed outside till his limbs were paralysed with frost and the howling wind had robbed him of his breath, was not fulfilled.

"Suddenly I was hit with full force by a realisation. His death would certainly be to my benefit, it would deliver the coveted contract into my hands. By now I was wide awake, all traces of my previous boredom disappeared in the twinkling of an eye. Outside it was still raging on, inside my head developed no less a jumble. Nevertheless, I was capable to form a plan, whose implementation I initiated without delay. The man was in his cups, therefore his sapped will should make it easy to be led."

"Led to do what?" Hawkes could not refrain from asking in a reproachful tone.

"Well, outside raged a storm, the crippling cold began to split trees, the door was framed of sturdy planks, its bolt had been forged by able hands, and don't you see, my competitor was fogged in by an alcoholic vapour. Need I say more?"

Hawkes sat up startled, while Renard hid his face behind both hands. Although they divined the connection, they still felt uncomfortably affected by his attitude. His callousness shocked them as much as the lurking, malicious look, accompanied by his startling admission, or rather the will to a deed of which his friends would have never thought him capable. That he was talking arrant nonsense was evident, no less the fact that his mind was plagued by a guilty conscience.

They recognised the rankling tooth, sharpened by evil hopes, rummaging snarling through his brain. It seemed that at times he was thrown off the regular path, as it were, mainly in a violent storm. Without expressing it, they hardly believed that their loyal, upright friend could really have hatched such an insidious plot, let alone carried it out. He imagined something that never happened. The uncertainty, augmented by alcohol consumption induced him to mistake fancy for reality. No doubt, he blamed himself over his failure not to have done more to save Kirkland. But intentionally causing his death? Not their righteous Ralph Mara, they silently agreed. He however had more to say:

"Now I waited impatiently for Kirkland's next outing. Seldom were my senses so acute, I heard and saw everything around me. I observed him constantly, nothing escaped me, all his movements were perceived and interpreted. When he showed no inclination for awhile to run outside, I tried to incite him. How? Well now, by sudden starts, bolting upright, enraptured listening while pointing a finger in suggestive mimicry.

"Next we could hear a tremendous crash. As if stung by a tarantula I jumped up, pretending to rush outside to investigate. Of course it was only a feint. As expected Kirkland beat me to it, he plunged blindly into the treacherous night. Hardly had he stepped outside, when I slammed the door shut and pushed the bolt home."

"Oh no," Renard groaned.

"Oh yes," sneered Mara without realising it.

He sounded like a man at the bottom of degradation.He kept on talking:

"Almost right after I heard insistent knocks and rattles outside, followed by loud calls. Kirkland then belaboured the heavy planks with kicks and fists, without of course budging the sturdy door. So it went awhile, perhaps for ten minutes. His ever more piercing, desperate cries I answered with earthy curses. I lambasted his knavery, an outrageous swindle, which with someone else's assistance he had perpetrated on me.

'Destroying my dreams riffraff?' I called out. 'Ha, ha, ha, now face the music which you have written yourself. A frozen contractor is surely of little use to Wabush Mines!'

Were they once more mistaken, or did their friend really gloat over their consternation? His cunning glances, as much as defiantly pursed lips, invoked an impression of being made wicked sport of. One thing was certain, Mara had lost his reason, nothing could have altered that assumption. What he disclosed bore all signs of murder most treacherous and perfidious. Hawkes wanted to raise objections, he intended to impel his friend to be silent, but he was unable to garner enough force and will to carry it out. Renard too allowed Mara to continue, although his report pained him deeply. Mara had more to say:

"So it went for awhile; from the outside resounded shrill, imploring calls, while inside I answered with curses and imprecations. Then suddenly it grew quiet, even the roaring storm seemed to abate. The next moment I was gripped by a realisation which raced like red-hot steel through my veins. Assuming Kirkland was found frozen to death at the door, while I twiddled my thumbs inside in warm surroundings. Would that not throw a shadow on me? I could be reproached with carelessness, nay, even with criminal negligence. After all, Kirkland's demise would serve my own needs.

"In the meantime I had fled to the furthest corner, hoping to distance myself from his whimpering calls. In a few leaps I reached the door, which I carefully opened. Kirkland was nowhere to be seen, nor could he be heard. My loud calls remained unanswered, only the wind hissed through the moaning, cracking treetops.

"A frantic fear now gripped me, as I considered the possibility he would somehow manage to stumble into the main camp, even though half dead, but nevertheless able to explain the circumstances. In no time had I thrown heavy clothes on and ran outside. Although not before grabbing an iron poker from a tray."

"What for?" Hawkes and Renard asked in one breath.

Mara stared at them quizzically, as if to read in their faces what he did not understand himself. He shook his head saying:

"That I don't even know today. Maybe for protection from my feeling of guilt, or for self-defence; who knows. First I walked three times around the building, rather trudged stooped in proximity of the walls. Driving snow hindered my vision to a degree that forced me to discontinue my search. My heart was pounding, sleep was out of the question, since my whole inside was aflame with anxiety, besides I felt the need to keep watch."

"In case Kirkland showed up again?" inquired Hawkes.

Mara gave no answer. Either he was not aware of the question, or he did not want to hear it.

"How did it end?" Renard asked, still harbouring a wish for a happy conclusion.

"As the newspaper says, he was found dead the next day in a snowdrift not far from the main camp."

"Dead?" interrupted Hawkes, which elicited a glance from Renard, expressing more than words.

Stupid question, it was meant to say. Mara gave no answer, he just squinted and continued:

"Everything else you know already, it pretty well happened as the newspaper writes. Of course there were questions directed at me, particularly by the police. Some could have been called pestering, others were routine, many seemed doltish, so much so, that it wrings a smile even today from my lips."

"They had you under suspicion perhaps?" inquired Renard.

"Indeed so, but rather because of a presumed nonchalance on my part. I should have done more to prevent his reckless excursions, they implied. Some, who never experienced a blizzard did indeed accuse me of gross negligence. Relatives even raised their voices to the authorities that I should be criminally charged. But nothing came of it, there simply existed not a vestige of proof."

The long narration had weakened Mara, he seemed to be fatigued and indifferent. He neither stirred nor blinked when outside a tree fell crashing to the ground. He remained seated, even though his comrades jumped up and ran outside.

Not much was said anymore, except Hawkes' statement that he believed the storm's eye started to point away from them.

An embarrassed silence now ensued, none knew where to direct their eyes anymore. What they had heard quite shocked them, despite a lingering belief, rather blind hope, that Mara mistook an inflamed imagination for reality. He felt culpable, if not responsible for his competitor's death, whom after all he had wished six feet under the earth. They nodded towards each other, as if to say:

"To wish someone's demise is quite unchristian, but not indictable."

Mara rose and disappeared in one of the bedrooms. Shortly after his friends too wished each other a good night's rest and went to their respective rooms, understandably quite dispirited. Their bedroom doors were left open, to receive the benefit of the warmth in the fireplace.

The wind rattled undiminished on everything in its path, whirling snow obliterated all visibility. But the log house was save and warm, no storm between heaven and earth could lift it from its foundation. Soothed by the belief that this blustery weather would blow itself out, making room for the customary autumn air, Hawkes fell asleep.

In the early morning hours he began to toss from side to side. His sleep was marred by gruesome dreams. He deemed himself marooned in a cave where, lightly dressed, he groped for warmth between frost ringed walls. He shivered from cold, and trembled from fear to find an icy grave in that narrow vault. He wanted to call out, pray for help, but only a moaning sound passed through his chilled throat. Even though he knew it was only an ugly dream, from which he could extricate himself, he felt paralysed from head to toe.

When he finally succeeded, half awake, half asleep to open his eyes, he immediately closed them again. The cold did not exist in his dreams, but in reality. The fire must have gone out, was his first thought, I must rise and restoke it. When his eyes opened completely, a realisation hit him like a violent blow. He now was wide awake.

A mass of snowflakes danced wildly through the living room, driven by a blowing wind. The heavy timbered entrance door stood wide open. Chilled to the bones, he levered himself from his bed, wavering between disbelief and anger. Blasted Ralph, he mumbled while his clammy hands groped for warmer clothes. Imprecating his friend, who probably rose to look outside again, he shuffled shiveringly towards the door, which he angrily slammed shut.

"What is the matter?" Renard inquired in an irritated tone.

His bedroom door was closed, therefore the cold did not affect him so much. Hawkes, who had in the meantime approached Mara's bed to give him a piece of his mind, answered stupefied.

"Ralph has disappeared!"

They searched all over, first in every nook of the house, then outside as far as one could see. No trace of Mara was found. Their calls, progressively louder and more insistent, remained unanswered.

After dressing more appropriately, the whole area around the house was diligently searched. Turns were taken to look further away. One of them always needed to remain close by the hut, at least within sight, while the other could venture deeper into the woods. Ralph Mara could not be found.

By daylight the weather changed, clear skies smiled at them, not a snowflake was falling anymore. The wind now whispered rather playfully in the branches. Shortly after the sun had climbed over the mountains, Mara was found. Crouching between two trees, head bowed, cold and stiff, half covered with snow, he seemed to keep vigil there.

Hawkes approached him first, he wrapped his arms gently around his friend, imbued by hope to render much needed warmth.

Suddenly an almost imperceptible shudder ran through Mara. With great difficulty he raised his head. A mysterious smile brightened his countenance, it wandered from lips to his brow, and then to both temples. In the next instant his head fell down abruptly. Ralph Mara had found redemption.

# The Promise

On a sunny day in April a young Native Indian appeared in the camp of the Onondagas, on Lake Otisko, in today's State of New York. He came on foot with a rifle over his shoulders, on his belt he carried the usual game bag, a knife plus a drinking horn. He approached chief Tekanawita's tent with firm steps.

"The chief has gone hunting with other braves," an elder advised, whereupon he declared: "You are not an Onondaga."

"Kajuga," came the curt reply.

No further inquiries were made, since it would have offended an Iroquois' custom, which said: 'The will to talk is my own, whoever besets me commits a theft.'

An invitation followed, which Mantinoah, the young wanderer refused with thanks.

"I will wait for Tekanawita."

The elder considered the stranger closer. He nodded satisfied, what he saw appealed to him at once. He thought of Hiramatha, his granddaughter, the unapproachable daughter of an inaccessible mother. None of the braves around were good enough for her, not even the sons of Tekanawita captured a raised eye from the beautiful, proud Hiramatha.

"Tekanawita may be gone for some time," said the elder.

"I wait," grunted Mantinoah.

Time did not matter to him. Like all Indians unvarnished by Europeans, he calculated in moons. Hours, days meant little to him. He squatted down beside the chief's tent without a word. Tekanawita had to return sometime, if not today, tomorrow maybe.

After a while a second elder joined them. He remained silent, because he perceived with the unerring feeling of uncorrupted men a predicament in the young Kajuga. To step between him and his thoughts would have been deemed a desecration.

"I seek refuge with you," Mantinoah announced finally.

The elder nodded, after which he called out to the others. They came closer. Women, old men, as well as some braves who had stayed behind for protection, showed their friendly intentions. He was accepted without further ceremony. It presented no difficulties, since he too belonged to the Iroquois Nation. Nobody inquired why he came, or how long he wished to stay. Later the chief, along with other returning braves, welcomed him like a brother. A tent was allotted him without delay, also a horse plus other necessities.

Spring comes early in the valley of the Onondagas. The wind, warmed by the expansive water of Lake Ontario, sweeps unobstructed over the valley. Gradually the world acquired gayer colours. The willows in the lowlands changed their golden-yellow inflorescence to a glorious green. The red buds of crab apples waited for the approaching day when they would be ablaze in a jubilant red-white lustre.

Spring had come, the beautiful blooming-time had arrived. Young unmarried women and girls now cast bolder glances towards the youths who rode wilder than ever on their horses.

Then came fall, with it appeared Georg Marsen, the new Indian agent. He took quarters in one of the wooden huts. The Indians called him Watias, but they paid scant attention to him. Only Mantinoah, the migrant Kajuga, showed inclinations to become closer acquainted.

Marsen welcomed the youth's attention, because he did not feel exactly cordially received by the Onondagas. They tolerated him, but with little enthusiasm. Their distant behaviour bothered him more than he was willing to admit. Particularly since there existed an element of disdain.

To be sure he could not, like them, gallop bareback in full career across the meadows. Privations, accepted by them with admirable equanimity, would have meant certain death to him. Forced marches while heavily laden, on an empty stomach would have surely done him in. And to what purpose should he do it, he asked himself, had fate not set other targets for him?

Winters between Lake Oneida and Lake Ontario can be severe, snowy and cold, but they are invariably short. Nothing much happened in the settlement, life followed its customary pace. One could hear the occasional cries of newborns, could see the radiant faces of newly-weds, or meet the sad countenance of a bereaved.

Marsen, the Indian agent, turned out to be a bright spot. He was reliable, in no way intrusive or imperious like his predecessor. Little by little the Indian's distrust waned. Particularly when they noticed his effort to learn their language. Their confidence grew as he progressed therein. Indeed it was astounding to see Marsen's knowledge in Onondaga develop. The Indians recognised this advancement as a sign of good will.

With Mantinoah, however, emerged a closer association. As the sun climbed higher, and spring was announced by the honk-honk of Canada geese, they considered themselves as friends. They exchanged gifts, hunted together, undertook swimming contests on the ice-freed lake, or sat silent at a campfire, satisfied with themselves and the other. Their friendship loosened tongues, slowly certain taboos were overcome.

Where Mantinoah hailed from, Marsen knew already, but why he came continued to remain unknown to him. He did not mind, an association of many years with Indians had taught him much. For instance that knowledge about others robs the relationship of its magic. But he liked to tease him, especially about his shyness with women.

"Mantinoah, my friend, what have you got against Hiramatha?" he asked one evening half in jest and half in earnest.

No Indian could have turned redder than the one questioned.

"Nothing, Watias, but why do you ask?"

"Ha, ha, ha, don't even try to deceive me, a blind man can see how you intentionally avoid her."

Mantinoah just shook his head, he was embarrassed, but he made no reply. Marsen's observation was of course right, the girl, pretty as a picture had obviously cast both eyes upon his friend. Why any youth, straight in body, of a radiant exterior, unattached to boot, should evade a beautiful maiden was beyond his understanding.

Hiramatha's intentions could hardly be misunderstood, her whole being changed when near him. Her customary stiff demeanour took on a noticeable softness. A bright sheen flitted over her face at the sight of him, which rendered it even lovelier than usual. She then resembled a wild rose, which in the whiff of a warm morning wind burst out in full bloom.

Almost two years had passed since Mantinoah's arrival in the camp of the Onondagas. He had settled down, indeed it was gradually forgotten that he belonged to the Kajuga tribe. This fact was never mentioned by him, nor did he show even once a yearning for his homeland on Lake Kajuga.

Hiramatha wooed him with womanly wiles, with the natural aptitude of a woman in love. She had noticed long ago his reciprocal feelings, although he would not, or dared not to acknowledge them. Well, patience was a virtue of the Onondagas. Whether child, woman or man, all viewed haste as an unworthy characteristic of an Iroquois. Rashness would be laughed at, if not punished with disdain. Life consists of many moons, they said, what does not happen today, might happen another time.

Nevertheless, she visited Marsen, the Indian agent on a raw day in March. She of course knew about his friendship with the recipient of her love. She came to draw him out. What to a brave was unbecoming, namely to be inquisitive, the tolerant Indians considered it not amiss in a woman.

Marsen had to smile when he saw her come, sort of traipsing along, because he was aware what she had in mind. But he knew his duty, it would have bordered on brutishness not to exercise it. He greeted her, inquired about her well being, expressed astonishment over her rosy looks, then invited her inside. After the usual pleasantries the conversation steered itself in the direction of their liking.

"Watias, where is your friend?" she asked kind of indifferently.

"Mantinoah? He went hunting," came the answer.

"Without his white brother?" she inquired.

"Yes, without me."

Just let her wriggle, thought Marsen, it is good to be on tenterhooks for a while. In spite of her youth, notwithstanding an inborn reserve, she finally asked the burning question:

"Watias, does Mantinoah show his heart occasionally?"

"I know his heart," he assured her.

"Does he tell you to whom it belongs?"

Marsen gave no immediate answer. He looked at the raindrops running down the window in little rivulets. He could not understand Mantinoah. Although he cast more than just one eye towards Hiramatha, he hid his feelings with unwonted taciturnity. Any allusion to her seemed to effect him unpleasantly, as if hurting. His guileless friend, communicative without reserve, open like the wide, verdant land, clammed up at the mention of her name. He then wrapped himself in his cloth with a pained air and grew silent like a mummy. Whether out of shyness, exaggerated awe, or profounder motives, he was unable to say. But he intended to find out. Hiramatha interrupted the silence.

"His heart is already given?"

"Yes it is," he admitted unhesitatingly, whereby he looked fully at her.

The flickering uncertainty over her face, a countenance pained by fear, yet lit by quenchless hope, moved him to add:

"Yes Hiramatha, to you."

The joy on her countenance illuminated the whole room, it rendered the streaming rain into a golden glitter. A gleam entered her eyes, bright like the rising sun, warm as the nights in July. She then left him to his own thoughts, for she had heard what she wanted to hear.

When Mantinoah returned from hunting he unreservedly shared his quarry with his friend Marsen, who took the opportunity to report the latest.

"Mantinoah, I have talked with Hiramatha, she is waiting for a word from you."

This time Mantinoah did not shrink back, nor did he wrap himself up, he only examined his friend silently. Marsen inferred from his countenance a wish to hear more. It suited him fine. Mantinoah's puzzling behaviour disquieted him considerably. Purposeful in everything like the rippling brook between the hills, bright and clear like the blackbird's o-ka-leeee over the dewy meadows, the young brave showed himself fickle when it came to winsome Hiramatha.

"Watias, I have no word to give," he announced modestly.

Marsen's patience, already stretched to the seams, was about to burst.

"But don't you want to marry her?" he called out indignantly.

"I do," came the reply.

"What hinders you?" Marsen asked louder than intended.

"I may not do it," groaned Mantinoah, obviously in the throes of a dilemma.

Avoiding Marsen's disbelieving, flabbergasted look, he murmured:

"Before the leafs on the trees turn green I shall be dead. That is why I can not marry Hiramatha."

Perturbed Marsen stood up. So, that was it, a face had appeared to Mantinoah. As once Minnehaha, the daughter of the old arrow cutter, he saw the mask of death and heard the voice of Pauguk. Of course he knew about these predictions which were often fulfilled. But it happened only to old men and women already near the end of their lives. This harbinger never appeared to young, strapping fellows. But making an attempt to talk him out of it would be futile, therefore he let it be.

Two weeks later Mantinoah showed up at Marsen's door, mounted on horseback in full regalia. Sitting upright on his steed, he stood silent and immovable. What a sight! flashed through Marsen's mind for the thousandth time. A picture of grandeur were horse and rider. As often before he admired the noble demeanour of the Indians. Man and animal seemed to be transformed into a statue of dignity.

"Watias, you are my friend," interrupted Mantinoah the silence.

"That I am," he was assured.

"I need your escort."

"Where to?"

"To Lake Kajuga, my homeland."

On the way Mantinoah began slowly to explain, haltingly at first, then with more and more fervour.

"Before the sun today disappears behind the treetops I will be dead," he related to a speechless Marsen.

"Exactly two years ago I became embroiled in a quarrel with my friend Tuskarare. He reproached me of lying, the most evil offence to a Kajuga. The squabble turned into a brawl, I slew Tuskarare."

Mantinoah grew silent, as if the memory had robbed his voice. Marsen interposed:

"You acted in self-defence."

"So the mind says, but reality speaks different. No Watias, I am guilty, my heart knows it. Inside of me burned a fire not to warm, but to destroy. My arm was commanded to exterminate, not to defend. I deserve to die."

Marsen still did not know where this would lead to, but he raised no objections. Obviously Mantinoah's conscience drove him back to the scene of the crime. Did he want to commit suicide there? Hardly, Marsen thought, because in all his years among the Iroquois he heard not a syllable of such a thing. Suicide was foreign to their nature, mental breakdowns were unknown to them. But he understood his charge's resolve; once something enters their heads, they will carry it out with certainty.

They finally came near a grove where Mantinoah stopped. He swung from his horse, after which he laid both hands around his mouth and send piercing cries towards the wood. He then listened without stirring. His horse also evinced not a sound, nor did it twitch a muscle. Soon similar calls resounded like an echo from the grove. Mantinoah's countenance brightened, traces of a smile appeared around his lips. He nodded imperceptibly.

Shortly after a figure stepped out from the little forest. It was a young Kajuga in full finery with a rifle in his hand. A hundred thoughts raced through Marsen's brain. Hardly had he dismissed one, when already three different ones assailed him. He sensed something which he could not name.

The two Indians took each others hands with such hearty greetings, which dispelled all misgivings of an impending evil. Maybe they just exercise a custom unknown to me, Marsen conjectured. There seemed no cause to worry, all malevolent intentions were precluded by this sincere joy over their meeting. In the next instant, however, his hopes were dashed. Mantinoah stepped up to him, serious yet relieved; he spoke:

"Watias, trusted friend, there is my horse, it now belongs to you. Take it back to the Onondagas, tell them Mantinoah died like a brave warrior. They need not hang their heads in shame, they granted an intrepid man a second home. Here is my belt, give it to Hiramatha, speak loud to her of Mantinoah, the young Kajuga, who did not tremble when death approached him with outstretched hands. Here Watias, take my game bag, my knife and horn, I need them no more. I must go, the great spirit is calling. Farewell."

Before Marsen could fully understand, Mantinoah stood under a huge oak tree. With his back against its trunk he waited calmly for the end. Like in a dream Marsen could hear the two young Kajugas' words of farewell. Rifle in hand, the other said:

"Mantinoah my friend, the sun begins to descent behind the trees, are you ready?"

A nod was Mantinoah's answer. The other continued:

"Exactly two years ago you slew my brother. We granted you a respite of two years, which time has now elapsed. Your promise to accept your punishment under this old oak, you have kept like a Kajuga, we are proud of you."

Marsen was about to step protectively in front of his friend, but it was too late. The unerring bullet met his aim. The hand which obeyed a saddened heart's command, did not waver. Mantinoah tried to raise his hand in salutation, but again it was too late.

# The Voice Of The Tulameen

The first letter arrived on a Friday. Addressed to herself, it came by regular mail, but without a sender's name. She immediately recognised the stamp as Canadian, the land which she had left six months ago. When she opened the envelope a frown disfigured her face, because it seemed to be empty. Just as she was about to throw it away, annoyed, but equally relieved, a small piece of paper fell out. More intrigued than vexed by now, she stooped to pick it up, thinking someone exercised his humorous propensities on her. When she read it however, all such notions disappeared quicker than they had manifested themselves.

'The voice of the Tulameen' it said, just that, nothing more.

Staring at the cryptic line, written in awkward block letters, questions raced through her head. What's the meaning of this, who sent it? 'The voice of the Tulameen' she read again and again.

Else Peters knew that river well, she had spent almost twenty years there, wandering from the snow covered Cascades to Princeton, where the Tulameen flows into the Similkameen. Puzzled, but also perturbed she turned the snippet every direction. She tried to fend off unwelcome memories, which nevertheless were unable to suppress a rising longing for the fabulous West, where the wind rustles through tall ponderosas high above the river of many voices.

She had crossed a mighty ocean to lay a distance between herself and bittersweet memories on that ever shifting river, boiling and roaring through gorges, as if intending to make the rocks crumble, then meandering peacefully through lowlands, beckoning to linger. She had returned to the place of her birth to efface all recollection from that eagle haunted place, but she sensed that these memories would follow to her grave.

With an indignant wave of the hand she shooed away these wistful thoughts, then tore up the paper and envelope.

"Unpleasant tidings?" she heard her father say.

As she turned around, startled by his sudden appearance in the doorway, she instinctively hid the paper shreds behind her back.

"No, no," she answered a bit annoyed over the disturbance.

"A message from your husband perhaps?" her mother, who had also appeared wanted to know.

Her round good-natured face had acquired an expectant expression. When Else shook her head vigorously, visibly peeved, the mother looked crestfallen aside. They were puzzled, indeed uneasy on account of their daughter's secretiveness concerning her husband. They knew him by name only, plus by Else's singular description a long time ago.

Shortly before the daughter's wedding in a far away land, they received news from across the ocean. She must have been spellbound then, uplifted by ringing jubilation, judging by the long and enthusiastic letter that reached them. Rolf Peters, her future husband, was showered with every eulogy under the sun, and adorned with layers of praise. From his manly stature to a lofty mind, everything was described in glowing details.

That was over ten years ago; now their daughter had come back, although shrouded in mystery and determined to conceal her past, certainly anything concerning her marriage. She arrived practically unannounced, but was welcomed just the same. After a continuous absence of twenty years, they were surprised by her sudden appearance, nevertheless overjoyed, albeit dismayed over her odd behaviour.

Mrs Reusle, solicitous as ever, asked one evening, after imps in the full-bodied wine had loosened tongues and lowered the threshold of reserve:

"Else, why did your husband not come with you?"

A clap of thunder from clear skies could hardly have caused greater consternation than this innocent inquiry. Else stiffened, she shifted uneasy to and fro, evidently confused and embarrassed. While one hand tugged at her clothes, the other was drawn across her brow repeatedly, attempting to wipe the unpleasant question out of existence. Her father scowled at his wife when he noticed his daughter's discomfort, although he too waited anxiously for an explanation.

"He – he could not," she stammered looking down.

Her mother, as a rule an understanding soul, felt offended. Her artless nature was unable to fathom how one could just push husband and duty into the background. Nevertheless, she tried to smoothen the ripples caused by her inquiry.

"Do understand Else, we sure would like to meet our son-in-law, in particular since he was described to us in such glowing terms," she remonstrated.

"Well my dear, he probably stayed behind for stringent reasons," the father defended her, while glancing reprovingly at his wife.

Mrs Reusle put a good face on a situation incomprehensible to her, although now as before displeased. She then asked:

"How long shall we be able to enjoy your cherished presence, Else?"

Her tone and airy countenance made her husband smile.

"Hm – hm, for quite a while if you don't mind," followed an evasive answer.

"Stay as long as you like. A month, a year, ten years or forever," her father encouraged in a booming voice.

That took place in the beginning. Now, six months later Else seemed burdened as ever by fears of an impending calamity. Some days one had the impression that she walked under a threatening cloud, which at any moment might burst and inundate her. Both parents were baffled, actually worried over their daughter's restlessness. Many a night they could hear shuffling steps on creaking boards above them.

"Like a prisoner's walk," Mr Reusle whispered to his wife.

"Our poor daughter can not sleep again," his wife said to him almost accusingly, as if it stood in his power to alleviate her plight.

Slowly however, the situation changed. In the absence of further messages from Canada, Else began to relax. Her spirits rose visibly, she even talked freely about her life in Canada's West, a place without parallel. Words failed her to describe her stay on the banks of the Tulameen, a river without equal among many spectacular streams. But not a word about her marriage or Rolf Peters, her husband, could be pried from her lips. Her moods now reached heights of scintillation, which were only dimmed upon the appearance of Karl Fischer, the letter carrier.

"Something for me today, Mr Fischer?" she called out the moment she caught sight of him.

"Sorry, Mrs Peters, nothing today," followed his regular answer.

Immediately lines of worry disappeared from her face, glints of gratitude entered her eyes, and a sigh of relief escaped her lips. Another carefree day stood in the offing. Soon after she could be heard humming through the house while helping with housework, or her father's many little projects. One could have thought there was a woman satisfied with life, a person content with her lot, who hailed the mornings and thanked the evenings for another happy day.

Autumn had closed in, harvesting was almost done, landscapes began to turn brown, and withered leaves covered the ground. Shorter, cooler days, as much as longer, cold nights presaged of harsher times to come. Birds of passage flocked together, people grew pensive and morose, the former spring in their steps was no longer there. Else too felt affected by the cloud-draped sky and barren ground. She gazed more and more at the horizon, expecting she knew not what. Something was missing, a vital part for this time of year was absent.

A burning desire to find that elusive element drove her out of the house. Tucking up her skirt she climbed onto a nearby hill, from where the entire region could be surveyed. As she stood there a breeze came up stirring the wilted leaves, as much as her imagination. When shortly after a gust of wind blew over the meadows, she suddenly knew what was lacking: it was the wind tossing up the Tulameen.

The second whiff seized her thoughts and carried them westward over the wide ocean to the green hills of Newfoundland. Onwards they travelled, across storm lashed lakes and unending prairies, now cold and barren, moaning in the grip of frost. Further her mind's eye hurried, to the foothills, then across the Rockies, where it lingered as if daunted by towering peaks.

But her thoughts wandered on, to the fabulous semi-arid region of British Columbia. She could almost see the seared land, burned by a relentless sun, parched by winds that bend the grass and chase balls of tumbleweed up and down the valleys. She could very nearly feel the pungent smell of flowering sagebrush in her nostrils, as much as nostalgia in her heart.

When she came back, her mother hailed her from afar:

"Else, Else, see what I have," she cried all excited.

"What is it mother?"

"A letter for you."

"For me, who from?" she asked with a sinking heart.

"Hm, I can't say, there seems to be no return address, but the stamp is Canadian," her mother said while turning the envelope every which way.

Else took it ungently out of her hands. With pursed lips and furrowed brow she tried to decipher the handwriting, which bore a resemblance to the previous one. Even the touch of the envelope felt similar. Indeed, she could guess its contents, but not the name of the sender. Annoyed, she put it away with a deprecating smile that she hoped would dim her mother's further interest.

"Are you not going to read it Else?" she was asked in surprise.

Imitating a casual wave with the hand, Else replied:

"Not now, I have other things to do."

Hardly however had she stepped across the threshold of her room, when she tore open the envelope with trembling fingers.

'The voice of the Tulameen' was written on a slip of paper as previously.

What did it mean, moreover who sent it? Slumping down on a chair and burying her head with both hands, she tried to control her emotions. Someone played a practical joke on her, or worse, tried to frighten her. But who? After a while she concluded there was only one man capable of such trickery. Hogart Peters, her brother-in-law was mean enough to perpetrate any misdeed against her, no matter how wicked or damaging.

Then on second thought, the letters could stem from her in-laws, a mischievous, embittered pair to be sure. But that seemed far-fetched, for both were prematurely enfeebled by malevolence, as much as bitterness over a botched up life. Having denied and suppressed their Swedish roots, they wilted before enough sap rose to render new life. Consequently they were neither grass nor hay, just withered pseudo Canadians, bent on punishment.

No, Else decided, although inclined to such chicaneries, her in-laws lacked the strength to carry them out. There remained only Hogart Peters, her brother-in-law, who might be sending these ill intentioned messages. But why it was done, moreover what aim and purpose it should fulfil, Else was unable to determine.

The voice of the Tulameen! how enigmatic it sounded, but also disquieting to a guilty conscience. Hogart meant to ruffle her, send ripples of trepidation into a mind already troubled. For some mysterious reasons he had chosen the name of Tulameen to disturb her equanimity, a river once beloved, but now abhorred. Did he intent to somehow injure her, perhaps thwart a return linked with inconveniences for him?

Well, she would go back and show him a thing or two. It was not so easy anymore to browbeat little Else. The image of a timid soul, shrinking like mimosa leafs at every breath of wind, existed no more. However, she did not cross the ocean as yet. No amount of prodding or self-encouragement was able to transform her intention to action.

After a while, taking heart again, she went for long walks with Anton Bleuer, a flame of her youth. Together they strolled through the city and hiked across the countryside. Every time while ambling through narrow streets of the medieval town, she felt a mighty hand tugging at her heartstrings. At the sight of expertly hewn and embellished portals, splashing fountains built by artistic hands, and frescoed buildings, tears of joy welled up in her eyes. Bleuer had to apply all his gift of persuasion to induce her to move on. She simply could not turn away from these ornate buildings, lovingly decorated by skilful hands. A breath of times past, a civilisation that would not easily repeat itself hovered around everything. It enlivened the spirit and soothed the mind.

"Does it not enthral you?" Else said rebukingly, since he seemed so indifferent.

"Not really, I see it every day," he answered casually.

"Just look at it," she called out while pointing all around.

"What do you see?" she added.

"Buildings, some statues, what do you see?"

"I see moving hands, urged by inclinations and guided by minds of their own. There is song and laughter embedded everywhere, mixed with profound devotion, and a will to create something enduring."

"Oho, I hear the talk of a philosopher," he teased.

She glanced at him appraisingly before asking:

"Have you ever been in Canada or America?"

"No, never, why do you ask?"

"For no particular reason," followed an evasive answer, for she was reluctant to admit why she had asked that question.

Her motives were ulterior, she would have liked to obtain his opinion about some shocking discoveries she had made in the world of plenty. But having not seen them himself, how could he ever believe her. Like many Europeans, he perceived North America to be rich, if not opulent with nary a trace of poverty. Reality would have horrified him, since in many places existed not only material deprivation, but also resignation and spiritual apathy.

"Tell me about your life in Canada, Else. Where do you live?" Bleuer asked.

"On the banks of a river with many voices, by the name of Tulameen. A truly changeable stretch of water that is. Tumultuous in spring when the snow melts, still wayward and boisterous in summer, then quieter, much tamer in the winter," she explained with rising enthusiasm.

She told him more about that huge country with pygmean aspirations, as she called it.

"But the country, not its people, remains unforgettable," she averred.

Without further prodding she described that immense land, stretching from ocean to ocean, warmed by the midnight sun and resounding from undaunted voices of the wilderness. She could have gone on for hours extolling its impressive features, that could haunt a person's memory forever.

However, she did not tell him all. Despite the country's captivation she never felt at home there. Her heart, that foolish, throbbing seat of emotion, never found fulfilment in this wild and beautiful land. Again and again it seemed to rise from her breast to soar above wind and waves, seeking surcease at the bosom of her ancestors.

"You see Anton, I was unable, unlike most immigrants, to cast off my heritage at the border and embrace a terrible strange way of life. Sooner could I have peeled off my skin, than my origin," she concluded.

And then, before they parted at her parent's house, she added these cryptic words with a deep sigh:

"Had I been able, or even willing to do so, my life would have been spared its greatest sorrow."

When Bleuer glanced at her, she silently averted his eyes and took leave.

Before Else crossed the threshold she sensed the different ambience. A suspicious silence hung in the air; her normally expansive parents appeared subdued, they strenuously avoided her questioning glances. Even her effusive greeting only received a curt reply. They looked out the window as if fascinated by something, for which reason they could not pay attention to her. The realisation hit her like a burst of chilly air. Another message from Canada had arrived! And so it had.

Running up to her room, she immediately detected the portentous envelope on the table. This time, however, it read different. When she tore it open she flinched as if dealt a blow.

"We know the secret of the Tulameen" she whispered, trembling all over.

The blood seemed to drain from her lips, when her glance fell on the calendar on the wall. Today was her wedding anniversary. She now felt certain of Hogart's hands in this, but how he could contrive to be right on the mark, seemed uncanny. Unless – unless he or an accomplice had taken up residence nearby. Racked by fear of the unknown, buoyed by the realisation that distance afforded some protection, she nevertheless locked the door and lay down to think.

What were his intentions, moreover, how much did he know. No doubt, his desire to lay hands on that extensive property in an excellent location, provided a powerful motive to a man of his ambition. But to be sure, that would take some wangling, unless – unless of course he were able to produce evidence which would render the inheritance invalid.

A wry smile escaped her lips when thinking thus, for she knew he was absent on that fateful day, away on business from early morning till late at night. She remembered when he came back, morose as ever, moreover irritated beyond measure, owing to his inability to lay blame at her threshold. Imputing is one thing, prove another. His sideways glances dripping with accusations, meant to intimidate her, missed their mark. To be sure, she would never forget them, no less than his blunt innuendoes. Missed their mark? Not entirely, she had to admit, when considering her frayed conscience lacerated even more by these messages.

"Just wait," she murmured under her breath, "I will show you all."

Returning was a must, otherwise peace would never again calm her mind. Hardly had she racked up enough courage to do so, when the voices from the Tulameen chilled her resolve. They rose from the canyon, as on that fateful day; quietly, hardly discernible at first, then louder, increasingly shriller, till her ears rang from those mournful cries. Covering both ears did not shut out these lamentations, the heartrending calls kept rising from the restless river. She could hear the wind pick them up, lifting them above tall ponderosa trees and drifting across land and sea. They soon filled the room with a chorus of accusations. She buried her head in pillows, hoping to stifle the sounds of eternal guilt.

Then she remembered her parents down below, who were surely waiting anxiously to receive word from her, at least a reassuring nod or smile. For a moment she considered telling them all, make them privy to her battle with her conscience, a losing feud to be sure, which dragged her inexorably towards an abyss of misery. But she decided otherwise; first her thoughts had to be put in order. Moaning she curled up tighter on the bed, trying to fend off ghosts of the past. A rueful smile rose to her lips at the memory of those sweet and bitter years on that legendary river. 'The voice of the Tulameen.' Closing her eyes she could see that wayward stream. Though far away, its course was now as then indelibly anchored in her mind.

On that lonely wind-blown plateau Else Reusle spent the happiest time of her life. On a cloudy day in spring, when the hills were aflame with yellow and red flowers, and the feral cries of eagles resounded from cliff to cliff, she met Rolf Peters. Not long after they walked hand in hand over the grassland, where they exchanged kisses under every flowcring shrub. A pungent smell hung over the plateau, which was resplendent under the warming sun, like their growing passion.

The whole world seemed young then, laughing, filled with zest like themselves. The Tulameen, swollen to its banks, vied boisterously with the roar of the wind. Whole trunks were pushed down river, the turbulent water pounced on rocks that would not move, splashing foam and spray all around. The river behaved like an enraged giant roused against his will, and was therefore bent on destruction.

Every day after work they wandered tightly embraced to a nearby bend, where the rushing river seemed undecided in which direction to flow. There they sat for hours lost in themselves, paying no attention to their surrounding. Only after the sun disappeared behind the mountains, and the coyotes started their piercing singsong, did they return.

It was in the fall, as the shadows grew longer, when the honk-honk of Canada geese high above filled the air, that Rolf Peters asked:

"Else, will you marry me?"

Hardly had the last word fallen from his lips, when the echo returned her jubilant 'yes.'

Her reveries were interrupted by a knock at the door. No doubt her parents, uneasy about her, stood outside. First she tore the offending message to shreds, then she opened the door. Her father, his kind face deeply lined, tried to smile while saying:

"Else my dear, your mother and I are beginning to worry about you."

"Was the news not good?" her mother asked solicitously.

Else did not say a word at first, she just stood there and stared at them as if paralysed. Tears then welled up in her eyes, visibly in anguish she collapsed on the bed.

"I'm at the end of my tether," she groaned. "I can go no further."

Her parents sat down and waited patiently till Else found enough composure to continue. They looked at her with concerned eyes, hoping that unburdening her mind will scare away the gnawing unrest within her. Else broke the silence:

"I will tell you everything, from the beginning of my wretchedness to the bitter end, which is now. Believe me, I can find no peace anymore, at night horrible dreams disturb my sleep, my waking hours are marred by fears of sudden calamities."

Then she said something that made her mother sob and her father's head bound up.

"My conscience is killing me by inches," she groaned.

They were too startled to respond immediately. First they both looked quizzically at the daughter, then bewildered at themselves, before Mr Reusle suggested:

"Perhaps sharing your sorrow will lighten your load."

"Yes Else, I believe it will," remarked her mother.

Else nodded, showing her willingness to do so.

Where should she begin. Best would be from the day after a lengthy argument, acrimonious to the hilt, when their relationship began to take a nasty turn. True, a discord festering more with time, had prevailed for a long while. She had ceased long ago to be the coddled darling of her in-laws, as much as the beloved of her husband. Although never expressed in words, the bone of contention arose from her inability, or as they called it, unwillingness to fully integrate. She was deemed aloof, a pretender who took on airs. When she reached that part, her father interrupted:

"But Else, you were a most unassuming girl, sometimes I even rebuked you for being too modest."

"I know father, but in that rough and ready region everybody is expected to fall in line, to be average, they call it."

When she noticed her father's wince, she had to smile despite her grim situation. He abhorred that definition, she knew. Then she told them of the silent struggle on both sides, which graduated from resentment to hostility, and finally to hate. Soon she stood alone against the whole town, including her in-laws as well as her esteemed husband, who had not yet openly turned against her. She had loved Rolf with a true heart, but his continual carping gradually smothered that deep affection. Her unwillingness, according to him, to be a true Canadian woman, was most disagreeable.

"You probably remember that arduous letter, describing my husband in glowing terms."

"We sure do," they practically answered in unison.

"I did not exaggerate, he was a most desirable mate, as could be deduced from my letter; believe me, my happiness was consummate."

"But not lasting, as we have reasons to believe," said her mother.

"I regret to say that was the case. To be sure, it took years for the disharmony to manifest itself to an unbearable degree. The signs must have been there long before I took any notice, for I was occupied with the endeavour to please my husband. I was young, and proud to wear the girdle of Venus, ready to please and serve my husband, while remaining cheerful and keeping myself attractive."

"Your husband must have been satisfied," interrupted her father.

"Surprisingly not. He, as much as the whole town took umbrage at the way I dressed and behaved."

"Oh, why should they?" Mrs Reusle asked, who not for a moment doubted their daughter's proper deportment.

"For one thing I refused to wear men's clothes; for another I tailored my own dresses and skirts, which proved too colourful for the womenfolks; and to top it all, I played chess and read books."

"They must have been peculiar people to take offence at that," mused Mr Reusle.

"Well, they still are."

"What did Rolf say to all this?" he asked.

"At the beginning he sided with me, actually he encouraged me to preserve my ancestral ways and language, but soon it became obvious it was only lip service, his heart was not in it. After my suspicion was roused I became leery and resentful, moreover openly scornful. That piqued Rolf to no end. His criticism grew more scathing, he now made fun of me in front of his cronies. Mimicking my accent in the company of silently applauding women, turned into a routine. By then I felt ostracised and unjustly treated, in particular by my husband."

Else then eyed her parents intently, her face took on an apocalyptic expression.

"You asked me why my husband did not come with me."

She chuckled as if amused.

"He couldn't, because he is dead."

When her mother approached with outstretched arms, she was rebuffed unceremoniously:

"Let me be mother, hear me out first," she remonstrated.

"Yes, let's do that," her husband agreed.

In all these years he was unable to reconcile himself to his wife's gushing ways.

Else continued her narrative. She told of times when doubts chafed at her mind, which soured her days and troubled her nights. Yet she strove to make the best of it, although her cuddling nature felt the chill that slowly crept between them. Their former chaffing and dallying gave way to constant bickering, ending in tiffs. Furtive, stolen kisses, over the years deeply ingrained in their habits, grew rarer, till finally they ceased all together. A gulf opened between them, which increasingly became more difficult to span.

Seeing her father nodding knowingly, she added:

"Differences in outlook, long treated with good-natured chuckles and banter acquired ominous aspects. Values, though dissimilar, long tolerated gracefully, if not esteemed, took on threatening dimensions."

A dismal loneliness overshadowed her life, aggravated by a sense of betrayal. Her in-laws practically avoided her entirely, while Rolf, although remaining polite, took on a painful unfriendly attitude towards her. Add to it an increasing frosty reception by the villagers, her reluctance to leave the house was understandable. That enmity, perhaps imagined, undermined her self-confidence. She grew insecure, defensive and easily offended.

"I felt misunderstood, vilified and shunned like one beset by leprosy."

"Could you not have moved with your husband?" her father asked.

"I discussed it with Rolf not only once, but several times. We should sell and move far away, I suggested, rather entreated, to Vancouver perhaps."

"He refused?" her mother interrupted indignantly.

"Absolutely, in no uncertain terms. To be sure I could partly understand his refusal, since even the most elaborate property in that remote area would probably not attract a single offer to buy. The last time when I alluded to it, he became almost abusive, calling me stuck-up, and worst of all cast aspersions on my mental state."

At these words her mother's eyes slowly filled with tears, she shook her head till reproving glances from her husband made her stop.

"Could you not have left your husband and start a new life somewhere else, perhaps even back here?"

"I played with that idea father, more than once, I can assure you. I also made an attempt, not too convincing, mind you, to mingle more with the locals, perhaps exhibit a more embracing attitude. But it should not be. Hardly had I made the first step towards its inception, when I began to stumble. I simply could not stomach their, how should I say, addictive devotion to mediocrity, which they veiled with the euphemism average."

"I should hope not," interjected her father incensed.

He was a professor trying to instil in his pupils a desire for excellence, as much as in his wife and daughter.

Before Else took up her narrative again, her facial expression changed. The dark shadows of resentment gave way to an unexpected radiance. One could feel an uplifting force at work that illuminated her whole being. She told them of the day when she stopped waiting for the sword of Damocles to fall; she got away from under it.

It happened in early April when her combative spirit suddenly returned. On a clear morning upon hearing the familiar honk-honk of Canada geese, she leapt out of bed, dressed and laced her shoes quickly, then ran out of the house after the geese till she reached the top of the hill. A strong scent from the never dying sagebrush rose from the high land. Chattering jays flew back and forth excitedly. Their saucy 'whee-ahh–chuck-chuck' followed by short bursts of scoldings, seemed like calls of welcome to her.

Every cry of an eagle, wild and free high above, removed a stifling band from her heart. The sight of rasping and wailing falcons soaring slowly around in circles, lightened her steps. When a pack of coyotes started to bark and sing across from a clearing, the magic of life began captivating her once more. It also roused her slumbering defiance.

When she came back, refreshed in body and mind, she was in a singing mood, moreover gripped by a long dormant desire for ventures. Feverishly she got to work. Forgotten were imagined wrongs, through the window flew homemade worries; out came cloth, scissors, twine and needles; she remembered that busy hands are the bane of brooding. She tailored dresses which were embroidered colourfully, cutting and folding them with intense care. Without exception eye-catching clothes came into life under her deft hands.

Colourfully dressed, graced by an upbeat mood, she often sat at the piano playing and singing songs of her childhood and youth. Her husband perceived these activities, as much as her stylish clothes and cheerfulness, as an effrontery, it affected him like a gauntlet flung squarely into his face. To his eternal shame he began whispering behind her back, besides denigrating her openly.

Then spring had arrived in all its glory. Else however, hardly noticed the splendour of colours covering the hills, as little as she heard the voices of a fully awakened nature. The fact could no longer be denied: her newly found courage did not last long.

She now shambled towards indifference, a sort of lethargy and acceptance of an unfortunate fate. Even the irrepressible voices of the Tulameen left her untouched. She wandered aimlessly around, deeply absorbed within herself, weighted down by gloomy thoughts, which she could not banish from her mind.

"For hours I searched the clear sky and blooming hills for a sign of encouragement. I pined for a friendly voice, a heartfelt word or just a well-meant glance to lighten that oppressive weight. A sincere smile or sign of understanding would have enlivened my sinking spirit in leaps and bounds. But it should not be. The wall of resentment, in part erected by myself, became more difficult to climb."

Her father was unable to contain his vexation any longer, he interrupted her with a screwed up face:

"But Else, why did you not write to us, we both would have rushed to your side."

Else looked up, then shrugged her shoulders before she said:

"That thought never entered my mind, after all I was a grown woman who had made her bed a long time ago. Anyway, listen a bit longer, I am getting towards the end."

"To the end?" inquired Mrs Reusle apprehensively.

Else glanced at her in a strange sarcastic way. One could have thought she was gloating:

“Yes, there is an end, in any case did I think so till recently, but I have my doubts now.”

Then she continued:

“My husband and I walked through the house like strangers, polite but unapproachable. We both nursed grievances that reached a bottomless pit, an abyss of no return. We associated less and less with each other. I can not say when the realisation hit me that he hankered for a separation, if not a divorce. You see, I no longer served his purpose.

“Some recent business ventures had brought him in contact with so-called highfliers, who considered themselves as sharks in the world of business. These men perceived women as trophies; stereotyped from their false hair to painted toenails these ladies were, or rather had to be. Rolf introduced me to a few, to show me I suspect, what a woman should look like that wishes to call a successful man her husband.

“I regret to say, all my good breeding could not prevent guffaws and scorn on my part, which hurt Rolf to the quick. These women resembled each other like lifeless dolls, sporting frozen smiles, actually gargoylean grimaces, which would have put Lucifer to flight. I can hardly describe their terrifying impression on me. I was certain they were remotely controlled like marionettes, albeit by invisible strings.

‘You want me to look like that? what an abomination, what a holy terror,’ I said to Rolf in my most crushing manner.”

Soon all intimacy between them took a flight over the hills. Else was still willing to continue their marriage, but not in that area. Too many harrowing memories lurked in all directions. Behind every tree it seemed, as much as on the grassland and hills, sneered mocking spectres at her. Even shadows cast by tall ponderosa pines looked ominous. Never again could she lead a life of peace among these ghosts of the past. Besides, too many bridges were pulled down, which the most adept hands could never reinstate. Towards Rolf she harboured conflicting feelings, vacillating between disdain and a lingering affection.

“One day in June I noticed a change in his deportment. He was more talkative than in the past months, moreover he spoke with a peculiar furred tongue. Despite being suspicious, the fact that he wanted to approach me at all, gave me a tingling feeling. He coughed like so, he breathed heavier and cleared his throat several times, and believe it or not, he even smiled at me while coming closer. Finally he made known his intention.

'Else, I have lately thought quite a bit about us,' he said haltingly.

'I too,' I admitted still on guard.

'We should have a serious talk,' he added, loud enough to drown out the clatter of dishes, which I pretended to wash.

'I am ready,' was my response.

"He let his eyes wander from me to the sun-drenched hills, then observed some cawing ravens nearby. The day was still young; like every morning the wind was not up yet, it hardly bent the bunch grass. It was a god given morning. Finally he said:

'Not here, I have taken a day off, it would be an ideal occasion to wander around a bit.'

"I was confounded but willing to go along. Under the rays of the warming sun we walked atop the rushing and gargling Tulameen to a destination I could well imagine. We hardly spoke a word, one seemed to wait for the other's conversation. All nature was astir, the wind gained strength, it started to move the ponderosa tops. We stopped at the bend where the river below roared and rushed from bank to bank, seemingly undecided in which direction to flow.

"What happened next I am unable to explain even today. Rolf made me uneasy, he cast strange glances at me, as if undecided of his steps. I watched him standing there, staring silently, thinking heaven knows what. Seeing him so tense my blood rushed and my pulse beat faster. The spot where we had spent so many happy hours, where my consent was given so jubilantly, took on a sinister aspect.

"Rolf too seemed distraught, clearing his throat again and again, while shuffling from foot to foot, breathing heavily, he stroked his face with fidgety hands. Suddenly he turned fully towards me; then in the next instant made a move as if to embrace me. This unexpected step, resembling more an attack under the circumstances, I repulsed with more force than intended. Pushing him back vehemently sent him staggering towards the precipice, over which he tumbled with a cry of terror from his lips."

"Good gracious," her mother exclaimed.

Even her sedate father was unable to hide his shock. Nevertheless, he managed to ask calmly:

"What happened then?"

"I was seized by a paralysing terror, standing there like rooted to the ground, unable to move a limb. Only one thought kept racing through my head: it had to be a nightmare which must be cast off. There I stood, hands outstretched to prevent my husband from falling, yet helpless to do so. Somehow I must have entered a world of fantasy, since even the noise from the river sounded different. Unreal, more like human wails, desperate cries for help.

"While frantically attempting to shake off this imagined dream, the mournful cries from below grew more intense, getting louder and exceedingly more heart-rending. It was a voice imploring for deliverance. Then I heard my name being called, again and again it assailed my ears, inducing me to cover them with both hands. But still these woeful, piercing lamentations were audible. Incredulous I shook my head, it could not be, no water, not even the wayward Tulameen could produce such sounds."

Else paused for a moment while contemplating her parents, who obviously sat on pins and needles. But they kept themselves in check, rather her father did. Her mother had more difficulties to remain still, she tugged at her clothes, moved from side to side, and seemed on the verge to burst out with questions or remarks. Only her husband's raised hand as much as his stern countenance held her back. Else picked up where she had left off:

"You may think me silly, a fumbling ninny all in a dither when presence of mind was advisable. But I was dazed, like mesmerised by these sudden unthinkable events. Eventually I plucked up courage and stepped closer to the edge. Clearly now I could hear my name being called, it was Rolf trying from somewhere below to drown out the rushing sounds of the river. I could hardly believe it, my husband was still alive, the roaring, tempestuous currents had not swept him down river.

“We started to make contact. I could not see him but heard his voice, provided he called out loud enough. He quick-wittedly had grabbed a protruding rock, he told me, where he was now half hanging, half standing, holding on for dear life.

‘How long I can hold out, I don’t know,’ he said, rather hollered.

“He was unable to move, he informed me, it would be impossible to climb up, consequently help from above was needed. Two or four strong arms, plus a stout rope could rescue him, he advised. He directed me to hurry to the next house and ask for assistance.

“I ran as never before towards the village. My heart was pounding wildly, my pulse throbbed furiously, in part because of exertion, but more so out of guilt. Sending one fervent prayer after the other to heaven, trying to suppress pangs of remorse, I plunged ahead.”

Mrs Reusle was unable to contain her anxiety any longer. No amount of reproachful glances from her husband could keep her quiet, she burst out:

“That poor man, what agonies he must have endured; and you too Else, it is terrible even thinking about. Tell us what finally happened.”

Else looked at her mother pensively, her whole demeanour expressed an inscrutable air, a mixture between anguish and defiance.

“I am getting there, but I don’t believe you will like it; no, I doubt that you will. But here it is. As I raced stumbling and panting along the path, wondrous thoughts began chasing through my head. Two contradicting voices arose: One, raising doubts, the other trying to be reassuring. Why did he want to come nearer, to embrace me, or push me down the canyon? Maybe he just intended to make a conciliatory gesture, after all we are still spouses. But no, his move was too sudden and brisk. So it went, malicious imps scurried around my ears, putting weird ideas in my head.

“Unwittingly I slowed down, then finally came to a halt. Not much was stirring in any direction, neither was another human being abroad. Only the wind moaned through the trees. Even the Tulameen beside me sounded different, quieter, but disjointed like the voices inside me, which burrowed like voracious worms through my mind. What did Rolf want from me, why growing so amiable all of a sudden, after all these years of coldness?

"Then the devil, tempting as ever, came out of the woodwork. Spurring me on, prodding, making my ears tingle with evil suggestions, tormenting my heart with mistrust, and finally a desire for redress. The recurring question arose: Why should I run for help?"

At these words her parents winced visibly. Her father looked pained at his wife, who bowed her head low. Both were bewildered, too stunned to even whisper. They waited in awed silence to hear the rest.

"Such thoughts and many others flitted through my mind. Was it not fate that spoke, did not destiny mete out a well-deserved punishment for ignominious deeds? What a deceiver this man turned out to be, how he betrayed his solemn vow to honour our marriage and stand by me in joy and sorrow; but he broke his solemn word, moreover abandoned me so shamefully that it still hurts today."

Else jumped up, more agitated than before she cried:

"I had to go back, although by now I was determined to lend him no hand of mine. 'Let him suffer, let him die,' I cried into the wind, which in the meantime had reached its usual force. I had reached this conclusion, dastardly it may sound, because he cowardly stabbed me in the back and assaulted my pride and character. Most infuriating I found his intention to turn me into a trophy woman, an inanimate monstrosity, rouged and paint splattered from head to toe, artificial and mouldable like a waxen doll. Ha, ha, ha and ha again, I shouted at the surging water below, let him crouch there for eternity or fall to the bottom of the river. There will be one scoundrel less, and no further harm done."

Her admission that she was prepared to leave her husband to his fate, disconcerted her parents beyond measure. They appeared to be shaken to the roots, which fact manifested itself through hunted glances in all directions, while their faces took on a shroud-like pallor. When Else noticed their piteous discomfort, she added defensively:

"You simply can not imagine the frame of mind I was in. I stood alone, surrounded by a sea of hostility, not a single compassionate soul was in that whole wide country to reassure me, not a single hand was proffered in friendship. My own husband had even conspired against me. Where, oh where could I have found comfort."

"With us," moaned her parents in unison.

Else was stuck for a reply, she just nodded her head as if to say:

"That is easy to say now, but then it all looked different."

She contemplated them closer for a moment, before she carried on:

"As I neared the bend I could hear Rolf calling from a hundred steps distance; he therefore was still alive."

Her mother now jumped up and clapped both hands over her face, she could stand the tension no longer. Her daughter looked at her with mocking and disdainful eyes that seemed to say: 'Just wait, there will be more.'

Her father too was barely able to disguise his consternation. He looked aghast at his daughter, not certain whether she still possessed all her senses. Else went on:

"Did I hear voices from heaven, or urgings from hell? I could not say then and now, I was simply unable to judge. But the recurring thought that the man in the clutches of death had for years shovelled a pit for me into which he tumbled himself, guided my actions. Destiny had spoken, it seemed to me, justice was meted out with twofold intensity."

An unexpected serenity now appeared on Else's face, which stood in marked contrast with her disturbing narrative. Not a trace of those fateful days marred her features, just calm surrender, a purifying renunciation graced her countenance. She gave the impression of a woman that rose beyond human judgement. Almost apathetically did she pick up again:

"His cries rose louder, more terrified over the banks of the Tulameen, that signified a nearing end. Covering both ears with my hands, I ran like a hunted doe uphill, then again towards the village. I wanted to gain time, nothing more I realised, as I went back, slowly, mind you, to the same spot."

"By all saints in heaven, you waited for your husband to fall," wailed her mother.

"I don't really remember. But listen to this; something most unusual happened, a phenomenon inexplicable to this day. Rolf's heart-rending screams, rising from the depth of a stricken heart, melted into the sounds of the Tulameen, the two became one. The rushing water between the rocks had lost its harsh, peremptory tone, as much as Rolf's piercing cries had lost their urgent, jarring effect. A sound as never before rose from the Tulameen, a new cadence filled the air, steeped in melancholy and soul-rending lament.

"The voice of the Tulameen had changed, all discord was gone, it had acquired a sound of harmony, albeit haunting, doleful. From thereon rang in my ears, still rings today, an imploring cry asking for deliverance. It was only the river's rush I now heard, accusing, as if I were responsible for its eternal imprisonment between its high banks. Miraculously Rolf disappeared from my thoughts, the Tulameen had swallowed him body and soul.

"Afterwards I was in a dither. Plagued by guilt, but never touched by remorse, I tried to persuade myself a dozen times at least, to make a report to the police. But for what end? After all I had perpetrated nothing indictable. True, I was remiss in some ways, but who could prove it in the absence of witnesses."

Else sighed deeply, then smiling ruefully she proceeded:

"All would have been well without the voice of the Tulameen. I found no peace, the plaintive tune from that fateful bend followed me day and night. Our house stood on a knoll where the smaller Otter River joins the Tulameen. The loud swirl and rush could be heard even with all windows shut.

"Many a night I could not sleep, a force stronger than reason drove me to that unforgettable spot. The need to listen to the mournful sounds down below was irresistible. Things got progressively worse, soon these voices filled my ears constantly; I was unable to flee from their reach. Added to that were my brother-in-law's biting remarks, not to mention his sneering sidewise glances.

"When a rumour started to circulate that Rolf was lured by me to that place for the sole reason to be flung to the bottom of the river, I had enough. My cup was filled to the brim, I packed up and left."

"It was high time," her mother agreed, while her father too expressed his approval.

"Ten wild horses could not have held me there anymore. At first I intended to move to Vancouver, maybe even farther to the West Coast, where billowing waves break thunderously over sand and rocks. That deafening clamour surely would drown out the voice of the Tulameen, I reckoned. But I rebuffed that idea, for in the meantime I had taken a dislike to the whole country. Moreover, my inquiries revealed that job opportunities there were scarce. Thus I decided to come back here."

Else fell silent, she had said all to lighten her heart, part of her load had been shifted on to her parents. They where at a loss for words, their quiet, moral world had received a severe jolt, their emotions were hurled onto a whirligig of dizzying speed, which they would have liked to send back across the ocean. Her father was first to break the silence:

"We are glad you came. Relax, all danger has passed," he consoled.

Else shook her head, then sighed and groaned between sobs:

"I can't, the voice of the Tulameen has found me again."